* * * * * * *

As Tracy came out of the barn after cleaning the stalls, she looked up at the clear blue sky. Again, she searched the sky with the hope of seeing at least a small cloud that would indicate there might be some moisture in the air. But there was none. It was obvious there was little chance of it raining today. With a deep sigh, she closed her eyes, put her hands on her hips and stretched in order to remove some of the stiffness in her back.

When she opened her eyes, Tracy noticed a cloud of dust off in the distance. It was rising up from the dirt road that led to the ranch. Although she could not see the vehicle as it was some distance away, it was easy to see the cloud of dust it kicked up for miles out on the wide open prairie. She wondered who could be coming out there to see her. She was not expecting anyone.

Tracy slowly walked toward the house as she continued to watch the cloud of dust move closer and closer. She shook her head in defeat when she finally was able to see the vehicle enough to identify it. It was Tom Norbert's car. He was the last person she wanted to see right then.

* * * * * * *

Other titles by J.E. Terrall

Western Short Stories	Western Novels
The Old West	Conflict in Elkhorn Valley
The Frontier	Lazy A Ranch (A Modern
Untamed Land	Western)
Tales from the Territory	The Story of Joshua Higgins

Romance Novels	Mystery/Suspense/Thriller
Balboa Rendezvous	I Can See Clearly
Sing for Me	The Return Home
Return to Me	The Inheritance
Forever Yours	

Nick McCord Mysteries
Vol – 1 Murder at Gill's Point
Vol – 2 Death of a Flower
Vol – 3 A Dead Man's Treasure
Vol – 4 Blackjack, A Game to Die For
Vol – 5 Death on the Lakes
Vol – 6 Secrets Can Get You Killed

Peter Blackstone Mysteries	Frank Tidsdale Mysteries
Murder in the Foothills	Death by Design
Murder on the Crystal Blue	Death by Assassination
Murder of My Love	

LAZY A RANCH

by
J.E. Terrall

ISBN: 978-0-9916232-6-6

This is a work of fiction. Names, characters, and incidents are either a product of the author's imagination or are used fictitiously, and any resemblance to actual persons, living or dead, is purely coincidental.

Printed in the United States of America
First & Second Printing / 2015   www.lulu.com
Third Printing / 2015   www.creatspace.com

Covers: Front and back covers photos taken by
        author J.E. Terrall

Book Layout/
Formatting: J.E. Terrall
             Custer, South Dakota

LAZY A RANCH

To
Debbie and Steve Carlson

CHAPTER ONE

Tracy Atwater, the daughter of Sam Atwater, stepped out onto the porch of the ranch house and looked over the prairie that made up most of the Lazy A Ranch. The morning sun was shining down on the rolling grasslands of central Montana just east of the Rocky Mountains. She slowly tipped her head back and looked up at the sky. It was a clear deep blue sky without a single cloud for as far as the eye could see. It was obvious to anyone that it was going to be another hot day without any rain to quench the thirst of the parched ground. Another day without rain meant another day closer to having to give up the ranch Tracy and her father loved.

She took a minute to let her eyes survey the dry prairie that made up most of the ranch. Tracy had been born and raised on the ranch, and it held a lot of fond memories for her. She had learned to drive a tractor, bale hay and herd cattle on the land as well as to ride a horse, rope a steer, and brand a calf. She had also learned to care for all the animals that lived on the ranch.

As she stood on the porch, she took a few minutes to think back to why she was there and what had brought her back to the ranch. Tracy's mother had passed away before she had graduated from high school. From the time of her mother's death, she had helped her father on the ranch until he insisted that she go to college, something her mother had always wanted her to do.

In the fall of the year after her graduation from high school, Tracy left the ranch for college with her father's blessing. After college she went to work in Great Falls,

Montana, at a local hospital as a registered nurse. She worked there until her father had a stroke that confined him to a nursing home.

Knowing how much the ranch meant to her father, Tracy quit her job and returned to take over the operation of the ranch. Unfortunately, things had not gone well for her. Now, at the age of twenty-seven, Tracy was doing whatever she could to keep the ranch going. It wasn't easy in a time of low cattle prices, and a drought that spread across almost the entire midsection of the country. There were several ranchers that had to give up ranching because they couldn't make it with all that was against them.

Tracy was a tall, nicely built woman with long light brown hair that gently cascaded over her shoulders, except when she had it tied back in a ponytail to keep it out of her face. Her eyes were a deep brown and sparkled when she was happy, although lately she had not had a great deal to be happy about.

Her shapely hips and long legs filled out the faded jeans she wore while working around the ranch. The long sleeved shirt she was wearing had been her father's. It didn't fit her all that well, but it protected her soft smooth skin from the harsh Montana sun while she worked side by side with the hired hands in the fields and pastures.

Tracy was feeling a bit depressed that morning, but she had every right to feel that way. The low price of beef and the last two years of relatively dry weather had put the ranch deep in debt. That alone would have made it hard enough for most ranchers, but there was the additional expense of the nursing home for the care of her father.

She had already let two of the four ranch hands go because she could not afford to pay their wages. She still had two men working for her, but she owed both of them two months in back wages. There was no doubt in her mind that they would eventually have to leave, too.

The extremely dry conditions had continued to plague the land well into late August. Most of the water holes used by the cattle she had left were drying up. The dry conditions were also affecting the amount of hay that would be needed to feed the cattle during the winter. If it didn't rain pretty soon, there would be little hope for her to make the payment at the bank come fall without selling off the rest of the herd. If that occurred, she would be forced to sell off the ranch itself. Without breeding stock, and no money to buy new breeding stock, the Lazy A Ranch would become a thing of the past. It would become the property of the bank. It would be sold to anyone who could afford to purchase it, or it would be auctioned off to the highest bidder. All the equipment would be auctioned off as well.

Tracy tried to think of positive things, but she found it very hard. All she could do was try to keep her head up and keep the place functioning as best she could. It was a wait and see situation. The only other thing she could do was pray for rain or some kind of miracle that would provide enough money to help her pay the bills. But even that was very unlikely to happen.

She took a deep breath and stepped down off the porch. As she walked across the yard toward the barn, she looked out at the pasture. The grass was brown and short. If she continued to feed the cattle on it much longer, it could take years before it would became a decent pasture again.

Tracy had always been an optimistic person, but it was very difficult to remain optimistic without even a small cloud in the vast blue Montana sky. There was not even a small patch of green grass for as far as the eye could see. She knew that rain would turn the buffalo grass green again very quickly, but there was no rain in the forecast, at least not for the near future.

Even without rain there was work to be done. Standing around wishing for rain was not going to get the work done. Tracy took a deep breath and headed for the barn.

Once inside the barn, she started working to care for the horses. She moved the horses out into the corral behind the barn, then spent the better part of the morning mucking out the stalls and putting out feed for them.

It was dusty and dirty in the barn. There was no way to clean the stalls in a barn and not get dirty. Sweat rolled down her face and mixed with the dust causing streaks of dirt on her face. By the time she was finished in the barn, she was hot, dirty and tired. She could use a bath, but her day and the work she had to do was not even half done. There was still more to do.

As Tracy came out of the barn after cleaning the stalls, she looked up at the clear blue sky. Again, she searched the sky with the hope of seeing at least a small cloud that would indicate there might be some moisture in the air. But there was none. It was obvious there was little chance of it raining today. With a deep sigh, she closed her eyes, put her hands on her hips and stretched in order to remove some of the stiffness in her back.

When she opened her eyes, Tracy noticed a cloud of dust in the distance. It was rising up from the dirt road that led to the ranch. Although she could not see the vehicle as it was still some distance away, it was easy to see the cloud of dust it kicked up for miles out on the wide open prairie. She wondered who could be coming out there to see her. She was not expecting anyone.

Tracy slowly walked toward the house as she continued to watch the cloud of dust move closer and closer. She shook her head in defeat when she finally was able to see the vehicle enough to identify it. It was Tom Norbert's car. He was the last person she wanted to see right then.

Tom Norbert was the son of the local banker who just happened to hold the lien on the ranch. Tracy had known Tom as far back as grade school. She remembered him to have been sort of a spoiled brat back then. During high school Tracy had dated him a few times, but they never seemed to hit it off very well. They just didn't seem to fit together for some reason. She knew he wanted her. He had even told her so as early as their junior year of high school. He considered her to be the most beautiful girl in the county, and she knew Tom liked having beautiful things.

At one time, she had liked Tom a great deal, but she wasn't sure how she felt about him now. It didn't really matter how she felt about him now. Her life was wrapped up in trying to keep the ranch in the family, and that would take all her time and effort.

Tracy remembered that Tom was good looking. He had been the captain of the football team. Most of the girls in town had tried to get him to notice them. He was tall with dark brown wavy hair and dark brown eyes. Tom was handsome and had a very nice smile, which would send all the girls into a swoon.

As for Tracy, she thought he was just a little too conceited and arrogant to suit her, although he had always been nice to her. The fact that his mother tended to look down her nose at Tracy and her father and thought of her as a poor little country girl, did little to help their relationship. Tom's mother didn't like her son going out with a poor rancher's daughter even if she was the most beautiful girl in the county. His mother always wanted him to marry some girl whose parents had influence. In other words, she wanted her son to marry into a family with money.

Tom's father was different. He liked Tracy and her father. He knew them to be good, honest, hardworking people. They were the kind of people that made the country great. They were also the kind of people he had built his bank around, and he respected them for it. He knew without people like Sam Atwater and some of the other ranchers in the county, he would not have as successful a bank as he had.

As Tracy watched Tom turn into the drive, she remembered a time when he had tried to get her into the backseat of his car. It was at the end of their senior year of high school and took place at the local drive-in theater. He had told her that he loved her, but she wanted no part of being one of his conquests in the backseat of his car. She had to slap his face to get him to quit mauling her. After her strong objections to his advances, he took her home and never asked her out again. In the fall of that same year, they both went off to college in different cities and hadn't seen each other for almost eight years.

When Tracy had returned to take over the operation of the ranch, Tom had been the first and only one to come and see her. He had asked her to go out to dinner with him shortly after she had returned to the ranch, but Tracy had declined his offer. She knew there was a chance that he had changed, but she was not ready to put in the time and effort she felt it would take to find out. There were too many other things on her mind to start up any kind of relationship with any man, especially with him. She had a lot to do since her father could no longer run the ranch. She didn't need anything that would interfere.

Tracy knew Tom had never married. It seemed strange to her that some beautiful young woman hadn't grabbed him up. After all, he was good looking, of that she had no doubt. He was also the son of one of the wealthiest families in the county. Tom could be very charming when he wanted to be, as she remembered.

As Tom stopped his big fancy sports sedan in front of the ranch house, Tracy realized she was not very presentable to be receiving guests, especially the banker's son. Her hair was in disarray with pieces of straw in it, her face was dirty and several strands of hair were falling over her face. Her jeans were covered with dust and dirt as was her shirt. There was also horse manure on her boots. She certainly didn't present the image of a successful rancher to someone she was sure was coming to the ranch on business.

Tom stepped out of the car and leaned against the top for a moment as he looked over the car toward Tracy. He looked every bit the part of the banker's son. He was wearing a dark suit and tie with a white shirt. He smiled as he looked Tracy over while she walked toward his car.

"Well, I see you've been working," he said with a grin.

"Yes, and I see you haven't," she snapped back with a sarcastic grin.

Tom straightened up and took off his suit coat. He casually tossed it onto the seat of the car then shut the door. As he walked around his car, he couldn't help but look her over. He could not get over how pretty Tracy looked, even in dirty work clothes.

"What brings you all the way out here on such a hot day? I would have thought that you would stay in your nice air-conditioned office."

"I was in the neighborhood on business," he replied in his usual casual, easygoing manner.

"Yeah, I bet," she replied with a note of sarcasm.

"No, it's true. I was over at Wilber Blaine's place. It seems he is planning on sinking another well."

"Well, I hope he has better luck finding water than some of the others who have tried around here."

Tracy turned and began walking back toward the house again. Tom moved up close to her and walked alongside her. He was tempted to put his arm around her, but quickly decided against it. He remembered that she had made it clear that she had no interest in him the last time he had seen her. He hoped to change that, but he would have to take his time.

"Since you're here, would you like something cool to drink?"

"That would be nice. Yes," he replied as they stepped up on the porch.

Tracy took a minute to bend over and take off her boots before going inside. She set them on the porch near the door. As she did, Tom did not hesitate to admire the way she filled out her jeans. She did have a nice figure, and he was not one to miss such things.

As she straightened up, Tom reached in front of her and pulled open the screen door. Tracy nodded a thank you then stepped past him. If nothing else, Tom was a gentleman, most of the time, she thought. Tracy went into the kitchen with Tom following along behind her.

"Have a seat," she said as she went to the sink and quickly washed her face and hands.

Tom sat down at the kitchen table and proceeded to watch her every move. He didn't miss the fact she had managed to keep herself in good shape. In fact, he thought she was better looking now than when they were in high school.

After Tracy dried her hands, she went to the refrigerator and took out a large pitcher of lemonade. She poured two large glasses almost full of the cool liquid. After putting the pitcher back and adding a little ice to the glasses, she took them to the table. She set one glass down in front of Tom and then sat down across the table from him. She looked over the rim of the glass as she took a sip of the cool liquid. She couldn't help but think how good he looked. Even on such a hot day, he hardly seemed to break a sweat. He always looked great whether in a suit or a pair of jeans.

"How's your father doing," Tom asked, his voice showing he really did seem to be interested in her father's health.

"He's about the same. There hasn't been any noticeable improvement, I'm afraid," she replied with a sad look on her face.

"That's too bad."

"Yeah."

"How are you doing?" he asked, hoping to get her to talk about herself.

"I'm getting along fine," she said with kind of a forced smile.

"I'm sorry to say this, but it doesn't look like you're getting along fine. I know you had to let two of your hired hands go."

Tracy looked at him. It angered her to think he was sticking his nose into her business.

"I don't see that that's any of your business," she said sharply.

"But it is my business. My father's bank holds the mortgage on this ranch. He is concerned that you might not be able to make your payment this fall," he said calmly.

"I see. So this is not a social call after all. You came out to check on your interest in the ranch."

"That's not entirely true," he replied.

"Oh. Then just why did you come here?" she asked sharply.

"I came to see you," he said as he looked at her.

"Sure you did. Well next time you come to see me, be sure you make it clear as to what your purpose really is," she said as she stood up and walked to the door.

"That's not fair," he retorted.

Tracy stopped in her tracks and turned around.

"What's not fair? What do you call what you're doing?" she said with a sharp note of anger in her voice.

"You are judging me by what I do, not on who I am or what I am."

"One thing I know for sure is that you are your father's son," she snapped back.

"And just what is that supposed to mean?" he asked, the anger building inside him.

"It means that it is too hard for you to separate the two. You can't just come here as a friend. You have to bring your job with you," she said sharply.

"I admit it is hard to separate the two, but I came out here to see how you are doing, and to see if there was anything I could do to help you," he said, trying to keep his growing temper under control.

"Right now, you can help me most by leaving," she said as she pushed the door open and held it for him.

Tom looked at her for a moment before he got up from the table. He slowly walked to the door and then stopped directly in front of her.

"I wish you would let me help you," he said calmly with a note of frustration in his voice.

"You can help me by leaving," she repeated as she looked into his eyes.

Tom hesitated for a moment as he looked into her deep brown eyes. She was upset with him. Upsetting her was the last thing he had wanted to do, but he had managed to do it anyway, and for that he was truly sorry.

Realizing that for him to stay any longer would simply upset her more, he walked past her. He continued on across the yard to his car. As he walked around to the driver's side, he stopped briefly before getting in to look at her standing on the porch. She had her arms folded across her chest, and the look on her face was one that he wished he had not seen. He could tell that she was angry and wanted nothing to do with him.

Tom had hoped that over the years she would have changed her mind about him. He had changed a lot from when he was in high school, and was hoping she would give him the chance to prove it.

Letting out a sigh of disappointment, Tom reached down and opened the door to his car. He got in and started the engine. He glanced back toward the house before he put the car in gear and drove off.

Tracy watched as Tom drove down the road that would take him back to town. The thought that his father's bank would own the ranch soon enough passed through her mind.

As she turned to go back inside, Tracy began to realize she had not been completely fair to him. She had treated him as if he was the villain, when she knew that he wasn't. He had done nothing to her. It certainly was not his fault that the ranch had fallen on hard times. And it wasn't really his fault for checking on the bank's investment.

She turned back and watched the cloud of dust that was kicked up by his car as he sped away. She knew that he could help her if she would simply let him, but she didn't want to be obligated to him.

Even so, she could not help but be angry with herself for running him off like she did. She wished she had handled things differently, but it was too late to worry about that now. What was said was said, and there was no taking it back.

Tracy began to wonder if Tom might have changed over the years. He didn't seem to be conceited or arrogant any more. Since she had returned to the Lazy A Ranch, she had run into him a couple of times in town. He had always been the perfect gentleman. He had only asked her out once. When she refused, he didn't try to push himself on her. Years ago that would not have been the case.

Tom had remained pleasant and polite to her on the few other occasions when they ran into each other. He had done nothing to her, and he had asked nothing of her. All he seemed to want was to help her and be a friend.

All she had done was to push him away. It occurred to her that if she continued to push him away, she might never find out if he had changed; and she might never find out if she still had feelings for him.

Maybe it was for the best, she thought. Even if she wanted to get to know him again, it would have to wait. The ranch needed her attention full time. She didn't have time for him. She was also reasonably sure his mother would still not like him spending anytime at all with her.

Tracy knew that Tom had gone to college right after graduation from high school. After getting his degree, he returned to work with his father in the bank. Her old school friends who still lived in the area had told Tracy that they didn't think he was dating anyone even though almost every available woman, and some who were not available, were trying to get him to notice them.

"If he was dating, it was no one from around here," they would say.

As soon as he was out of sight, she turned and went back into the house. She sat down at the table, picked up her lemonade and sipped a little from the glass. She was not able to get Tom out of her mind. The one thing she had noticed was he looked very distinguished and very handsome in his well-tailored suit.

CHAPTER TWO

Tracy sat at the table mentally beating herself up over not giving Tom the benefit of the doubt. His reason for coming to the ranch may have been as innocent as he said. Maybe he had been there just to visit and to offer her whatever help he could give her. God knows she could use all the help she could get.

Then again, maybe she had been right all along. Maybe he had been there to check out the property in case they did have to foreclose on the ranch. Whatever his reason, she had treated him badly.

The more she thought about it, the more she wished she had treated him differently. She had not been fair to him. After all, his father did have an invested interest in the ranch, and he had every right to protect that investment.

Tracy's thoughts were suddenly interrupted by the sound of someone at the door. She turned and looked through the screen door to see one of her hired hands, Jacob Adams, standing there looking down at his feet and holding his hat in his hands.

Jacob Adams was a tall lean man with a good deal of gray in his thick head of once dark brown hair. He wore a long handlebar mustache that curled up on the ends. His skin was tanned and wrinkled, and appeared to be as tough as shoe leather from years of working outside in the unforgiving weather and the harsh Montana sun.

He wore his jeans tucked inside the tops of his well-worn cowboy boots. There was a utility knife that he kept razor sharp neatly tucked in the top of his right boot as well. The long-sleeved plaid shirt he wore had seen better days.

The color was faded and there were patches on the elbows. The neckerchief he wore around his neck had been washed so many times that the color was almost gone.

From the look on Jacob's face, whatever it was he had come to say must have been very serious. The usual sparkle in his brown eyes was not there, and the smile was gone from his face.

"Come in, Jacob," Tracy said with a smile. "Would you like a glass of lemonade?"

"Thank you, Missy, that would be nice," he said as he opened the door and stepped into the kitchen.

Tracy smiled to herself as she got a glass out of the cupboard for Jacob. Jacob had worked for her father for many years and had called her "Missy" for as long as she could remember. She sort of liked the name and liked the way he said it.

She filled a glass with lemonade and ice, and then topped off her own glass. As she turned around, she noticed Jacob had not sat down. He was still standing just inside the doorway with his hat held firmly in his hands as he watched her.

"Why don't you sit down and relax a little bit, at least while you have your lemonade," she suggested.

"Thank you, Missy," he replied as he reached out and pulled a chair out a little way from the table.

Tracy watched him as he turned the chair around and sat down on it backwards. She reached across the table and set the glass of lemonade in front of him, then sat down at the table across from him. Jacob reached out, picked up the glass and took a couple of big gulps of the cool liquid.

She knew he had something on his mind, but she also knew he would tell her what it was in his own good time. Jacob was one of those people that could not be rushed, and it would be a waste of time and effort to try. That didn't mean that he was lazy, far from it. He was a hard working ranch hand.

Jacob set the half-empty glass back on the table and crossed his arms over the back of the kitchen chair. He sat staring at the glass for some time as if he was trying to gather his thoughts. After a little while, he slowly raised his eyes up and looked at Tracy. His eyes were sad and tired looking. He was a quiet man and didn't like to cause problems, but today was the day he had wished would not have come. He took a deep breath and let out a long sigh before he spoke.

"I don't rightly know how ta say this, Missy," he said softly as he looked at her.

"We've known each other for a long time, Jacob. Why don't you just say what's on your mind. You can say anything you want to me, you know that."

"Yes, I know," he said as he looked back down at the glass again.

Tracy could see that Jacob was having a hard time gathering his thoughts, or picking his words. Whatever it was he had to say, she knew it had to be important for him to take so long at it. She also knew it was not easy for him. Finally he looked up at her again.

"I'm sorry, Missy, but I gotta quit," he said with a look of sadness in his eyes.

Tracy looked at him as if she was almost in shock. A tear began to form in the corner of her eye then slowly slid down her cheek. She had been halfway expecting it, but it didn't make it any easier for her to hear when it did come, especially after Tom's visit just moments ago.

"I'm sorry, too," she replied sadly.

"I got done all I can ta make it easier for you, but I need my pay. I know you ain't got it, so there ain't no sense in discussin' it. I need ta move on. I've been offered a job over at the Clausen Ranch over west of here. I told them I'd take it. I'm sorry, Missy," he said with a note of regret in his voice.

"I'm sorry, too. But I understand, Jacob. You shouldn't feel bad. You have to do what is best for you. I'll send you what I owe you as soon as I can," she promised.

"I know you will. I ain't worried none about that, Missy," Jacob said as he started to get up.

"Please, Jacob, finish your lemonade," she said hoping he wouldn't leave so soon.

Jacob looked at her for a moment, then sat back down. She watched him as he picked up the glass again and drained the contents. She knew that without Jacob, she and the one remaining ranch hand were going to have to work even harder just to keep the place going.

"I know this will make it harder for you, but I have ta pay my bills," he said as he set the empty glass on the table and stood up.

"It's all right, Jacob. I understand, really. I just wish I could pay you."

"I'll work out the day for you, but then I gotta leave," he said, his eyes showing how hard it had been for him to make the decision to leave.

"Thank you. I appreciate that."

Tracy watched him as he turned and walked out the door. It was a sad time for her. She had known Jacob since she was a little girl. He was like family to her. Seeing him go like that was hard on her. It was almost like losing an uncle.

Tracy sat at the table looking at the empty glass across the table from her. Tears were running down her cheeks as she thought of the ranch without Jacob. It would be almost like having a ranch without cattle. He had been as much a part of the ranch as anyone.

"Come on, girl, pull yourself together," she said to herself as she tried to shake off the feeling of being defeated.

Tracy knew there was work to be done. She also knew it all might very well be in vain, but she wasn't defeated. Not yet, anyway. There was still some hope, however small, that things would work out.

The cattle in the east pasture had to be moved to the north pasture before they destroyed what little grass was left. They also needed to be moved to where there was more water. The north pasture was the only place left on the ranch where there was still water in a couple of the wells. The old windmill in the north pasture still worked and would pump the life saving water up from underground and into the troughs at the base of the windmill.

If she and her one remaining ranch hand could get all the cattle to the north pasture, the cattle might be able to survive until the rains came. It was a long shot at best, but it was the only place left that gave her any kind of hope of saving the ranch.

The old barn in the north pasture was in pretty bad shape, but it would provide at least a little shade for some of the cattle. It was the only place where hay was still stored. If she remembered right, the old barn still had a lot of hay left in it. She knew there was not enough to feed the herd through the winter, but it was enough to keep them fed until fall if she was careful. Maybe by then there would be enough hay in the fields that it could be baled and used to feed the cattle through the winter.

Tracy was dreaming. She knew that. It was a one in a million chance at best. It would take a lot of rain and sunshine. It would have to come at just the right times, and in the right amounts to restore the pastures and hay fields enough to be able get a cutting before winter.

The time had come to stop dreaming. It was time to get to work and move the cattle. She knew that it would take most of the day just to get them rounded up and headed toward the north pasture. It would be best if she were to get started while she still had Jacob around to help.

Tracy emptied her glass, then picked up the other glasses on the table. After putting them in the sink, she turned and went back outside. As she headed across the yard toward the barn, she began to look around. She saw Jacob putting a saddle on one of the ranch horses. She had talked to him about moving the cattle the other day. It sort of surprised her that he was getting ready to help with the move, but she was glad he was.

As she was walking across the yard, she also saw her other hired hand, William Strong, or Will as he liked to be called, go into the barn. He was leading a horse back into the barn.

Will was a big man, almost six foot three, and weighed in at close to three hundred pounds. Even as big as he was, he was not fat. He carried his weight well, considering his size. He had broad shoulders and a strong barrel chest with a fairly narrow waist. Will wore a thick heavy beard that was as dark brown as his eyes. His arms were big and muscular, and covered with dark brown hair. He was far from what most women would consider handsome, but he was polite and a hard worker. Some might refer to him as "a mountain of a man", and he fit the analogy well. Will was a loner and very seldom went into town even when there was something special going on like the Fourth of July Barbeque and a parade. He took orders well from both Jacob, whom he considered to be the foreman, and from Tracy, his boss.

Tracy knew only a little of Will's background. He didn't have much of an education, maybe fourth or fifth grade at the most. He was considered to be a very dangerous man by some of the locals. He had spent several years in the Montana State Prison for killing a man with his bare hands. Tracy didn't know what the whole story was, but she trusted her father's judgment. Her father would not have hired Will if he thought for one second that he was a danger to anyone on the ranch.

Her father had hired Will about six years ago while Tracy was in college. No one else in the area would have anything to do with him. She thought it was probably because they were afraid of him. Tracy had kept him around at Jacob's request when she returned to take over the ranching operation. Up until recently, she had not worked with him very closely. With Jacob leaving tomorrow, she was going to have to depend on him, provided that he would stay on. She had her doubts he would stay on once Jacob left. After all, she owed him almost three months in back wages.

Tracy walked up to the barn as Will was coming back out. She had wondered why he had taken a horse into the barn, as he would need one to help Jacob round up the cattle.

"Howdy, Boss," Will said as he reached up and touched the brim of his well worn cowboy hat.

"Why did you take that horse back into the barn?"

"I won't need him 'til dark," he replied, the look on his face showing how confused he was by her question.

"I thought we were going out to round up the cattle. We have to move them to the north pasture in the morning."

"We got 'um all rounded up, Boss. Jacob and I done that yesterday whilst you was busy," he said with a slight grin.

"You did," she said with a smile.

Tracy was very pleased that Jacob and Will had taken it upon themselves to round up the cattle and get them ready to move. It meant she was not going to have to spend two days in the saddle getting them rounded up, then another day moving them halfway across the ranch.

"Yeah," he replied, pleased that she approved of what they had done. "All you and I have ta do is move 'um ta the north pasture tomorrow."

"That's great, but I just saw Jacob ride out of here. Where was he going?"

"He said he'd take the first watch. He's goin' to keep 'um close ta the waterin' hole for the night so we can take 'um to the north pasture first thin' in the mornin'. He said that he ain't goin' ta be here ta help. Did he quit, Boss?" Will asked with a worried look on his face.

"Yes, he did. But I don't want you to worry. He had to do what he had to do."

"I ain't worried none. I understand, Boss," Will said, but Tracy knew he didn't understand at all.

Tracy was hesitant to talk to Will about Jacob's leaving. She was afraid that Will might take it to mind to do the same. If she lost Will, there would be nothing she could do but sell off the rest of the cattle and then sell the ranch. With things the way they were, the drought and all, she doubted she would be able to get enough out of the ranch to pay off the debt against it. Like it or not, it was time to have a talk with Will.

"Will, I need to talk to you," she said not sure how she was going to explain things to him in a way he could understand.

"I know, Boss."

"You do?" she asked wondering what it was he thought he knew.

"Sure I do. I've known for some time that Jacob was goin' ta quit. He told me the other day that he's gotta leave for a new job," he said flatly.

"Yes, that's true. But I would like you to stay on if you can," she said, worried that he would leave, too.

"I'll stay," he said without a second's hesitation.

"Do you understand that I won't be able to pay you for a while?"

"I ain't got much use for money no how. I sure ain't got no place ta go," he said as he looked at her with sad eyes.

Will didn't have any place to go. No one in the area would hire him because he was an ex-con. Nobody wanted him around because they were afraid of him. Nobody seemed to care why he had killed a man, or that he had paid the price for what he did. It only mattered that he did what he went to jail for.

"I want to thank you for sticking with me, Will. When you get done with your chores, you can come up to the house to eat your meals. I may not be able to pay you for awhile, but I can sure feed you," she said with a smile.

"I'd like that, Boss. I ain't had no home cookin' in a long time," he said with a smile.

Tracy looked at Will and smiled at him.

"Thank you, Will. When you get through with your chores, you come up to the house for dinner."

"Yes, Boss," he replied with a big grin.

Tracy could see the excitement in his eyes. At that moment, he reminded her of a great big teddy bear.

Tracy returned to the house. She had heard about Will's appetite, and she wasn't about to give him any reason to leave. With all the other ranch hands gone, she had to count on Will to do all the heavy work.

* * * *

That evening, Will came up to the house. He had never been in the ranch house before. He had eaten all his meals with the rest of the men in the kitchen at the end of the bunkhouse. And when there was only Jacob left, he ate with Jacob.

Will was a little nervous when he put his big feet on the porch. He wasn't sure it was a good idea. He thought about turning around and going back to the bunkhouse, but he knew there was nothing for him to eat there. No one had ever taught him how to cook for himself. He could fix a couple of things. He could cook enough to get by if he had to, but nothing anyone would want for a steady diet, including himself.

Tracy heard the sound of Will's big feet as he stepped up on the porch, but she didn't hear him knock on the door. She went to the door and found him just standing there looking at the door.

"Come in, Will," she said with a smile as she pushed open the screen door.

Will looked at her. He still felt a little uncomfortable about going into the boss's house for dinner, but he didn't have much choice if he wanted to eat.

Will reached up and took his big cowboy hat off and held it in both hands in front of him as he walked into the kitchen. He could smell the aroma of freshly baked bread and of simmering apples and cinnamon on the stove.

Tracy turned and walked over to the stove to stir the cooking apples. When she turned around, she saw that Will was still standing just inside the door with his hat in his hands. He was watching her every move.

"Sit down at the table, Will," Tracy told him and pointed to the chair where she wanted him to sit.

"Thank you," he said politely

"I hope you are hungry."

"I am, Boss."

"Good. I have a good meal for you."

Tracy served up a big meal of meat, potatoes, vegetables, biscuits and apple cinnamon dumplings for the big man. She sat down across the table from him and watched him eat while she ate. There was no mistake that Will had a healthy appetite. He almost wiped out all the apple cinnamon dumplings.

After dinner, Will thanked her and left the house. But before he left, he asked Tracy what time she wanted to get started in the morning. She told him at sunrise and bid him goodnight.

Tracy watched the big man walk off across the yard. She wondered if the two of them could keep the ranch going. Will had been good company for her, as she was feeling a little lonely. He didn't talk much, but just by being there he had given her some small measure of hope.

As soon as he was gone, Tracy cleaned up the kitchen and put things away. It was getting pretty late if she was to get up and get some food packed for tomorrow's cattle drive to the north pasture.

Tracy took a quick shower and got ready for bed. She was tired, but she wasn't sure if it was because of the worry or the hard day's work she had put in. All she knew was that tomorrow would be another long hard day. She set the alarm to go off before sunrise so she could pack up some food for them to take along. Her head no more than hit the pillow and she was asleep.

CHAPTER THREE

The alarm next to Tracy's bed went off at the time she had set it, but she was not ready to get up. She rolled over with a slight moan. With a great deal of reluctance she reached out and shut off the alarm. It was still dark outside; and she wanted more than anything to simply roll over and go back to sleep, but she knew she could not do that.

Unenthusiastically, she swung her legs over the side of the bed and sat up. The floor was cool under her bare feet, but she didn't mind. It was a welcome relief after so many hot days without rain.

She stretched and ran her fingers through her hair. Yesterday had been hard on her, both physically and emotionally. It had drained her of her energy like no other day had done for a very long time. But no matter, today was a new day. Another day that had to be dealt with in the best way she knew how. With what she knew had to be done, it was not a day she was anticipating.

Tracy stood up and walked across the bedroom to the bathroom. After removing her cotton nightshirt, which looked more like a long T-shirt, she stepped up to the shower and turned on the water. Although she had taken a shower last night, there was no doubt a cool shower would help wake her up and help her face the long day ahead.

As soon as the water was flowing at a temperature she was sure she could stand, yet not too cold, she drew back the shower curtain and stepped into the shower. Her breath caught when the cool water hit her naked body. It was a little cooler than she had expected, but not so cold she needed to warm it up.

It took only a few seconds for her to get used to the cool water. After a little while it began to feel good running down her skin, almost refreshing. She leaned back and let the water flow over her head, her face and down over the smooth curves of her body. She would have liked to have stayed in the shower longer, but it was going to be a long day. To delay the start of it would only make it seem to last that much longer.

Tracy shampooed her hair and rinsed it. She then took the soap and washed her body. The water felt so good on her skin that she took several extra minutes to rinse off. Reluctantly, she shut off the water, stepped out of the shower and wrapped herself in a large towel. She went into her bedroom, drying herself as she walked into the room. She finished drying herself off, and then dried her hair with a towel. Tracy tossed the towel over the top of the hamper in the corner of the room to dry.

She went to her closet to pick out what she was going to wear for the long dusty trail drive to the north pasture. Opening the closet, her eyes first fell on a couple of very nice looking dresses she had not worn since she left the city. She knew they looked good on her, but she had no need for them while herding cattle. She doubted that the cattle would care what she wore. As she looked at them, she wondered if she would ever have the opportunity to wear any of them again.

Tracy let out a sigh and pushed the dresses out of the way. She then took an old shirt out of the closet she often wore when she would come out to the ranch on holidays and vacations to help her father. It was a shirt she would never have thought of wearing in the city, but it was very appropriate for today's work on the ranch. The cuffs were worn and the color was faded, but it still had some wear left in it.

She tossed the shirt onto the foot of the bed and took out a pair of jeans that were worn thin in the seat and the knees. They still had some wear left in them, too. It would not be long before they would look like the ones the kids liked to wear in the city. She smiled to herself as she thought how ridiculous that was, but it was true. If her jeans had holes in the right places, she would be right in style with the city kids.

Tracy shook her head as she realized she was wasting time. She had work to do and she had better get a move on. Will would be waiting for her, and she didn't want to keep him waiting. After all, she needed him. She quickly dressed and left the bedroom.

Tracy went to the kitchen and quickly began packing up some grub for the trip to the north pasture. She had no more than filled the saddlebags when she thought she heard someone at the back door. Cautiously, she went to the door and opened it. Standing on the porch was Will with his hat held in front of him with both hands.

"Morning, Will," she said as she looked at him.

"Mornin', Boss," he replied shyly.

The look on Will's face made her wonder if everything was all right. She wondered if she might have told him something yesterday that she had forgotten about by morning, or that he may have misunderstood.

"Is there something wrong?" she asked.

"No, Ma'am. I was just wonderin' if I was supposed ta come up ta the house for breakfast?" he asked shyly.

"Oh, of course," she replied with a smile. "Come in."

Tracy held the door open while Will moved on past her. Once Will was inside the house, she went to the kitchen. She hadn't even thought about feeding him breakfast. Tracy had not been prepared to make breakfast.

"I didn't think to ask you what you like. How about a thick slice of ham and some eggs, and a few biscuits left over from last night?"

"That sounds good, Ma'am," he replied with a smile.

As Tracy got out a frying pan and put it on the stove, she hesitated. She was still a little nervous about him being alone in the house with her, considering his past. It was still dark outside and there was no one to help her if he decided to do her harm. Then there was the fact she didn't really like having him standing there watching her every move. It made her nervous. Tracy turned and looked at Will.

"Are the cattle still gathered up around the water hole?" she asked, trying to make casual conversation while getting things ready to make breakfast.

"Yes, Ma'am."

"Did you put bedrolls on the saddles? It will take us all day to get them moved to the north pasture. We'll be staying there tonight."

"Yes, Ma'am," he replied again, sort of pleased with himself that he was one step ahead of her.

"Did you saddle a horse for me?"

The look on Will's face suddenly went blank. His jaw dropped open and his eyes got as big as saucers. He had done everything to get ready to go except saddle a horse for his boss. It was something so simple and obvious, but he had not thought to do it.

"No, Ma'am," he replied sheepishly.

"I'll tell you what, why don't you go saddle a horse for me and bring it up to the house along with the one you're going to ride. And don't forget to put a bedroll on the saddle for me. By that time I'll have breakfast ready," she said with a smile.

"That's a good idea, Boss. I'll do it right away," Will replied as he quickly turned and left the kitchen.

As soon as he had gone, Tracy went to work preparing breakfast for Will and herself. She was glad he would not be standing there watching her while she fixed it.

The breakfast was simple, but it was good for them and there was plenty to it. She had it fixed and ready to serve by the time Will returned to the house. They sat down to eat.

Will didn't say anything while he busied himself eating. He was not sure if conversation was a part of breakfast or not, not that he was the talkative kind when he had a choice between eating and talking. The one thing he didn't want to do was say something that might cause him to have to fix his own meals, or to eat alone.

"Will, do you know the short cut my father used to take when going to the north pasture from here?" Tracy asked.

"You mean across Spiny Ridge?"

"Yes. Across Spiny Ridge."

"No, Ma'am. But I hear tell it's a hard trail ta travel," he replied as he looked up at her.

"Too hard to take the cattle that way?"

"I ain't never took no cattle that way. Your father used it for gettin' between the north and east pastures in a hurry. Weren't none of us allowed ta use it. I don't even know where it starts. Them cows is already not in the best shape. We could lose some if we try goin' that way," he said, looking a little worried that she might insist they take the short cut.

"We can't afford to lose any cattle," she said thoughtfully. "I guess we'll take the long way."

Tracy noticed a slight smile come over Will's face as he let out a sigh of relief. She got the impression he was pleased with her decision. Tracy was sure Will would have gone through Spiny Ridge if she had insisted, but he wouldn't have liked it. Will reminded her of the old cowboys who rode for the brand and did whatever they were told without question, like it or not.

Tracy looked over at Will. He had cleaned the large plate in front of him, and there were only a few biscuits left in the bowl. He had eaten very well, even using his last biscuit to wipe up the last few morsels on his plate. She was satisfied that she had done her part to make sure he was well fed.

"Did you get enough to eat?" Tracy asked him.

"Yes, Ma'am," he replied. "You cook good enough ta make a fella wanta stay on just for the food.

"Thank you," she said with a grin as she stood up.

Tracy picked up her plate and took it over to the sink. As she turned around, she noticed that Will had stood up and was picking up his plate. She was a little surprised to see the big man was so willing to help her in the kitchen.

"You don't need to help," she said.

"I ain't got nothin' ta do 'til we leave. If I help, we can get goin' sooner," he suggested.

"Okay, I'll wash and you can dry," Tracy said, agreeing with his logic.

Tracy smiled at him, then turned and started to run water in the sink. As she prepared to wash, Will cleared the rest of the table.

"You'll need ta tell me where ta put thin's," Will said.

"Just put the clean dishes on the counter," she replied as she started washing. "It will be faster if I put them away."

"Yes, Ma'am," he replied.

It didn't take very long before they were done. Tracy couldn't help but think that Will was a very special sort of cowboy. A lot of the cowboys she had known over the years wouldn't be any help at all in the kitchen. They would think it was woman's work, not to be done by man.

It was then she remembered he had gone to jail for killing a man, but she had to wonder what the man had done to cause Will to become so violent. After working so closely to him, he didn't seem to her to be the violent type. He was rather slow in his ability to think which made her think it would have taken a lot to get him mad.

Once they were done in the kitchen, Will took the saddlebags and went outside while Tracy hung the dishtowel up to dry, put the clean dishes away and turned off the lights. When she went outside, she found Will sitting in the saddle ready to go to work. She was sure that work was all the big man knew.

"Ready to get started?" Tracy asked as she untied the reins to her horse.

"Yes, Ma'am," he replied.

"Well, I guess we best get a move on," she said with a smile after swinging up into the saddle.

Tracy reined her horse back and swung it around. She kicked the horse gently in the ribs and it started off at a gallop across the yard. She looked to her left and there was Will, riding a little behind her as if he was following the boss. Tracy smiled to herself then motioned for him to come up beside her.

As they rode out toward the east pasture, Tracy looked up at the sky. Off to the east the sky was a light blue. Off to the west the sky was still dark and the morning star could still be seen as clearly as if it were the middle of the night. To anyone else it would have been an almost perfect morning with its clear skies, a cool morning breeze and the promise of plenty of sunshine. But to Tracy it was the kind of morning that promised another day of hot, dry weather that would make the already drought conditions worse on the ranch.

By the time they were getting close to where the herd had been gathered, the sun was starting to spread its light across the wide open plains. As they came over a little rise in the vast prairie, they could see the cattle gathered around a watering hole.

As they approached the cattle, it was easy to see why the cattle had to be moved. The grass had been eaten so short by the cattle that there was so little left it would not be long before they would starve. The nearby watering hole had very little water left in it. It would be completely dry within a couple of days if the cattle weren't moved.

Tracy reined up and Will stopped beside her. She sat there looking at the cattle for a minute or two before she looked over at Will.

"I think we should go over that way," she said as she pointed to where she wanted to start.

"We can start moving them slowly away from the watering hole. There may be a few that will not want to leave, but we will have to make them," Tracy added as she looked at Will.

"Yes, Ma'am," he replied.

"Let's move them slowly. We don't need to cause them any more stress than necessary," she reminded Will.

Will simply nodded his head and gently nudged his horse forward. As the two of them slowly moved closer to the cattle, they spread out away from each other. They didn't want to scare the cattle and have them run off in all directions. If that happened, it could take hours to get them together again. With only the two of them to move the cattle, they needed to keep the cattle calm. More importantly, they needed to keep them bunched up and moving.

Except for one or two that tried to run back to the watering hole, they were able to gently nudge the cattle away from the watering hole and off across the open pasture toward the north pasture. Those that tried to stay at the watering hole were quickly rounded up and gently but firmly pushed back in with the others.

By mid morning, the sun was starting to give Tracy some idea of how hot it was going to be. Tracy had seen a couple of small dust devils off in the distance, but she was too busy keeping the cattle moving in the right direction to pay much attention to them.

By noon, Tracy was already hot and tired. The shower she had taken earlier in the morning may have helped her start her day, but she was already feeling dirty and sweaty as if she had not taken a shower for weeks. Her throat was dry and felt like it was full of dust and dirt.

As her horse moved along with the cattle, she reached for the canteen on her saddle. Without stopping, she opened the canteen and put it to her lips. She took a mouth full of the lukewarm water and washed it around inside her mouth before swallowing it. Even though the water was not cold, it felt good and seemed to wash some of the dust and dirt from her mouth. She closed the canteen and hung it back on the saddle horn.

They didn't stop for lunch. There was no time for that. They had to get the cattle to the north pasture before sunset if they planned to keep them together.

After a while, she pulled back on the reins of her horse, stopped and stepped out of the saddle. As she took her canteen off the saddle horn, she could see Will about a hundred yards away rein up his horse and look toward her. She was sure he was wondering if she was having trouble with something.

She removed her hat and held it upside down in one hand as she poured some water in the hat. Her horse drank the water quickly. When it was finished, she tipped her hat over and poured what little water was left inside over the horse's head. The horse shook its head as if in appreciation. She then hung the canteen back on the saddle horn and returned to the saddle.

Once she was back in the saddle and back in position to keep the herd moving, she saw Will stop and get off his horse to give it some water. She smiled as she watched him take a drink, too.

It was early evening when they finally crested the last hill and started down toward the old barn and the watering troughs. At this point there was no need to keep the cattle together. There was water and food for them there and they knew it. They could smell the water and began moving faster toward the watering troughs.

Once they reached the barn and the watering troughs, Tracy stepped out of the saddle. Since one of the troughs was along one side of a corral, she put her horse inside the corral. She took the saddle off her horse and put it over the fence, then removed the bridle and put it over the saddle.

Neither she nor Will had eaten since breakfast. It had been a long day and they were both feeling very hungry and tired.

"Will, would you mind taking care of the horses while I fix us something to eat?" Tracy asked as he rode up next to the corral.

"Okay, Ma'am. I could sure use somethin' ta eat before we head back," he said as he stepped out of the saddle.

"We're not going back tonight," she reminded him. "It's too late to get back before it gets dark."

Will looked at her as if she had lost her mind. What would people think if she spent the night out there with him? He wasn't sure it was a good idea.

"You mean we're stayin' the night, here, together?" he asked looking a little confused.

"Sure," she replied. "The horses need a bit of a rest and the cattle aren't going anywhere. They have grass and water. Tomorrow we'll put some hay out for the cattle to help them get their strength back."

"Yes, Ma'am," he replied, still not sure about this.

"It's okay, Will. I'll sleep in the hayloft and you can sleep on the ground floor of the barn," she explained.

"Okay," he replied, but he still didn't sound too convinced that it would be okay with anyone else.

While Will got the cattle settled down and took care of the horses, Tracy cleared a place in the corral where there wasn't anything but dirt and built a small fire. She was careful not to let the fire get very big as a range fire would not only cause a lot of damage, it would certainly mean the end of the ranch. There was hardly enough grass for grazing without burning it off.

She fixed a basic meat, beans and biscuit dinner like they did out on the open range in the old days. It wasn't fancy, but it tasted good and filled the stomach.

By the time dinner was over and everything had been cleaned up, it was already dark. Tracy was tired and so was Will. Tracy bid Will goodnight then took her bedroll and went into the barn. She climbed up into the loft and spread her bedroll out on the hay. She removed her boots and laid down. The last thing she heard was Will on the ground floor of the barn rustling around as he made himself a place to lie down for the night.

Tracy's last thoughts were of Will and his concern about being out there overnight with her. She smiled to herself as she thought about it. She had been nervous earlier about being alone with him, but after spending the day working with him, she was no longer afraid of him. Besides, she was too tired to worry about what anyone else might think.

CHAPTER FOUR

Even as tired as Tracy was, she spent a good deal of the night tossing and turning. Just before dawn she was awakened by something moving around inside the loft of the barn. She opened her eyes and began slowly looking around, but it was still too dark for her to figure out what, or who it might be. The only light that was filtering into the barn was from what was left of the three-quarter moon in the early morning darkness. The last thing she wanted to do was frighten an animal that might panic and bite her; so she laid very still for what seemed like forever.

Unable to hold still any longer, she slowly turned her head to look over her shoulder. There in the faint shadows she saw the outline of a large man against the opened loft door. Seeing a man so close to her in the dark caused her chest to tighten with fear, and her breath to come in short gasps. In the dark, the figure looked very intimidating, even dangerous.

"Who is it?" she demanded nervously, hardly able to get the words out.

"It's me, Ma'am," Will replied.

"What are you doing up here? You scared the hell out of me," she said as she sat up.

"I was just checkin' on you, Ma'am. I heard you tossin' and turnin' up here. I was just makin' sure you was all right," he said, not sure if he had done the right thing or not.

"I'm fine and I don't need you checking on me. Go back down the ladder," she said with as much authority in her voice as she could muster.

"Yes, Ma'am," he replied softly.

Tracy could see his shadowy figure in the loft door suddenly disappear. For a few seconds she wasn't sure if he had really gone back down the ladder. It wasn't until she heard his footsteps on the hard dirt floor of the barn that she was convinced he was gone.

She laid back down and let out a sigh of relief. Tracy had not expected Will to come up into the loft. If he had actually been up in the loft for the reason he said, she had spoken to him rather harshly; but he had scared her.

Tracy tried to close her eyes in the hope of getting a little more sleep before the sun came up. Sleep did not come to her, even after she could hear what sounded like Will snoring again.

Having Will suddenly appear in the loft only a few feet from her, had shaken her more than she wanted to admit. Tracy didn't know why she was so afraid of him. He had been as nice to her as anyone she had ever met. He had even helped her with the dishes before they left the ranch house.

After giving it some thought, it occurred to her that she was still afraid of him. The reason being was that she was afraid of the unknown. She began to think that maybe he was in the loft for no other reason than to check on her and make sure she was all right. He seemed to be the sort of man who would protect a woman from harm, not the sort who would inflict any harm on a woman.

Tracy really didn't know very much about Will. What little she did know was not all that clear. For one thing, she had no idea what had caused a man who seemed to be as gentle as Will to become so violent that he could kill a man with his bare hands. She vaguely remembered hearing that he had killed the man over a woman, but she had no idea what the circumstances had been.

It also occurred to Tracy that she was still not one hundred percent sure she should trust Will, but what choice did she have? She didn't have the money to pay for any more ranch hands. The ones she had had already quit because she couldn't pay them, except for Will. Up to now she had no real reason to fear him, but that didn't seem to matter. Everything she knew about him she had heard from those who were afraid of him. She wasn't even sure how much of what she had heard was true.

Tracy laid on the bedroll and listened to every sound in the early morning hours as she thought about Will. She could identify some of the sounds like the cows chewing hay close to the barn, the horses in the corral shuffling around in the dry dirt, and the ruffle of wings of an owl that had made his home in the rafters of the barn only to have its peace disturbed by the humans who had moved in.

It seemed like it took hours before the sky to the east began to get lighter indicating the sun would be up soon. When the sun started spreading its golden glow over the land, Tracy felt she should get up. It was then she remembered that she needed to fix Will his breakfast.

Tracy stood up and brushed off what dust and hay she could from her clothes. She was wishing there was some place for her to take a shower or a bath, but the only place to find water out there was in one of the watering troughs next to the two wells that were still able to produce water. What few creeks that ran across the pasture had already dried up or had nothing but mud in them. She knew she would have to share the troughs with the cattle and the horses if she wanted to take a bath in them, a thought that didn't appeal to her.

Letting out a sigh of disappointment, she gathered up her bedroll and draped it over her arm as she walked toward the ladder. Before starting down the ladder, she looked down. She could see Will near the base of the ladder. She watched him as he picked up a square bale of hay and carried it outside. He seemed to carry the bale of hay with such ease that it reminded her of his strength. As soon as he had gone outside with it, she climbed down the ladder.

Tracy took her bedroll outside, shook the dust and bits of hay out of it and then draped it over the corral fence to air. She then went to the same place in the corral where she had built a small fire the night before and started another fire.

It wasn't long before the smell of bacon and eggs and hot strong coffee began to fill the warm morning air around the barn. Squatting down next to the fire, Tracy stirred the scrambled eggs. They were almost ready. She looked around but did not see Will anywhere in sight. He had put out some hay for the cows and had fed and watered the horses. She also noticed the cattle had not spread out very far. As long as they had food and water there was no need for them to wonder off in search of it.

"Will," she called out. "Breakfast is ready."

It was only a matter of a few minutes before he came around the corner of the barn and into the corral. He had a smile on his face as if he was glad to see she was not mad at him and that she had made breakfast for him. He picked up a plate and a cup from the saddlebags hanging on the fence and walked over close to the fire. He knelt down and held out his plate while Tracy filled it with bacon, eggs and two large biscuits. She then poured him a cup of hot coffee.

Thank you, Ma'am," he said.

Will stood up and walked over to a bale of hay just inside the barn door where he could sit down out of the morning sun to eat his breakfast. He immediately began to eat.

Tracy filled a plate for herself, filled a cup with coffee and then went into the barn. She sat down on a bale of hay a few feet away from Will and began to eat. Neither of them talked while they were eating.

Tracy glanced over at Will every once in awhile. He was shoving his food into his mouth and chasing it down with coffee. He didn't seem to be enjoying his meal. It was more like he was eating because he had to in order to do his work. It wasn't long before he was draining the last couple of drops of coffee from his cup.

"Will," she said to get his attention. "There's no hurry."

He looked at her as if he didn't know what she meant.

"You can take your time eating if you want. The cattle are fine and there is nothing you have to do that can't wait until you finish eating," she explained.

"Is it all right if I have some more coffee then?" he asked shyly.

"Certainly. Help yourself," she said with a smile.

Will stood up and walked over to the fire. He poured himself another cup of coffee, set the pot back next to the fire and returned to the bale of hay. He then sipped at the hot liquid in his cup, taking his time.

Tracy relaxed over her second cup of coffee, too. She knew she had a long ride back to the ranch house to get her father's one-ton stake truck, go into town for supplies and then return with them. It would have been nice if Jacob had stayed on just one more day. It would have saved her having to make the ride back to the ranch house for the truck and supplies. She could have taken the truck into town, picked up the supplies and then met Jacob and Will at the north pasture barn. It would have been impossible to herd the cattle with the truck and one rider on horseback.

"I guess I had better get started back for the supplies," Tracy said as she poured out what little coffee remained in her cup.

"You be careful," Will said.

"You, too. I'll be back by dinnertime. You should have plenty to eat until I get back."

"These cows ain't goin' ta want ta wonder off very far with water and food here," Will said. "They don't need much watchin'."

"That's good, because I want you to ride the fence line and check it out. If we have any fence down, do what you can to repair it," she instructed him.

"Yes, Ma'am. I'll get on it as soon as I get cleaned up around here," he replied.

"Good. You be careful out there. I won't be back until late, probably just before dark," she reminded him.

"Yes, Ma'am."

Tracy walked across the corral and untied her horse from the corral rail. She was glad Will had saddled the horse for her, but she really didn't want to get back in the saddle so soon. It had been a long ride yesterday and she was feeling it. Putting her butt in the saddle again was not her idea of the best way to spend the day.

The fact that she would be able to take a bath and wash off the dirt and dust when she got back to the ranch house didn't pass through her mind unnoticed, either. All Tracy could think about at the moment was getting back to the ranch house and climbing into a nice cool bath. It would feel so good to sit in a tub and soothe her sore muscles.

Reluctantly, she walked her horse out of the corral. She slipped her foot in the stirrup and swung herself into the saddle. As she sat in the saddle, she turned and looked back over her shoulder. She noticed that Will had already put out the fire and was putting things away. All was well except for the long ride back to the ranch house.

Tracy nudged the horse in the ribs with her boots and started off across the prairie. She let the horse trot for a little while in the clear, cool morning air, but as the temperature quickly rose, she slowed the horse down. There was no need to kill the horse just so she could get to a bath, she thought.

As she rode across the prairie, she took time to look around. Her heart sank as she thought about how it could very well be the year the ranch went under. One look at the sky told her there would not be any relief from the drought today. There was not a single cloud in the sky, and there was no breeze to indicate that some much needed rain would be blown in anytime soon.

The prairie grasses were as brown and lifeless as she had ever seen. They were short and brittle. There was almost nothing left for the cattle to eat. Even if rain did come, it might very well be too little and too late. What they needed was a steady rainfall that would last several days and soak into the dry lifeless ground.

Even the hay fields were not looking good. They had gotten one early cutting and it hadn't been very much. If they didn't get at least two more fairly good cuttings, or one excellent cutting before winter set in, there was little hope of having a ranch by next spring. Hay was scarce all over the northern part of the country. Many of the ranchers that could afford it were shipping it in from other parts of the country where hay could be found.

Tracy hated to use the hay that had been stored in the old barn, but what choice did she have. There was none in the area to buy; and even if there was, she didn't have the money to buy it. If things didn't change soon, she would have to sell off the remaining cattle and then sell the ranch.

The ride back to the ranch house took a lot less time than the ride out to the north pasture since she didn't have to herd a bunch of cattle that didn't want to go. It was quite a relief to see the ranch house in the distance. She knew it would mean a cool bath.

As she rode toward the ranch house, she noticed a pickup truck parked in front of the barn. At first she thought it might be Jacob. She wondered if he might have changed his mind about going to work for the Clausen Ranch. But as she got closer she began to realize the pickup truck was too new and too nice to belong to Jacob. In fact, it looked like a brand new pickup truck.

Tracy began to wonder who had come by the ranch and what they wanted. She knew that her questions would not be answered until she got to the ranch house. Tracy set her horse into an easy trot.

Just as she rounded the corner through the fence, she saw a man come out of the barn and walk toward the pickup. He was wearing jeans, boots and a work shirt as well as a cowboy hat. Since he had his back to her, it took her a minute or two to realize that it was Tom Norbert. She wondered what he was doing nosing around in her barn.

As he stepped up to his pickup and opened the door, Tom heard the sound of a horse trotting toward him. He immediately closed the door and turned around. He saw Tracy coming toward him. He smiled.

Tracy rode up to the barn and stopped. She stepped out of the saddle and wrapped the reins over the top fence rail. She then turned and started walking toward Tom with a determined and angry look on her face. She was not happy to see him there.

"What are you doing here?" she asked rather sharply.

"Whoa. I heard that Jacob quit and went to work somewhere else. I thought you might like an extra hand for a day or so," he said with a grin.

"I do need an extra hand, but aren't you afraid of getting your hands dirty."

"Wait a minute," he said sharply. "I know how to work on a ranch just as well as you. I came out to give you some help."

"Help with what. Inventory the ranch so you know what you can sell to get your money out of it," she said.

"That's not fair. I came out to help you. That's all. If you don't want my help, all you have to do is say so. You don't have to be nasty about it," he said, his voice showing how angry he was getting.

"I don't want your help," she said sharply, then turned around.

Tracy started toward the house. She wanted help more than anything, but not from him. With him there had always been a price, and she was afraid of what that price might be.

Tom stood there for a second before he ran after her. When he caught up with her, he grabbed her by the arm and swung her around. After grabbing both her arms, he held her out in front of him and looked into her eyes.

Tracy stared into his eyes. She could see the anger in them as he looked at her. She knew he wanted to say something to her, but she wasn't sure what. She was afraid to say anything as she felt she had pushed him too far already.

Suddenly, he pulled her up against his broad chest and leaned down and kissed her hard on the lips. She could feel the strength in his hands as he pulled her up against him. She could also feel her breasts pressed against his strong chest and the heat from his lips as he pressed them hard against hers.

Tracy knew she should push him away, but she couldn't. In her mind she wanted to, but her body wouldn't let her. Instead, she let him kiss her and let the feel of his strength flow through her entire body.

Just as suddenly as he had grabbed her, he let her go. Without a single word, Tom turned sharply and marched off toward his pickup. When he got to his pickup, he got in and started the engine. It was only a matter of seconds before he stepped on the gas and the pickup truck sprang to life. The tires threw dirt out behind the pickup truck as he sped toward the road.

Tracy just stood there in the ranch yard watching as he drove through the gate and out onto the road. Slowly, she reached up and touched her lips with the tips of her fingers. It was strange, but she could not ever remember being kissed like that before. Her lips still burned with the fiery passion he had shown in his kiss even though he was gone.

In a daze, she turned toward the ranch house and slowly started moving toward it. She never once took her eyes off the cloud of dust that Tom's truck was kicking up as he sped down the dirt road toward the highway to town.

When she got to the porch, she saw Tom's truck disappear behind a hill. Tracy stared off across the land toward the last place she had seen his truck. For several minutes after he was out of sight, she was unable to put the feel of his body as he held her against him, or get the fire of his kiss out of her mind.

All of a sudden, she realized where she was standing. She swung around and looked to see if anyone had seen her reaction to his kiss. Tracy quickly became conscious of the fact that there was no reason for her to feel embarrassed. There was no one around to see what had happened. In fact, she wasn't sure what had happened. All she knew was that she was feeling something, something very different from anything she had ever felt before.

Tracy turned back around and went up the steps to the porch. She took one last look in the direction Tom had gone before she went inside the house. Tracy went to the refrigerator and took out the pitcher of lemonade. She then walked to the cabinet and got out a glass.

Tracy held the pitcher of lemonade in her hand for the longest time as she stared at the cupboard directly in front of her. Her mind was so confused and so mixed up she could hardly think. It slowly began to creep into her consciousness that she had liked being kissed by Tom. His kiss had touched her deeply. It had touched every nerve in her body with its burning passion.

Tracy mentally shook herself. She knew it would do no good to think like that. She had too many things to do and too many responsibilities to let herself get involved with the likes of Tom Norbert, of all people. Besides, she was convinced that any relationship with him was destined to end in heartbreak and bad feelings on both sides.

Tracy suddenly realized that she had not taken care of her horse, and that she was standing there with a pitcher of lemonade in one hand and a glass in the other. She didn't even remember getting the lemonade out of the refrigerator.

She turned back around and put the pitcher back in the refrigerator. She then left the ranch house and started walking back toward the barn. As she walked across the yard, she resolved that she would forget what had just happened, and she would put Tom out of her mind immediately. Yet, she found herself looking off toward the road where he had gone as she walked toward the barn.

Her resolve to forget about Tom didn't work very well. All the time she was taking care of her horse, she could not get the look in Tom's eyes just before he kissed her out of her mind. They reminded her of the eyes of a predator, hungry and ready to devour her.

Deep in her heart she knew that to forget him, and the way he had kissed her, would be easier said than done. Even at this moment, she could not get him completely out of her mind. A cool shower and some soothing time in a cool tub might help, at least a little, she thought.

After taking care of her horse, Tracy returned to the house and went directly to the kitchen. She once again picked up the pitcher of lemonade from the refrigerator and was about to pour herself a glass, but stopped. She stood silently staring at the wall in front of her. Her mind would still not let go of her image of Tom's face after he kissed her and before he let go of her. It was etched in her mind like a design etched in glass.

Tracy set the glass and the pitcher of lemonade down on the counter without pouring any of the cool liquid into the glass. She turned and walked toward her bedroom in sort of a stupor.

Once in her bedroom, Tracy stripped off her clothes without thinking about it. Her mind was too occupied with thoughts of Tom to allow her to know what she was doing. She left her clothes in a pile on the floor as she turned and walked into the bathroom.

She turned on the shower. After making sure the water was cold, she drew back the shower curtain. Although she was unable to think clearly otherwise, there was no doubt in her mind that what she needed was something to help her get Tom off her mind, and a very cold shower seemed to be the answer.

Tracy stepped into the shower. She let out a cry and took in a deep breath as the cold water hit her naked body. She had not expected it to be so cold that it made her want to jump out of the shower, but she didn't. Instead, she stood there shivering while the cold water splashed down on her head and cascaded down the smooth curves of her body. It took her a little while before she could stand in the shower and still keep breathing.

Once she had adjusted to the cold, she reached around and took the soap from the wire basket hooked to the showerhead. She began washing away the dust and dirt of yesterday's cattle drive and the long ride back to the ranch house. She only hoped it would also wash any thoughts of Tom from her mind as well. It felt good as she rubbed the soap over her cool skin.

With the combination of the cold water and the soft fragrance of the soap, she began to slowly unwind. She had not realized how much internal conflict Tom had caused her by kissing her so hard.

As she rubbed the soap over her arms where Tom had held her, she could sense the feeling of them as if his strong hands were still holding onto her. That alone began to awaken the feeling of his warm lips pressed hard against hers. She could not help but close her eyes and replay in her mind what had happened to her when he kissed her. She reached up and touched her lips as she thought about it, unable to let the sensations she had felt leave her mind.

Suddenly her eyes flew open and her fingers moved quickly away from her lips. Although her heart liked having him kiss her, her head was telling her not to let him ever get that close again. He had touched her soul and it frightened her.

"Damn you," she said out loud, cursing Tom for awakening feelings in her that she had wanted left buried deep in the recesses of her mind.

Tracy quickly rinsed the soap off her body and stepped out of the shower. She grabbed a large towel off the rack and dried her face. As she began to dry herself, she could see her reflection in the full-length mirror on the back of the door. It startled her at first, as if someone had suddenly shown up unexpectedly in the bathroom with her. It caused her to stop and look at herself for a minute.

What she saw in the mirror was a full-grown woman with firm full breasts, a narrow waist, flat stomach and smooth shapely hips that tapered into long shapely legs. She could hardly believe what she was seeing. There was no doubt in her mind that the person she was looking at in the mirror was all woman, a real woman.

"Why do you act like a silly school girl when you look like a woman? Why do you fall apart when you are around that man?" she asked herself, not even able to mention his name for fear all the feelings she had for him would come rushing back again.

She had no answers to her questions. There was something about him that she could not seem to resist. Even in high school she had difficulty resisting his advances, but she had managed to keep him at arms length most of the time back then. Why was she having so much trouble now? By all rights, she should be smarter and in much better control of herself and her future, but that didn't seem to be the case. She certainly didn't feel as if she was in control of anything at the moment.

There was no doubt Tom Norbert was handsome, but he was more than that to her. He was strong and well educated. He wasn't some macho cowboy that had to prove how good he was at everything to anyone who challenged his ability to be a man.

From what Tracy had seen of him after she returned to the ranch, he had grown up a great deal. If anything, he was better looking than before. He seemed more confident in himself, and he was more of a man than most of the single or married men she knew. He didn't seem to be so possessive, selfish or conceited as he had in high school. She began to realize that she had not given him much of a chance to show her what he had become over the years.

Although, she found him attractive, as most women would, he was still a banker. In fact, he was the banker who held the lien against the Lazy A Ranch. That made having any kind of personal relationship with him not only difficult, but it made it impossible as far as she was concerned. To have any kind of a personal relationship with him under their current situation was to ask for it to fail.

"Get it together," she said as she took one last look at her reflection in the mirror.

Tracy left the bathroom with the towel wrapped around herself. As she walked into her bedroom, she still could not get Tom completely off her mind no matter how hard she tried.

Once in her bedroom, she dressed in a nice pair of jeans that hugged her hips and shapely behind. She picked out a blouse that even she thought looked good on her. After slipping into her good boots, she grabbed up her purse and started out the door.

CHAPTER FIVE

Tracy went around to the side of the house where her father's old stake truck was parked. She got in and put the key in the ignition. The truck didn't start the first or even the second time, but it did finally start. She put the truck in gear and pulled away from the house. She drove out onto the road and started for town to get the supplies that Will would need in order to stay out on the north pasture with the cattle. While he was there, he would fix fences and make sure the cattle were taken care of and safe from predators.

It was almost thirty miles to the nearest town. Close to fifteen miles of the trip into town was on dirt and gravel roads. With the dry conditions, even driving slow would produce a dust cloud that could be seen for miles.

The drive into town was not easy on such a hot day. The air conditioning in her father's old stake truck was broken. She had not had the time nor the money to get it fixed. To say the least, it was an uncomfortable ride. By the time she pulled up and diagonally parked the truck in front of the local grocery store on Main Street, she felt as if she had not had a shower for days.

As she got out of the truck, she looked across the street toward the bank. She wondered if Tom was in his nice air-conditioned office, or if he had decided to go somewhere else. It was then that she saw his new pickup truck parked in front of the bank. She bet he had air conditioning in his truck and that it worked. It better, she thought to herself, because the truck was a shiny black pickup. It was not the best color for days like they had been having, hot and dry.

* * * *

At that moment, Tom happened to glance out the tinted glass window of his office and saw Tracy as she turned to go into the grocery store. He had not seen her while she was looking at his office or his pickup truck.

As he watched her go into the store, he thought about how good she looked in jeans. He could not think of any other woman he had ever met that looked so sexy in jeans.

Tom thought about going across the street to the store and talking to her, but he had second thoughts on the idea. After what had happened earlier at the Lazy A Ranch, he had some reservations about confronting her in public. He didn't want the same kind of scene they had had at the ranch played out again in front of the whole town. The one thing he remembered about her from high school was that she had a temper; and from the way he had been treated at the ranch, she still had it.

He turned back away from the window and tried to return to his work. He found it hard to concentrate on anything as thoughts of Tracy continued to plague his mind. Tom had not planned to be in the office today. In fact, he had planned to be out at the Lazy A Ranch helping Tracy with her chores, but that hadn't worked out. With nothing else to do when he returned home from the ranch, he changed into what he usually wore to the bank and went to his office. He figured that working would help him get Tracy off his mind.

The idea had worked for a little while, but it went up in smoke when he saw her in town. He couldn't believe how much of a distraction she was for him. Tom was finding it very hard not to think about her. For all the good it was doing him to be in the bank, he might as well have gone fishing. He would have accomplished just as much, maybe more. Even if he didn't catch any fish, at least he would not have been there to see her, he thought.

Tom got so frustrated because he could not concentrate on his work that he slammed the file in front of him closed and pushed back away from the desk. Tom leaned back in his chair, put his hands behind his head and looked up at the ceiling. He spent the next few minutes watching the old fashioned ceiling fan slowly turn around and around and around as he wondered how it was that she had that kind of an affect on him.

While watching the fan his mind drifted back to when he had dated Tracy in high school. He remembered that he had liked her and thought she was the most beautiful girl in the world. He had wanted her more than anything, but she always refused his advances.

Tom remembered the time Tracy had slapped his face when he tried to get his hand under her blouse. She had slapped him so hard that he wanted to cry. He wasn't sure if it was because he was angry that she had turned down his advances, or if he was ashamed of himself for trying to force her to make love to him. Either way, it had been embarrassing and it was something that he would never forget. In fact, he was so embarrassed that he had had a hard time working up the nerve to apologize to her. He remembered coming home from college one weekend in the hope of seeing her so he could apologize to her. It had taken him a long time to work up the nerve to ask her to forgive him and give him a second chance. But when he went to see her, she had already left for college.

As Tom thought about that night, he wondered if that one incident had ruined any chance he might have had with her. He had to admit that he had been rather conceited and arrogant when he was younger. However, his time at college had changed him and made him realize that he had nothing to be arrogant or conceited about.

The years he spent away at college had instilled a good deal of confidence in himself. He had learned that people have feelings, and they should be respected. It had also showed him that he had left behind the one woman that he had ever loved. He had not realized how much he really loved her until he didn't have her around anymore. He missed not being able to see her every day.

He had moved back to his home town after college and taken a position at his father's bank in the hope that she might someday return. The day she returned was the first time in several years that Tom thought there might still be hope in the world. He quickly found out that she had never married and she didn't have a boyfriend. Tom was also hopeful that she would start going out with him again.

The one depressing thought was that Tom knew even if Tracy did start going out with him again, he would have trouble with his mother. He was well aware of what his mother thought of the Atwater family, and of Tracy in particular. She had told him enough times. She believed that Tracy was not good enough for her son, and that the Atwater family was below them. Tom may have grown a lot while at college, but his mother's dislike for the poor ranchers of the area had only gotten worse over the years.

His mother had always been afraid her son would get Tracy into the back seat of his car and end up having to marry her. If that happened, she just knew it would put a blemish on the Norbert family's good name forever.

Tom's mother was pleased when her son went to a different college than the one Tracy decided to attend. Tom's mother was sure he would find a nice, well-educated girl from an influential family at college to marry. She was surprised and disappointed when Tom had decided to return from college in California to work in his father's bank without having that perfect girl to marry. She was even more surprised when Tracy returned to take over her father's ranch. Tom's mother had hoped that the ranch would be sold; and she would never again have to see "that Atwood girl" again, as she called her.

Since Tracy had returned to the area, Tom's mother had started worrying about him getting back together with her. Since he had not married, his mother wanted her son to marry Mr. Slocum's daughter. The Slocums were well off from oil found on their ranch. The Slocums didn't get their hands dirty raising cattle any more. They had money, and that was all it took to be in the good graces of Tom's mother. The Slocum girl was pretty and a few years younger than Tom. She had only a couple of years of college at a local community college, but she was from the "right family".

* * * *

Tom turned and looked out the window again. He could see Tracy coming out of the grocery store with a couple of large grocery bags. He straightened up and watched her every move as she loaded the bags of groceries into the truck.

When Tracy went back inside, Tom continued to look at the truck. He wanted more than anything to talk to her and explain why he had been at the ranch that morning. If he could only get her to sit down with him and listen to him for just a couple of minutes, he would make her understand that he wanted nothing more than to help her and make life a little easier for her.

His thoughts were interrupted when he saw her come back out of the grocery store again with a couple more bags. He watched her as she glanced over at the bank before getting into the truck. Tom was sure she was wondering if he was in his office. He knew Tracy would not be able to see in his office because of the dark tinted windows.

Tracy had glanced up at the window of the bank. She thought about going over to Tom's office and telling him that she was sorry she had run him off. It only took her a second to decide it might not be a good idea. She didn't want to stir up the same emotions again that she had managed to get under control, so far.

She put the bags in the truck and got in. Tracy reached down and turned the ignition key. The truck made a funny growling noise followed by a loud bang. After that the truck motor would not even turn over, it simply groaned as if in pain. Tracy tried it again and again, but the truck refused to start. In frustration, Tracy hit the steering wheel.

"Damn," she said as she slumped over the steering wheel almost in tears.

It was obvious her father had not taken very good care of the old truck, but then she had not done anything with it, either. She had not had the money to take care of things. The result was what should have been expected, but why did it have to happen now, at that moment.

Tom could see from his window that she was having some kind of problem. He wasn't sure what it was, but she was obviously very upset about it. It didn't take him long to figure out that she couldn't get the old truck started.

Without even thinking about it, he got up and started out of the bank. But when he got to the front door, he stopped. She had made it clear she didn't want his help. He was sure she couldn't afford to get the old truck fixed, and it was too far to walk back to the ranch. Like it or not, she needed help from someone.

Tom decided it was time to help her even if she didn't want any help from him. He pushed open the door of the bank and went out onto the street.

As Tom started across the street, Tracy caught a glimpse of him in the rearview mirror coming toward her. She let out a long sigh as she wondered what else could possibly go wrong today. He was the last person she wanted to see right now.

Tom stepped up to the driver's door and looked inside at Tracy. She had her hands on the top of the steering wheel and her forehead resting on her hands.

"Is there anything I can do to help?" he asked, his voice showing nothing but kindness toward her and his willingness to help if he could.

Tracy slowly raised her head up off her hands and turned to look at him. She had tears running down her cheeks. She asked herself, why was he always coming to her rescue?

Tom reached into the pocket of his suit coat and pulled out a clean white handkerchief. He handed it to her. From the look in her eyes, he was sure that she was tired as well as frustrated. Keeping the ranch going had to be difficult enough for her; but with the added facts that her father was so ill in a nursing home and that the hired hands had quit, it was not hard for Tom to understand why she looked so tired.

Reluctantly, Tracy accepted the handkerchief from him and wiped the tears from her face. She then leaned back and let out another long sigh.

"What can I do to help?" Tom asked again.

Tracy looked at him. The expression on his face showed her that he really was concerned and he did want to help. She had hoped it would not come to this, but what else could she do? She had to get the supplies out to Will, and Tom was the only one who seemed to be willing to help her.

"Can you get my truck started?" Tracy asked, the tone of her voice showing that she was really pleading for help.

"I don't know. Move over and I'll give it a try."

Tracy scooted across the seat so Tom had room to get in. She watched him as he looked at the dash of the truck and reached for the ignition key. She knew if he started the truck she would be so embarrassed that she would want to die. But if he didn't get the truck started, how was she going to get the supplies to Will?

Tom turned the key and the old truck made a grinding noise that didn't sound good at all, and the truck did not start. In fact, it sounded very expensive to Tracy. She looked at Tom hoping he would be able to start it, but deep down knew it was not going to start.

Tom turned and looked at her. He didn't want to have to tell her there was no way anyone was going to get the truck started. It sounded to him as if the timing chain may have slipped or was possibly broken.

"I'm sorry," he said. "I think it's the timing chain."

"Is that serious?" she asked, hoping he would say it was nothing, but deep down she knew better.

"I'm afraid so. It will probably take a couple of days to get it fixed."

Tracy turned her head and looked out the windshield of the truck. Tears came to her eyes and began to roll down her cheeks again. How was she going to get the supplies to Will in the north pasture? It was the last straw. She could no longer control her emotions and broke down and cried openly.

Tom had always hated to see her cry. He waited while she slowly gathered her emotions and tried to get them under control.

"What can I do to help?" Tom asked once again.

Tracy turned and looked at him. The last thing she wanted was to ask him for help, but she really had no choice. If she didn't get the supplies out to Will, he would have nothing to eat. If he had nothing to eat, he would leave her to go to work someplace else, just like Jacob and the others had done. There was nothing else she could do but ask for his help.

"I need to get these supplies out to Will in the north pasture. Do you know someone who would rent me a truck for a day or two?" she asked knowing that there was no place to rent a truck around there even if she had the money.

"You can take my pickup," he said without thinking.

"I can't take your new truck, and I can't ask you to run these supplies out to Will."

"You don't have to ask. I'm offering you my truck. You can take it. It's right over there and the gas tank is full. I'll get your truck to Les's garage and have him fix it," Tom said.

Tracy just looked at him. She couldn't believe he would loan her his brand new pickup truck. He would never let her drive his car in high school even when he was with her.

"I can't afford to fix it," she said, frustration showing in her voice before she started to cry again.

"Don't cry. I'll take care of it," he promised.

"I can't ask you to do that," she said.

"You didn't. Take my truck. You can keep it until yours is fixed. When your truck is fixed, I'll bring it out to the ranch for you," he said in the hope she wouldn't be so damn stubborn that she couldn't see she had no choice in the matter.

Tracy looked into his eyes. She wanted to believe him. She wanted to believe he was not asking anything of her. It was too good to be true, and she knew what that meant. She also knew she really didn't have a choice. It was either take him up on his offer, or walk the thirty miles back to the ranch.

She turned and looked out the windshield of the old truck. Tracy knew that the truck was hardly worth fixing, but she could not afford a new truck.

Suddenly there was a hand in front of her holding a set of keys. She looked up and saw Tom offering her the keys to his new pickup truck. For the first time in a very long time she felt as if she was trapped. She could see there was no way out.

Reluctantly, she took the keys from him. He smiled at her as he reached back, opened the truck door and got out.

"Let me help you get your groceries into my pickup," he said as stepped back so she could get out of the truck.

"I can't just leave my truck here," Tracy objected.

"I'll take care of it. Now get your things together and put them in my truck," he insisted.

Within a few minutes, Tracy had all her things inside Tom's truck. He then opened the door on the driver's side for her. Tracy got in the truck, then turned and looked at him. She was seeing him in a little different light for the first time. Maybe he had changed, she thought as she closed the door.

After starting the truck and feeling the air conditioning come on and start to fill the cab with cool air, she began to feel a little better. She smiled at him as he stood beside the truck.

"Thank you," she said.

"You better get going," Tom said with a smile.

Tracy put the truck in gear and backed out of the parking space. She glanced at him as he stepped up on the curb and turned to watch her drive away.

Tracy looked in the rearview mirror as she drove down Main Street toward the edge of town. She could see Tom as he stood on the curb and watched her as she drove away in his new pickup truck. She had to wonder what was going through his mind now that he had let her have the use of his truck, but she couldn't worry about that now. She had to get the supplies to Will or he would have nothing to eat.

CHAPTER SIX

The trip back to the ranch was much more comfortable in Tom's air-conditioned truck. However, Tracy's mind was not on her comfort at the moment. She had convinced herself there was going to be a price to pay Tom for letting her use his new pickup truck. The long trip back to the ranch gave her plenty of time to think about all the different ways he might like to collect it.

It wasn't long before she arrived back at the ranch. Now it was time to get busy. There was a lot of work to be done before she would be ready to head back out to the north pasture. Tracy began by taking the supplies out of the pickup and repacking them. She packed some of them in metal boxes that were used to keep the small critters from getting into the food. Some of the food was packed in well-insulated metal boxes with dry ice to keep the food from spoiling in the summer heat.

Once the repacking was done, she loaded the supplies back onto the truck. She got a couple of large containers and loaded them on the truck. She then filled them with water for drinking and cooking. Now she was ready to head out to the old barn in the north pasture where she had set up camp with Will.

The work of loading the truck had been hard. Tracy decided she would have a glass of cold lemonade before setting out. She went back inside and poured herself a glass of lemonade then stood at the door looking outside as she drank it.

Her eyes drifted to Tom's pickup truck. She began to think about the rough ground she would have to cross just to get to the north pasture. Tracy was reluctant to take Tom's new truck out in the field, but what choice did she have. She was sure the truck was probably Tom's pride and joy as it had all the bells and whistles that anyone could put on a full size pickup truck. The last thing she wanted was to be responsible for causing any kind of damage to it.

"It's a four-wheel-drive truck, for crying out loud. It's designed to work and go places without roads," she said to herself as she shook her head in disbelief.

She finished her drink and put her glass in the sink before going out to the truck. Tracy got in and started down toward the pasture gate. She stopped and opened the gate, then got back in the truck. After driving through the gate to the other side of the fence, she stopped again, got out and closed the gate. Returning to the truck, she took a minute to look out over the pasture. There was not a single cow for as far as she could see, as well it should be. They had moved all the cattle to the north pasture.

As she got back in the truck, she smiled at herself. She had been taught from the time she was a little girl to always close the gate after going through it. The opening and closing of gates had become such a habit that even when it was not necessary she still did it. She then started off across the pasture.

Tracy quickly discovered that Tom's new truck could handle the rough pasture much better than her father's old stake truck. The ride was smoother, the pickup had more power and it was a lot more comfortable to ride in than her father's truck. It was certainly a lot more comfortable than riding a horse. The air conditioning made the trip across the open grasslands a far more pleasant experience than the old truck had, not to mention the fact it was cleaner.

When she came down off the hill above the old barn in the north pasture there was still plenty of daylight left. She could not see anyone around. The horse Will had been using was nowhere in sight. When she got to the barn, she parked the truck next to the corral.

As Tracy got out of the truck, she noticed the truck was very dirty. It was covered with a thick coat of gray dust and dirt from the gravel roads and from the dry fields she had driven across. She smiled as she wondered what Tom would think if he could see his truck now. It had been spotless when she left town with it. She thought it might be a good idea if she washed it before she returned it to him.

Tracy took a look around. She quickly saw that the cattle had started to spread out as they looked for places to graze, but then that was the whole idea. The pasture could support the cattle if they spread out, plus it offered them a couple of places to get water.

The fact Will was not around didn't bother Tracy all that much. She knew he was used to working until dark, and he was supposed to be riding the fence line. She would not worry about him until the sun was about to set. He should be back by then.

Tracy went to work building a fire in the corral so she could start fixing dinner. She put a pot on the fire and started to fix a thick stew made with plenty of meat, potatoes and vegetables from the supplies she had picked up in town. She used an old cast iron Dutch oven to make biscuits. It wasn't long before the aroma of her stew and fresh biscuits began to fill the air.

As the sun began to get low in the west, she began to wonder where Will was. She had been sure he would return before dark. She had told him that she would be back to fix him dinner.

Since her stew was ready, she moved it to the side of the fire to keep it warm and made a pot of coffee while she waited for Will. She was growing a little nervous as she looked out over the prairie hoping to see him, but saw nothing but wide-open spaces.

When it had finally gotten dark, she found it hard to see. The only lights to see by came from her fire, and from what little light the half-moon in the clear sky was able to spread over the land. She had decided she should keep the fire going as a light for Will to home in on just in case he had gotten lost in the dark.

Time passed slowly as she paced up and down along the barn and kept watch out over the prairie. He had been gone for far too long to her way of thinking. There were a dozen or more reasons she could think of for Will not to have returned to the barn before dark, none of them good.

It was well past ten and still no Will. She got to thinking about what she would do if she had been out on the range and couldn't get back to the camp before dark. She thought that if she was not hurt in any way, she might camp out for the night and wait until daybreak so she could see her way back. It eased her mind a little to think that Will would probably do the same thing.

Suddenly, she thought of one way to find out if he was prepared to spend the night on the open range. If his bedroll was in the barn, he wasn't prepared for an overnight out there. It may be hot during the day, but it could get a bit on the cool side at night.

Tracy went into the barn and looked around. Will's bedroll was gone. She let out a sigh of relief that he was at least prepared for a night on the ground.

Even with that small bit of relief, she was still worried about him. He was not the brightest person she knew, but she was sure he would know what to do if he was lost and couldn't see his way back. She was also sure he had spent many nights out on the prairie before. The only thing she wasn't sure about was how many of them he had spent alone. Usually, he was with one of the other ranch hands, someone to fix him a meal.

Then she began to think that he might have
misunderstood her and thought she was not going to return
until tomorrow. If that was the case, he would not worry
about getting back tonight. He did have enough to eat if he
wanted to fix something for himself, she remembered. As
long as he was not hurt, he would be all right, she told
herself.

That thought gave her some measure of peace of mind,
but she thought she should at least go up on top of the hill
and see if she could see light from a campfire. Tracy started
up the hill behind the barn. The weather had cooled off
some and it had turned out to be a rather pleasant night.

The walk to the top of the hill was not very long, but it
gave her a chance to look around. The sky was clear and
filled with stars. The Milky Way was easy to see in the clear
Montana sky. It was easy for her to understand why some
people called Montana "Big Sky Country". The sky did
seem to be bigger.

When she reached the top of the hill, she stopped and
looked out over the prairie. Even though it was dark, she
could see hints of lights off in the distance. For the most part
she could figure out whose lights they were. Most of them
were the yard lights at the ranches of her neighbors, some
almost ten miles away.

It crossed her mind that such a clear night should be
shared with someone, someone special. One thought led to
another and before long she found herself thinking of Tom.
She began to remember how she felt when Tom pulled her
up against him and kissed her hard on the lips.

She shook her head in an effort to put him out of her
mind, but her body would not allow it. No matter how hard
she tried, she couldn't get out of her mind the feel of his lips
against hers, and the feel of his hands holding her tightly
against his chest as he kissed her.

"Damn you, Tom," she cursed, not wanting to get emotionally involved with him.

Tracy seemed to have no choice in the matter. Tom was going to be on her mind no matter what she tried to do to prevent it. She quickly decided that since Tom was not around, it would do no harm to let her feelings for him run their course. Maybe if she did, it would help her get him out of her system, though she doubted it.

She sat down on the top of the hill and closed her eyes. Tracy let her mind wonder wherever it wanted to go, and it wanted to go to thoughts of Tom.

The first thing that came to mind was a mental vision of him. What she saw in her mind's eye was what she had seen in the rearview mirror of his truck as she drove out of town, the last time she had seen him. She was watching him as he disappeared from sight.

She remembered how nice he looked in his lightweight summer suit of tan, a white shirt and a dark brown striped tie. His wavy dark hair gently ruffled by a soft breeze. The look on his face had shown her that he was concerned for her. There was no doubt in Tracy's mind that he was one very handsome man, one who could take her breath away. In fact, he had proven that by kissing her.

She remembered that kiss. In fact, she couldn't forget it. It had haunted her mind from the very beginning. She had never been kissed like that before. Even though it had been a kiss that he had given in anger, it had penetrated her very being. Her entire body had reacted to it as if it had no choice.

She could remember the look in his eyes just before he kissed her. She wasn't sure if his look was one of anger or of passion, but she knew from the kiss that even he had a hard time controlling his feelings for her. That meant she would have to be very careful around him. It would not take very much for them to fall all over each other.

Tracy had to shake herself back to reality. She had enough of thinking of Tom. In fact, it was beginning to frighten her a little. All it did was make her more nervous about being around him. She knew in her own mind that nothing good could come of it. It would just cause her more problems if she were to get involved with him now, or at any time for that matter. She had a ranch that she was trying to save. It was all she could handle at the moment. It was going to take all her time and all the energy she could muster.

Tracy let out a long sigh, stood up and then turned. She started back down the hill toward the old barn. A glance at her watch told her it was now past midnight. It was hard for her to believe she had been sitting on top of the hill for well over an hour thinking about Tom.

It suddenly occurred to her that Will was still not back. She hadn't realized it until that very moment, but she had not thought of him for over an hour.

Tracy returned to the barn. She was beginning to feel tired and hungry. Once she was at the barn, she found her stew was still warm. She decided Will would probably not be back tonight, so she might as well go ahead and eat and then get some rest. Besides, there was nothing she could do about him now. She dished up a good sized helping of stew, sat down on a bale of hay and began to eat.

She was almost finished with her stew when she thought she heard something. It was hard to see anything outside the corral. The small fire lit the inside of the corral fairly well, but that was about it. There was what sounded like a horse moving slowly toward the corral, but she couldn't see it. She hoped it was Will.

Tracy stood up as a horse came around the corner of the barn. Sitting in the saddle was Will.

"It's good to see you," Tracy said relieved to see him. "I was worried about you."

She wasn't sure if she was relieved it was Will instead of someone else, or if she was relieved to simply know that he was all right. She watched him as he rode into the corral. He looked tired.

"Weren't no reason ta worry, Boss. Am I too late for supper?"

"No, of course not. There's plenty of stew for you," she assured him.

Tracy watched as Will got off his horse. He tied the horse to the top rail of the corral and walked over to the fire. Tracy dished him up a big portion of stew, put a couple of biscuits on the plate and handed it to him. He didn't wait until he had a place to sit down. He started eating as he walked over to one of the bales of hay to sit down. He was obviously very hungry.

Tracy poured him a cup of coffee and took it to him. She had a dozen questions to ask him concerning why he was so late getting back to the barn, but she decided they could wait until he had a chance to get something in his stomach.

"I was getting worried about you. Where were you?" she asked as soon as he set his plate down.

"I was out ridin' the fence," he said.

"I didn't mean you had to ride it all in one day," she said with a smile.

"I didn't. I found some tracks over by a place where the fence was down."

"What kind of tracks?"

"From a pickup truck, I'd guess. One like that new truck you got there," he said as he looked at her.

"Oh. That truck belongs to Tom Norbert. He loaned it to me when Dad's old truck wouldn't start while I was in town," she explained.

"Oh," he replied.

Tracy knew he was probably wondering how she could afford a new pickup truck when she couldn't pay his wages. Her explanation seemed to have cleared that up for him as he seemed to relax a bit, and the tone of his voice was not as sharp.

"Did you come in from the north side?" he asked.

"No. I came in from the ranch house, from the south," she replied. "Were the tracks on the north fence?"

"They came in over near where Spiny Ridge runs close ta the property line," he explained. "I'd guess it was a hunter that come through the fence, but I didn't see no one."

Tracy had to think about that. She knew there were a number of antelope and deer on the ranch, but it wasn't hunting season and no one had asked to hunt on her property. In fact, the ranch was posted for no hunting. She didn't like strangers on her land any more than her father did. If they came to the ranch house and asked, she would normally let them hunt on the place, but only during hunting season and only in areas away from the cattle.

"I guess we best keep an eye out," Will said as he stood up.

"Yeah," she agreed.

She watched as Will walked over to his horse. As soon as she realized that he was going to take care of his horse, she began to clean up around the campfire. It was getting pretty late and she needed to get some rest.

As soon as Tracy was done cleaning up the area, she went to the trough and dipped out some water. She returned to the campfire and poured the water over it. The last thing she needed was a range fire.

The thought of a range fire made her think about what Will had said about strangers being on her property. The last thing she wanted was some stranger starting a fire. It would certainly put an end to the Lazy A Ranch.

She understood there was nothing she could do about it tonight, but first thing in the morning she would head back to the ranch and call the Sheriff. He should be aware of the fact that there were trespassers on her property. He might even have one of his deputies come out and take a look around, but right now she needed to get some rest.

Will had taken care of his horse and turned it out in the corral behind the barn when she went into the barn. Just as she was about to start up the ladder, Will came into the barn.

"Goodnight, Will," she said.

"Goodnight, Boss," he replied.

Tracy climbed the ladder to the loft of the barn. She walked over to the end of the barn and looked out over the prairie from the loft door. She wasn't looking for anything special, just looking.

After giving out a long sigh, she turned and walked back to where she had laid out her bedroll. She laid down on it and closed her eyes. She was very tired as it had been a long day, but she didn't fall asleep right away. Her mind gave her one more look at Tom and how handsome he was before it allowed her to drift off to sleep.

CHAPTER SEVEN

Tracy woke with a start due to a noise she heard in the barn below her. Her eyes flew open and she looked around. At first she thought it might be Will "checking on her" again, but she quickly discovered that the sun was already up and she had slept in longer than she had intended. It soon became clear that the noise that had awakened her was Will, all right, but he was getting ready to go out to check on the cattle and ride some more of the fence line.

Tracy needed to get up and fix breakfast for him. She scramble off the bedroll and pushed her feet into her boots. She then quickly pushed her hair back away from her face before going down the ladder. When she reached the bottom of the ladder she noticed that Will had already saddled his horse and was almost ready to head out.

"Will, wait," she called out to him.

Will had just put his foot in the stirrup and was about to swing up into the saddle. He stopped, took his foot out of the stirrup and turned around to look at Tracy.

"Yes, Ma'am?" he asked wondering what she wanted.

"Don't go without your breakfast," Tracy said.

"I got to get to work, Ma'am. It's already past sun up," he said.

"The cattle are doing fine, and the fence can wait until you've had your breakfast," she insisted.

"Yes, Ma'am," he said, then turned and tied his horse to the corral railing again.

Tracy went right to work building a fire and getting some coffee going. As soon as the fire had burned down to cooking size, she fixed him a couple of thick slabs of ham and half a dozen eggs. While they were cooking she made some biscuits in the Dutch oven for him to take with him. The biscuits were ready by the time he was finished eating.

"I want you to take a couple of these biscuits and some ham with you for lunch," she said as she wrapped them up and handed them to him.

"Thank you, Ma'am," he said as he took them.

She watched him as he put them in his saddlebag.

"You be careful out there," she added.

"Ma'am, will you be here for dinner?"

By the look on his face, Will was hoping he was not going to have to cook his own dinner.

"I'm not sure, but there is some beef stew in the cooler. I'll put some biscuits in with it. You can make your own coffee, can't you?"

"Yes, Ma'am."

"Good. If I'm not here, all you have to do is warm up the stew and make yourself some coffee."

"If you don't mind my askin', where you goin'?"

"I'm going over and take a look at those tracks you told me about last night. I would like to see where they go. Depending on what I find, I may go back to the ranch house and call the sheriff to tell him about them."

"That'd be good. You want me ta go with you ta check out them tracks?"

"No, I don't think that will be necessary."

"You take care out there," he said as he reached up, touched the brim of his hat and nodded as if to indicate that he understood. He swung his horse around and rode out of the corral.

Tracy stood at the gate and watched him as he rode out of the corral and out across the prairie. She couldn't help but think about how much help he had been to her, and how lucky she was that he hadn't left her like the others, not that she blamed the others for leaving. She would have done the same thing if her boss didn't pay her.

As soon as he was out of sight, Tracy turned around and began cleaning up the dishes. As she was scrubbing out the Dutch oven, her mind drifted to what Will had told her last night about the tracks he had seen. She had gotten the impression that Will thought that the tracks may have been made by Tom's pickup, but she found that hard to believe. Tom couldn't have had the truck for more than a day or two before he loaned it to her. It would have been hard for him to go out there and run around on her land with it. Besides, what would he be doing out there anyway? It wasn't like him to go onto someone's property without getting permission first.

The more she thought about it, the more she convinced herself it had to have been a truck with the same or a similar kind of tires. After all, there had to be hundreds of trucks with tires like those on Tom's pickup truck. That would certainly explain why the tracks looked the same.

By the time she was finished cleaning up, her mind had taken her in all sorts of twists and turns. She even remembered that she had found Tom nosing around inside the barn. He had come out to the ranch on the pretext of wanting to help her. She remembered that she had accused him of taking inventory because he was so sure she was going to lose the ranch. Now she was beginning to wonder if maybe she had been right.

When it came to Tom, she didn't seem to know what to think. The only thing she had to go on was what she had known about him years ago. She still hadn't found out what he was like now that he had grown up. About the only thing he had done now that he wouldn't have done back in high school was let her drive his truck.

He had said he came to the ranch to see her, and he returned the next day and said he wanted to help her. The kiss he had given her when he was angry with her didn't do a thing to help her decide what his motives really were for coming to the ranch. The fact he came dressed as if he was prepared to work simply caused her to be more confused.

Then there was the fact that the ranch was so close to going under, and his father's bank held the lien on it. The fact that he just happened to work for his father did a lot to make her think he might have an ulterior motive for being at the ranch, other than to visit her.

It slowly began to creep into her mind that she might not have been fair to him. She had no right to think he had come to the ranch for any reason other than for what he had said. He had done nothing to suggest he wanted to do anything other than help her. It also occurred to her that she could never remember him ever lying to her. That alone was a big plus in his favor, she thought.

With all that had happened, Tracy was feeling somewhat confused and a little overwhelmed. With all the pressures of running the ranch when there was nothing to make her really believe she had any kind of chance in the world of saving it, and with her father in the nursing home slowly draining what little resources the ranch had left, what was she to think?

She sat down on one of the bales of hay. Tracy put her head in her hands and began to cry. She knew it would not change anything or make her situation any better, but she couldn't help herself. In a way, she wished she could get some help - - help from someone who would help her make the decisions that had to be made and take some of the pressure off her. At times it was getting to be too much for her to handle alone.

After a good cry, she looked up and took a deep breath. She knew that crying was not going to help. She had to keep on going even if there was little chance of her saving the ranch. Her father had taught her that she should never give up on her dreams. And her dream was to keep the ranch.

It was then that she remembered the tracks Will had reported to her. Maybe they weren't from Tom's truck. Maybe it would be a good idea to find out where the tracks went. There was nothing that had to be done right now, at least nothing that couldn't wait. She had Tom's truck and it wouldn't take her long to find out where the tracks went.

Tracy got into the truck, started it and headed off across the prairie to where she might find the tracks. From there she could find out where they went and, maybe, find out who had made them.

* * * *

It was early in the morning and Tom was already sitting in his office in the bank. However, his mind was not on work. He was leaning against the window and looking out as Les, the local tow truck driver and mechanic, was hooking Tracy's old stake truck up to his tow truck so he could take it to his shop. Les had already told Tom that the truck was hardly worth fixing, that there were too many things wrong with it. Tom had told him to take it to his shop, and he would let him know what to do with it after he had a chance to talk to Tracy about it. In the meantime, Les was to just check it over and put together an estimate on the cost of fixing it. Tom assured Les that he would pay for the estimate.

Tom was thinking about Tracy and how hard she was working in her effort to keep her father's ranch from going under. The problem with the truck was just one of many hurdles for her to get over. He had to wonder how much more she could take before she would give up and give in. He knew he could help her if she would let him.

Tom knew Tracy was under a lot of pressure, and it had taken a lot for her to accept his offer to use his truck. Tom smiled to himself when he thought about the fact that she had finally let him help her, even if it was in a small way. It gave him a certain amount of satisfaction and hope in knowing he might have won a little ground with her. Maybe since she let him loan her his truck, she might give in and give him a chance to really be of help to her.

Just then Tom's thoughts of Tracy were disturbed by the sound of the door to his office opening. He turned and looked toward the door as his mother walked in. He straightened up and walked around in front of his desk.

"Hello mother," he said, his voice sounding as if he were disappointed she had come to see him.

"Good morning, dear," she replied with her ever present smile.

"What brings you here at this hour?"

"I have a meeting at the church this morning. I thought I'd take a moment and stop in to see you. It's been a long time since you have come over for dinner with your father and me," she said as if he were a small child she was scolding.

"Mother, it's only been a few days."

"I know, but it seems like you are getting too busy to come and see your mother any more."

Tom knew it was not the dinners she had missed having with him. It was her lack of knowledge of what he was doing and who he might be seeing that she missed. He knew his mother to be one of those people who had a need to know everything that went on in her son's life. That would have been fine with him if that was where it ended, but Tom knew better. He knew his mother to be a very manipulative and controlling person. She had to be the first to know everything that went on, both inside and outside the family. It was the one thing that bothered him about his mother. Like it or not, she was the town's nosiest person. The hardest part for Tom was that everybody in town knew it.

"When can your father and I expect you for dinner?"

"I don't know. I'm pretty busy this time of year."

"Too busy to spend a little time with your mother?" she asked as if hurt by his comment.

Tom never liked it when his mother played the role of a martyr. It was always hard for him to tell her no, even though he knew that all she wanted to do was to pump him for information and control his life.

"No, of course not," he replied with a slight hint of irritation in his voice.

"Well, then we will expect you tonight for dinner at seven o'clock sharp," she said with a satisfied smile.

"Yes, mother," he replied, the tone of his voice showing that it was easier for him to give in to her than to fight with her.

"Oh, by the way, isn't that the Atwater girl's truck across the street that is being towed away?" she asked with a certain self-satisfying grin.

"Yes, mother. You know it is."

"What is that supposed to mean?"

"It means that you know darn well that it's Tracy's truck," he replied, getting a little tired of playing her silly little games.

He really wanted to tell her that she didn't have to spend all her time looking down her nose at Tracy and her family. But he knew it would do no good to say anything more to his mother. She had made up her mind that the Atwaters were beneath their station in life, and that they were just poor ranch folks who would never amount to anything.

The one thing his mother never seemed to be able to understand was it was those poor hard working folks like the Atwaters that kept her in the finer things that life had to offer, and that she had become accustomed to and expected. Most of the time the poor ranch folks in the county worked hard and paid their bills on time. It was only once in a while when times got tough like the past two years with not enough water that it was hard for them to meet their obligations to the bank on time.

"Speaking of trucks, I didn't see your new truck out in front of the bank," she said as she looked at Tom as if expecting some sort of an explanation.

Tom didn't want to tell her that he had loaned it to Tracy while her truck was getting fixed. He also thought about telling her that he had just left it at home that day, but he didn't want to lie to her, either. Besides, she probably knew that the truck was not parked at his apartment.

"I brought my car today," he replied without further explanation.

"Did you bring your car today because you let 'that Atwater girl' use your new truck?" she said as she looked at him with knowing eyes.

Tom didn't like the way she referred to Tracy as "that Atwater girl", but it would accomplish nothing to get into an argument with her. He knew that his mother knew he had let Tracy use his truck so there was no sense lying to her. He was well aware of the fact that news spread pretty fast in the town.

The gossips in little towns were often better than the telephone service, and certainly better than the newspaper for disseminating information, even if the information was wrong. The only problem with the 'gossip line', as it was often called by some of the locals, was that the information it spread was wrong more times than it was right.

"Yes, as a matter of fact I did let Tracy use it. She can use it until her truck can be repaired," he replied a little more sharply than he had intended.

His mother just stood there and looked at him. His statement had obviously upset her, but he wasn't sure if it was because he loaned Tracy his new truck, or if it was because she was losing control of what her son did. It was most likely because she was losing control of her son, he thought.

Tom's mother had been very happy when he had returned to work in his father's bank. He was sure it was because she would be better able to keep track of what he was doing. He knew she had been very upset with him when he had refused to live in his parents' home. Tom had decided he would like it a lot better if he got an apartment of his own until he decided if he was going to stay or not. His years of living by himself while in college had given him the kind of freedom and independence he had not had when he lived at home. He wanted that when he returned to his hometown. He was a grown man and he didn't need, or want, his mother directing his life.

Living by himself also made it harder for his mother to keep track of his every move, although she tried. She had not been able to admit to herself that she never had very much control over what he did in the first place, but she never seemed to give up trying. Even now she was trying to control his life and who he chose to see.

"I'm really disappointed," she said very calmly.

"Why, mother?" he asked bluntly.

"Well, there are several very nice girls who are available and would love to go out with you if you would simply ask them."

"Are you saying Tracy is not a nice girl?" he asked, knowing very well he was daring her to say anything against Tracy.

"Well, ah, no. I'm not saying that at all," she stammered.

"Then what are you saying, mother?"

She just stood there and looked at him. She wasn't sure what to say. He had never challenged her before, and she didn't have any idea what to do, or what might come of it. The last thing she wanted was for him not to talk to her at all.

If that happened, she might find that she had lost what little control she felt she had over her only son's life. She didn't want to be completely left out of his life.

"I'm sorry, but I have to go to my meeting at the church," she said, then quickly turned around and left his office in a huff.

Tom was angry with her for her narrow mindedness. But as soon as she was gone, he was sorry for the way he had spoken to her. He wished he could have taken back what he said, but it was too late. He would have to tell her that he was sorry later, even though at the moment he didn't really feel all that sorry. He loved his mother in spite of her being nosy and her efforts to control his life, but she didn't make it easy.

As he turned around and started back around his desk, he glanced out the window. There was an empty parking space in front of the grocery store where Tracy's truck had been. Tom let out a sigh and sat down at his desk. He didn't feel much like working, but there were several loan applications sitting in the "In" basket on the corner of his desk that needed his attention.

He took up the first one on the pile and opened the file. It had been a tough couple of years for all the ranchers in the area. There had been little rain and not a great deal of snow in the mountains to keep the creeks and rivers full. Times were tough all around. There were more requests for loans than usual, and most of the loans were for money to drill wells for water or for money to buy more hay. Hay was not only getting hard to find, but it was also getting very expensive. It was up to Tom to decide who should get the loans and who should not. Those who ran their ranches most efficiently were the best candidates for loans. Even so, it was hard for Tom to keep emotion out of the business of making loans.

Tom leaned back in his chair and closed his eyes. He thought about how hard it was for Tracy, and he thought about how hard it was going to be for him to refuse loans to people he had known most of his life. He knew there would be some he couldn't justify giving a loan to based on what he knew about their ability to repay it.

Tom's thoughts were suddenly interrupted by the sound of a light tapping on the door to his office. He opened his eyes and looked toward the door. He saw his father standing in the doorway. He wasn't sure he liked the look on his dad's face. He didn't look like he was very happy.

"What's up, Dad?" he asked.

"Do you mind telling me what you said to your mother?" he asked, then looked at Tom while he waited for a response.

"Nothing that she hasn't heard a hundred times before," Tom answered with a sigh of annoyance.

"She was upset over something, but she wouldn't say what. I thought maybe you could tell me since she just came out of your office."

"It's the same thing as always. She wants to run my life and decide who I should see."

"She's just trying to look out for you."

"I know, and I didn't mean to upset her; but I will see who I want, when I want."

"Okay, son. I'll have another talk with her," he said as he shook his head. "Not that it will do any good."

"She wants me to come to dinner tonight. I don't think I want to right now."

"I understand. I'll tell her you had some business to do for the bank. She won't like it, but she'll accept the excuse," he said with a smile.

"Thanks, Dad."

"I do wish the two of you could find some common ground to talk about once in a while," he said.

"So do I," Tom replied.

"How are you coming on those loan applications?" he asked.

"This is not going to be easy. Some of these ranchers are already in hock up to their necks. Adding more debt is not going to help them. They would have to have the best year of their lives next year to just keep their heads above water," Tom said with a tone of frustration in his voice.

"It's not an easy job being in the business of making loans, is it?"

"No, it's not," Tom agreed.

"Well, I'll leave you to do your job. I'm sure you will make the right choices," his dad said with a grin.

"Thanks."

"Oh, by the way. Are you planning on making a loan to Tracy Atwater?"

"No," he answered. "What makes you ask?"

"I was just wondering. I saw them tow her truck away, and your mother said that you loaned her your new truck. Do you think that was a good idea?"

"Yes, I do," he replied. "And no, she has not even asked for a loan."

"Well, I'll leave you to your work," he said as he looked at Tom for a moment before turning around and leaving his office.

Tom looked at the door for several minutes before he got up from his desk. He walked over to the door, looked outside at the secretary who was sitting at her desk.

"I would like it if I am not disturbed for the next couple of hours," he said to her.

"Yes, sir," his secretary replied with a knowing sort of smile.

Tom stepped back inside his office and closed the door. He returned to his desk and sat down. He let out a long sigh as he again opened a file containing a loan application and all the supporting documentation.

CHAPTER EIGHT

It took Tracy a little over an hour to drive to the north fence line from the barn. It was a bumpy ride across the north pasture, but the new truck handled it well. When she got to the fence line, she turned and drove along the fence toward Spiny Ridge.

Spiny Ridge started at the northeast corner of the ranch, and ran in a southwesterly direction. The ridge actually cut diagonally a little over halfway across the Lazy A Ranch, making the land that was available for pasture and for hay into the shape of something like a large out-of-shape horseshoe. It came close to splitting the ranch almost in half.

The ridge itself was over a mile wide in some of the narrower places and over three miles wide at the widest. It rose up out of the prairie to over a hundred and seventy-five feet high in some places. From a distance it looked something like the backbone of a giant Dinosaur. It put the ranch house on one side of the ridge and the north pasture over twenty miles away on the other side. If they could have driven the cattle straight across the ridge, it would have saved them more than fourteen miles of herding the cattle from the east range around the end of the ridge to the north range where the barn was located.

It wasn't long before Tracy found a place in the fence that looked like it might have been cut and then repaired. Tracy stopped the truck, got out and began to look around. She immediately began to look for tracks in the dry brown grass. It didn't take her but a couple of minutes to find them. From the looks of the tracks, a vehicle had been driven through the opening and on across the prairie.

She was sure that she was at the place Will had said he found a hole in the fence. After taking a closer look at the fence, she could see from the tool marks on the barbed wire that it had been recently cut and then repaired.

Based on what she could see and what Will had told her, Tracy figured that someone had cut the fence and driven through the opening. When Will came along, he fixed it. That part all made sense. But why would anyone cut the fence to come onto property that was posted?

A quick look at the tracks showed her the vehicle that had come onto the ranch had to be bigger than Tom's truck. When she compared the tracks with those left by Tom's truck, it was easy to see that it had a wider track as well as wider and much heavier treaded tires. She could see from where the vehicle turned that it had only four wheels so it was not a semi-truck, but rather a single unit type of truck with four very large tires.

Tracy smiled to herself. She was relieved to know that it had not been Tom's truck. It gave her hope that what Tom had been telling her was the truth.

She couldn't think of anyone around who might have a vehicle big enough to make the kind of tracks she had found. Most of the local ranchers had full-size pickup trucks like Tom's or ones with tandem axles and more than four tires.

Tracy knew only too well that cattle rustling was not a thing of the past as many people seemed to think. It was still big business, even today. She instantly began to worry about her livestock. If cattle rustlers were in the area, she needed to notify the sheriff as soon as possible. She could not afford to lose any cattle to rustlers.

She quickly got back in the truck and started it. As she started to put the truck in gear, she looked out the windshield. Tracy could make out the tracks in the dry grass. She felt the need to know where the big vehicle had gone. The tracks indicated the truck had gone back out the same way it had come in, but where had it gone while it was on the ranch? If it were rustlers, were they scouting out the prospects of stealing some of her cattle? It was certainly possible, but why leave so many tracks and not repair the fence when they left? It would certainly cause anyone who found it to be suspicious that something was going on.

Tracy could see the tracks went straight toward the ridge. All she could think was that the rustlers had gone to hide in the rocky ridge, but that didn't make a whole lot of sense to her. It had to be over a mile from the fence to the ridge. If they had been scouting that part of the ranch, they would know the cattle were a long way away from the ridge. She had to wonder if they had seen Will riding fence and decided to hide in the rocks until it was dark and then get out before they were spotted. Again, that was a possibility.

The one thing she knew for sure was she was going to have to keep a good watch over the cattle. So far they had stayed fairly close to the old barn, but once they got spread out they would become easy for rustlers to steal if they were not watched all the time. She also knew that keeping a close eye on her cattle would be hard to do with just Will and herself to watch them, especially if they began to spread out to find enough to eat.

Tracy swallowed hard and put the truck in gear. She started out slowly moving along side the tracks left by the larger vehicle. Her original thought that the vehicle had gone to the ridge seemed to be proving right. The tracks led right straight toward the ridge.

Once she got close to the ridge, she noticed the tracks turned and ran parallel to the ridge. She found several places where the vehicle had apparently stopped, but why? There didn't seem to be any reason to stop where they had.

As she continued on, she found several more places where the truck had apparently stopped for some reason. At one place Tracy stopped and got out. She looked for tracks and found several made by men in boots, but they weren't cowboy boots. What she saw were the boot prints of work boots, heavy deep treaded work boots. They were not the kind of boots one would wear if he were riding a horse, and not the kind of boots most ranch hands around there would wear.

One set of boot tracks led to a rock that was easy to climb up on. She climbed up on the rock and looked over the other side. There she discovered a small area of dry grass, no more than five or six feet in diameter. In the middle of it was a hole.

She climbed down off the rock and walked over to the hole to investigate. Tracy stood staring at the hole for several minutes. She discovered that the hole was only about five or six inches in diameter and not very deep, maybe two feet deep at the most.

There were boot tracks all around the hole. She could not understand why anyone would want to dig a hole there. It wasn't big enough or deep enough to hold any useable amount of water, and the ground was hard and dry. It also troubled her that whoever had dug the hole hadn't even bothered to refill it. A horse or cow could break a leg stumbling into it.

She turned around and started to return to the truck, but stopped when she got to the top of the rock. She could look down and see where the truck had made a big circle as it turned around and headed back to where it had come from.

The whole thing was strange to her. Why would someone come onto her property, dig a shallow hole less than six inches in diameter, and then leave? What were they after? What did they think they would find, or what did they dig up? Or had they planned to bury something there and changed their mind. She also wondered if similar holes had been dug at other places where the big truck had stopped.

Tracy was confused and wasn't sure what she should do. The one thing she was sure of was she should notify the sheriff that someone had been on her property that didn't belong there.

She got back into the truck and started off across the pasture toward the old barn. It took her less time to get back to the barn than it had taken her to get to the fence. The truck handled very well going across country.

As she approached the barn, she remembered hearing about the short cut from her father that went through the ridge to the ranch house. From what her father had told her, it was not wide enough for a vehicle but a horse could get through. The only problem was she didn't have a horse. The only horse out there at the moment was the one Will was riding. The horse she had been riding was in a corral back at the ranch house.

She remembered that she was supposed to bring several horses out to the north pasture barn so they could change horses from day to day so as not to wear them out. The only course of action was for her to drive the truck back to the ranch house, call the sheriff and then return to the north pasture with some horses.

Tracy looked around but could not see Will anywhere. He had ridden off in the morning to do what he had been told, that was to ride the fence line. She wanted him to know what she was doing. Then she remembered she had told him that he could warm up some stew if she was not back in time for dinner.

She decided she might as well drive back to the ranch house and call the sheriff. She would try to get back to the old barn before it got too late. If she cut through the ridge on the way back, with a little luck she could get everything done and get back before it was time for dinner.

Tracy took off in the truck to go back to the ranch house. As she drove across the open prairie, she decided she would make a second call while she was at the house. She would call Tom to find out what he could tell her about her truck. Tracy was sure he had been right, that the truck was going to be in the shop for at least three days and probably more like a week. She had to admit she didn't mind having the use of a new truck. The only thing was she wished it wasn't Tom's truck.

Tracy couldn't help herself as her thoughts turned to Tom. Without realizing what she was doing, she reached up and touched her lips again as she thought about the hard kiss he had planted on her when he was angry with her. She could even remember, and almost feel, how it sent little tingling sensations through her body.

The sudden jolt caused by hitting a rut brought Tracy quickly back to reality. She realized she was not paying attention to what she was doing, or she would have seen the rut. It was a good thing the rut was not too deep. If it had been deep she could have damaged Tom's new truck.

Tracy quickly brought the truck to a stop before she chastised herself for letting her mind wonder. She was especially upset with herself for letting Tom occupy her mind so completely that she could not concentrate on what she was doing.

"Get it together," she said out loud. "You can't be doing this to yourself."

Tracy leaned forward and put her head on her hands on the steering wheel. She was finding it very hard not to think about Tom and all he had done for her. She began to think that one reason she couldn't get him off her mind was because she was in his truck. Another reason might be the fact that she kept thinking about what he was going to ask of her in return for the use of it?

She began to think she was going to "owe" him big time for what he had already done for her. That thought didn't set very well. But the more she thought about it, the more she began to realize Tom had asked her for nothing. The only thing he had ever asked of her since she had returned to the ranch was to go out to dinner with him. She had turned him down and he didn't press the issue. All he had ever done was to be there for her, even when she had been nasty to him.

Tracy tipped her head back and looked out of the windshield. She had been rather cruel to him. It made her feel like she really needed to have a long talk with him. She needed to apologize to him for the way she had treated him when she really didn't have any reason. Even with the way she had treated him, he still came through for her when she needed it the most.

"I've got to call him when I get back to the ranch," she said to herself.

Tracy put the truck in gear and started on across the prairie, again. As she drove, she thought about what she would say to him and how she could make it up to him for the way she had acted. Maybe she should let him take her out to dinner once she got things settled down on the ranch.

Then it occurred to her that because of the way she had treated him, he might not want to take her out to dinner. She couldn't blame him if that was the way he felt. She smiled to herself as she thought the way to avoid having to go out to dinner with him was to ask him to have dinner with her at the ranch.

"That would work," she said to herself as she drove on toward the ranch house.

* * * *

It was mid afternoon when she arrived at the ranch house. Tracy parked the truck in front of the house and went inside. She immediately went to the desk and picked up the phone. She placed a call to the Sheriff's Office and told the dispatcher what she had seen and what Will had told her.

The dispatcher said she would send out a deputy to investigate and get back to her.

She explained to the dispatcher she would not be at the ranch house for very long, but that she would be returning to the north pasture very shortly. The dispatcher told Tracy the deputy would contact her in the north pasture at the old barn sometime late that afternoon or first thing in the morning.

As soon as she was done with that call, she placed a call to the bank in the hope of finding Tom in his office. Tom's secretary quickly transferred her call to Tom.

"This is Tom Norbert, may I help you?"

"Hi," she said.

"Hi, Tracy," Tom said, immediately recognizing her voice. "How's it going?"

"That's what I called to find out. What is happening with my truck?"

"I had Les take a look at it. I'm sorry to say it doesn't look good. He said it will cost more to fix than the truck is worth," he said, the tone of his voice showing he was wishing he had better news for her.

"Oh."

Tom could hear the disappointment in her voice in just that one word. He was sure all she needed was one more thing to go wrong, and she would probably break down and cry. He decided he would try to brighten her spirits.

"Are you enjoying my truck?" he asked, trying very hard to keep the sound of his voice light and pleasant.

"It's a very nice truck," she replied, her voice soft.

"I guess I don't have much choice but to get the truck fixed," she added. "Did Les say how much it is going to cost to get it running again?"

"Tracy, the truck is not worth fixing. It would be just a waste of money to fix it," he said, hoping she would not get too upset with him for saying so.

"I can't afford a new truck. I'm not even sure I can afford to fix the old one," she said, her voice showing her frustration.

"Tracy, you can use my truck until we can work something out. Besides, I use my car most of the time for business anyway," he said, his voice trying very hard to show her that he meant what he said.

"I don't know how long it will be before I can get it fixed."

"It's all right. I know you have a lot to do and a lot on your mind. Don't worry about the truck for now. When you get into town, or when I have some time to come out to the ranch, we'll talk about it. Until then, just enjoy the truck."

The sound of his voice gave Tracy the impression he really meant what he said. She couldn't believe he was so willing to let her have his truck for an indefinite period of time. It crossed her mind that the day would come when he would want payment for it, but what could she do. She needed the transportation now, well, at least she would in a couple of days. Right now, she needed to get some horses out to the north pasture.

"How is everything else going?" Tom asked.

"I called the Sheriff's Office. It seems we might have rustlers scouting around on the ranch," she said as if it was an everyday affair.

"Rustlers?"

"Yeah. Will found some tracks from a rather big vehicle in the north pasture. It came through the fence, but I think they're gone. We'll just have to keep a closer eye on things."

"You want me to take a couple of days off and come out to help you keep watch over the place?" Tom asked, his voice showing his concern.

"Thanks for the offer, but I think Will and I can handle it. Besides with the sheriff prowling around, I don't think they will stick around very long."

"Is Will staying on?"

"Yes, why?"

"Tracy, I don't want to alarm you or anything, but are you aware of his background?"

Tracy could hear the concern in his voice.

"Yes. My father told me about him some time ago."

"I'm not sure I like it very much that you're out there alone with him."

"I don't think that is any of your concern," she said as she began to think that he was trying to run her life already.

Tom could hear the change in her voice that indicated she was not about to be told what to do.

"I know you run that ranch, it's just that I worry about you. And before you get your dander up, I'm not trying to tell you what to do," he added quickly. "I just wanted to make sure you know about him."

"I know about him. He has been working very hard and has not given me any reason to believe he will do anything differently," she said in an effort to get Tom to stop worrying about her.

"Okay, but I'm still worried about you,"

"If you want to worry about me, worry about how I'm going to keep this ranch going."

As soon as she made her comment, she wished she hadn't. Without thinking about it, she had opened the door for him to provide her with a solution to her biggest problem. The last thing she wanted was for him to be telling her what to do.

Tracy let out a sigh knowing the damage had already been done. It would do her no good to tell him not to worry. At that point, she felt she was already obligated to him. He had done nothing but try to help, and she knew she was in need of his help. It was just that help from him might have too high a price tag, and it might not be in the form of money.

"I've got to get back out to the north pasture with some horses. I'll talk to you later," she said.

"When?"

"When I get back to the ranch house again."

"When will that be?" he asked hoping she would give him something to look forward to.

"I'm not sure, but if you want your truck it will be parked in the barn. You're welcome to come and get it."

"I won't need it," he replied.

"Well, just in case you do, it will be in the barn. I've got to go. I want to get back to the north pasture before dark."

"You be careful," Tom said.

"I will," she replied then hung up the phone.

As soon as she hung up the phone, she sat in the chair staring at it. For all the problems she had dealing with Tom, she actually felt a degree of pleasure in knowing he was worried about her.

She tipped her head back and closed her eyes for a few minutes. While she did, she let her mind wander. It seemed to want to wander in the direction of Tom Norbert.

As she thought about him, she remembered how it had felt when he held her up against him, and how his lips had felt against hers. She couldn't believe how much trouble she was having trying to forget about it. It seemed the harder she tried to get him out of her mind, the more she thought of him.

"It was just a kiss for crying out loud. Come on girl, get it together," she said to herself as she opened her eyes and stood up. "You're not a little school girl any more."

Shaking her head, she went into her bedroom. She took off her clothes then went into the bathroom to take a shower.

When she was done, she dressed in clean work clothes and headed for the barn.

After getting several horses ready to take to the north pasture, she climbed in the saddle. As she started out of the yard, she looked over at Spiny Ridge. With her horses in tow, she thought she might be able to find her way through the rocky ridge. It would certainly save her a lot of time in the saddle.

Confident she could find her way, she started off across the pasture toward the ridge. She had never been across the ridge before, but it never crossed her mind that she might not be able to find her way into Spiny Ridge.

Once she was close to the ridge, she led the string of horses along it looking for an opening in the rocky cliffs that would give her a place to take the horses across Spiny Ridge. She watched the time very carefully as she rode along. Although she had started out with a hint of confidence in finding her way across the ridge, it was slowly melting away with each passing hour. The longer she waited to go back, the later it would be when she got to the barn in the north pasture.

CHAPTER NINE

Tracy had no idea how far she would have to go along the ridge before finding the trail that led back into the ridge itself. She had heard her father talk about a trail that wound through the ridge, but she had never seen him actually use it. She had seen her father ride along the base of the ridge, but she had never seen where he went into Spiny Ridge.

Suddenly, Tracy came upon a narrow opening in the rocks. She stopped for a minute to examine it. There was no indication it was the way her father had used, but it looked like it could be. The trail into the rocks was just barely wide enough for one animal at a time to go through.

As she looked up, she noticed the dull gray rocks seemed to jut almost straight up toward the blue sky. It must have been fifty feet or more to the top from where she sat on her horse. Going in there would be like going into a very narrow canyon, and it could prove to be a box canyon. It could also prove to be difficult to turn around if it ended in a rock wall. There was nothing to indicate it went anywhere. There were no tracks on the floor of the canyon to help her decide if it was the entrance into Spiny Ridge.

Tracy had no idea where the narrow trail would lead her, but she hoped she could find her way to the other side of the ridge. If she could, she would save herself a lot of time in getting back to the north pasture. It was time to make a decision. Either go for it, or turn back and take the way she knew.

She took a deep breath, swallowed hard and then nudged her horse in the ribs. He reluctantly moved forward into the narrow canyon. The gloomy gray rock rose up on both sides of her blocking out the sun. The narrow pathway into Spiny Ridge gave her no choices as to which way to go. Once she was in the canyon there was no turning back. If she decided to go back, the only way out would be to back the horses up, and that became an even less pleasant thought the further she went into the canyon. She knew that she would have to back the horses up one at a time, and that could take most of what was left of the day.

The trail wound around and around, first turning right, then left, then right again and so on. Some of the turns were almost too sharp for the horses to make. It was not long before Tracy began to wonder if she might have missed a turn somewhere along the way, or had entered into Spiny Ridge at the wrong place. The more she thought about it, the more she realized there hadn't been any place to turn off, and she knew of no other place where she could ride into the rocky ridge. If that was true, then she had to be on the right trail.

All of a sudden she made a turn and her horse sort of stepped out of the narrow canyon she had been trapped in since she first entered Spiny Ridge. She reined up and looked around. Her mouth dropped open in disbelief. She could not believe what she was seeing.

That last turn had taken her out into a valley that was surrounded by a wall of dull gray rock. The valley was a flat open area that had the greenest grass she had seen for a very long time. It was almost belly deep on her horses. It was as if she had crossed over into another time zone or to another world entirely. It was like no place she had ever seen before. Yet, one look at the sky told her that she was still in Big Sky Montana.

Although the valley was only about a mile wide and looked to be a little over two miles long, the lush green grass made it seem so much bigger. The first thing to cross Tracy's mind was there had to be a spring somewhere feeding the field with water for the grass to be so green and thick.

She sat in the saddle as she continued to look around. It was amazing. It was like an oasis surrounded by dull gray rock walls that seemed to reach up to the sky. On the far side of the valley near the rocky outcroppings there appeared to be a grove of trees. There were only about four or five of them, but the trees were large and provided a great deal of shade. With such large trees, it had to be where the spring that fed the little valley was located.

She nudged her horse forward at a walk as she started across the field toward the trees. Tracy continued to look around in amazement. She had never seen anything like it. She began to wonder if there were other valleys like it in Spiny Ridge. The ridge had certainly looked to be long enough from the outside.

When she got to the trees, she found them to be large oak trees, a type of tree not normally found in that part of Montana. Their branches were filled with big leaves that shaded the grass under them. It felt cool under the trees, a stark difference from when she was leading her horses through the narrow canyon that brought her to the valley. It had been unbelievably hot with the sun reflecting off the gray rock, yet it was comfortable under the trees.

Tracy swung her leg over the saddle and stepped down onto the ground. She immediately began looking for a place to tie the horses. When she glanced at them and saw that they were quite content to stay right there and eat on the rich green grass, she simply tied the reins to the saddle and let them graze.

She spent the next little while looking for the source of the water that was giving life to the valley. Tracy could not find anything anywhere around the trees that would help her understand why it was so green there when just a mile or so away it was as dry as could be.

It was so refreshing in the cool of the big oak trees that Tracy decided to take a few minutes and sit down under one of them to relax. As she sat down, her thoughts turned to her father. She had to wonder why he had never told her about the place. Why had he kept it a secret?

When Tracy could not answer her own questions, she thought of her father in the nursing home. She knew he would not be able to answer any questions for her, either.

She could see where the horses had pushed down the tall grass, so it was easy to see where she had come into the valley. It was very important to know in case she couldn't find the way out the other side and had to go back. The question now was how to find her way out of the valley and into the north pasture.

Tracy stood up and began looking for a way out of the valley, a way out that would take her to where she needed to go. There was no time to scout out the entire valley. She needed to get the horses to the barn in the north pasture before dark.

She looked up at the sky and was able to figure out which way was north. She walked up to her horse, untied the reins from the saddle and stepped up alongside the horse. After putting her foot in the stirrup, she swung her leg over the saddle and sat down on it. She then began to lead the horses toward the rock wall on the north side of the valley.

As she moved closer to the north side of the valley, she was unable to see an opening. When she got to the north side, she had to make a decision on which way to go. She decided to work her way north and east along the wall. It wasn't until she had traveled some distance along the wall that she began to worry. She had been unable to find any way out of the small valley except the way she had come in.

It was beginning to get late. If she didn't find a way out of the valley very soon, she might get trapped in the valley for the night. She decided that it might not be the way her father had gone to get through Spiny Ridge. She felt there had to be some other way. Either that or she had gone the wrong way along the northeast wall of the valley.

Tracy decided it was best if she went back the way she had come. She would have to come back some other time to find the trail her father had used.

She began riding back along the wall toward the trees. There she could pick up the trail left in the tall grass, which would show her how to get back to the narrow canyon she had used to get into the valley.

Once Tracy arrived at the narrow canyon, she reluctantly guided her horses back into the narrow canyon. She wound her way back to where she had entered Spiny Ridge. It wasn't long before she came out of Spiny Ridge and onto the dry open prairie. From there she could see the ranch house.

Tracy let out a sigh of disappointment as she started moving the horses along the outside of the ridge. She had hoped she could save a lot of time by cutting across the ridge, but it had not worked out that way. She had lost a lot of valuable time, almost half the day.

As she pushed on toward the end of the ridge so she could turn toward the north pasture, she vowed she would find the shortcut someday. It caused her to wonder if it wouldn't be better if she tried to find her way through the ridge from the other side.

As Tracy moved across the pasture, she looked up at the sky one more time. There were still no clouds and no chance of rain. It might not be the best thing for her to be out there alone after dark, especially if there were rustlers roaming around. Although it was too hot to run the horses very far, she nudged her horse and led the others across the north pasture toward the old barn at a good walk.

The sun was just beginning to set in the western sky when Tracy came over the rise and could see the north pasture barn. In the corral was the horse Will had been riding. She could barely make him out as he stood leaning against the corral looking off in the direction they had come with the herd.

In the waning hours of light, she had gone to the wrong hill, which put her a little ways behind the barn. As she rode down the hill, Tracy saw Will turn around and look up the hill toward her. He watched her all the way to the corral. When she turned into the corral with the string of horses, she could see the concerned look on his face. She drew up to the corral fence and swung out of the saddle.

"Did you come through Spiny Ridge, Ma'am?" he asked almost before her foot touched the ground.

She looked at him. Tracy didn't want to have to tell him she had tried but couldn't find the way. She also didn't want to tell him what she had discovered in Spiny Ridge, at least not for the moment. Even if she did tell him, she wasn't sure he would believe her. She decided that it would be better not to say anything about it for the time being.

Tracy knew her father had kept what was in Spiny Ridge a secret. For what reason, she didn't know. She decided to keep the secret, too, at least until she had some idea of what it was she had found.

"Ah, no. I went around the hill because I didn't want to spook the cattle up there," she said as she pointed to a large number of cattle grazing on the side of a hill. "We're having enough trouble keeping weight on them without making them run by riding through them," she added.

"Oh," he replied, not really sure if he believed her or not.

Tracy looked around and saw that Will had not started a fire to cook his dinner. It was time to change the subject to something Will would certainly understand. He had probably been waiting until the last minute to warm up the stew, hoping she would get back to fix him something to eat.

"Would you mind taking care of the horses while I start dinner?" she asked.

"No, Ma'am," Will said with a smile.

Will's smile, and his eagerness to take care of the horses told her that she had been right. He was waiting for her to get back to fix dinner. While Will took care of the horses and turned them out in a small corral behind the barn, Tracy started a fire for dinner.

It wasn't long before she had a fresh pot of coffee going and the frying pan was on the fire. Will had the horses all fed and watered by the time Tracy had dinner going. When she looked up and saw Will watching her, there was no doubt in Tracy's mind that he was ready to eat.

"How did it go today? Did you get very far on the fence?" Tracy asked as she stirred the stew in the deep frying pan.

"It went okay. I got as far as the northeast corner before I had ta head back."

"Good. Did you have any problems?"

"No, Ma'am."

"Any more places where the fence had been cut?" she asked.

"No, Ma'am."

"Good," she replied as she took the frying pan off the fire. "I guess dinner is ready."

Tracy spooned a big helping of stew onto a plate and added a couple of biscuits. She then handed it to Will. Will took the plate willingly and walked over to the same bale of hay he had been sitting on to eat his meals. Tracy poured two cups of coffee and took one over to him. After filling a plate of stew for herself, she moved over next to the barn door and sat down to eat.

It was dark by the time they had finished eating and she had gotten everything cleaned up. Although Tracy was tired, she needed some time to think. She put another piece of wood on the fire, then stood up.

"I think I'll go for a walk up the hill. Even if it is dry, it's still a beautiful night," Tracy said.

"You want me ta go with you, Ma'am?"

"No. I don't think that will be necessary. I can find my way back."

"Okay. I think I'll get some sleep," Will replied as he turned and started into the barn.

"Goodnight, then. I'll try to be quiet when I come back," Tracy said as she turned and walked out of the corral.

The sky was clear and was quickly filling up with stars. It would be only a little while before the moon would come up over the horizon and give the countryside a pale yellow glow. She liked the peaceful quiet nights. It seemed to make things look better than during the day. She knew it was probably because she couldn't see the dried up grass and empty watering holes.

The walk up to the top of the hill gave Tracy time to think. One of the things she thought about was the valley she had found. It was clear that her father must have known about it. After all, he had been in and around Spiny Ridge a hundred times. As far as she knew, he had found a way to cross the ridge. She hadn't found it yet, but was determined to find a way if it took her all year.

One of the questions that kept spinning around in her head was why had her father kept the little valley a secret? What was he trying to protect? It made no sense to her to keep the little valley a secret. It occurred to her that it could prove to be the salvation of the ranch. She didn't know how, but it was possible.

Had he found something else in the valley or in the ridges that he was afraid to let anyone know about? There was always the possibility he had found something, but he had a stroke before he could tell anyone.

Tracy knew that none of the hundred or more questions running through her head were going to get answered. Her father had been unable to speak since his stroke. Whatever he knew about Spiny Ridge was locked up in his head. Unless he got better and regained his ability to talk, it would remain locked in his head forever. That was unless she could discover for herself what he had found.

Unable to come up with any logical answers, her mind turned to the cut fence, the truck tracks and the hole dug in the ground. The more she thought about it, the less she believed whoever had dug the hole were cattle rustlers. They had to have some other interest in that land. Her belief in that was confirmed by the fact whoever had come onto her property had done so without permission.

She began to wonder if someone else knew something about Spiny Ridge that she knew nothing about. What had the hole been dug for? It was not deep enough to indicate if there was water just below the surface. When she had looked into the hole, it was just a hole dug in the dry dirt. It proved nothing, at least that she could see. What were they looking for? Was it a hole to put something in, or had they taken something out? Was it some kind of geological test for something?

Tracy knew oil had been found in the county, but it was way over on the eastern side of the county where the land was much different. All the drilling and sampling that had been done on the western part of the county had proven worthless, as far as she knew. Nothing of any value was ever found. Even water had been hard to find.

When she reached the top of the hill, she sat down and pulled her knees up to her chest. She wrapped her arms around her legs and looked out over the prairie toward Spiny Ridge. Thoughts of the little valley returned to her mind. It was green and lush, yet she had not found the source of the water that would make it that way. She knew no matter what, she would someday return to that little valley and spend some time exploring it. But she also knew it would have to wait. There was too much to be done to save the ranch.

Tracy pictured the little valley in her mind and thought it would be really nice to live in a valley like that, one that was always green and cool. She had to laugh at herself for thinking that. To live there would be very difficult. Everything would have to be packed in on horseback. In the winter, the narrow canyon would fill up with snow and make it impossible to get in or out. Tom's truck could not get back in there, the trail was too narrow and had too many sharp turns that the truck would not be able to make.

The thought of Tom made her wonder what he was doing tonight. It crossed her mind that it would be kind of romantic to be sitting on the hilltop with him. Tracy quickly tried to shake that thought out of her mind. The last thing she needed was to get involved with him, but it proved hard for her to forget him. After all, he had helped her when he really didn't have to. He had helped her even though she had not been at all nice to him.

Getting Tom out of her mind was not easy. She was beginning to realize how much he had rattled her senses when he held her and kissed her. She slowly went over all he had done for her since she had returned. Yet, he had not once asked anything of her except for a dinner date which she had refused. Even so, he had still been there when she needed help the most. The only one she knew who did things like that was Hopalong Cassidy, and Tom was no Hopalong. He didn't even have a white horse. The thought of him being a Hopalong Cassidy caused a smile to come to Tracy's face.

However, the smile faded away when Tracy began to realize how much she owed him. As they say, she owed him big time. She also realized there were a lot of things in the way of them having any kind of lasting relationship. Tracy knew what his mother thought of her and her family. It was hard enough making a relationship work, but when there was interference from a close family member it became almost impossible. Tom's mother would do everything she could to make life miserable for them, at least for her. Past experience had taught Tracy that Tom's mother was good at making life miserable for someone she despised.

Then there was the fact that the ranch was in debt up to the top of its fence posts. The fact that the debt was owned by Tom's father's bank didn't help any, either.

When she tried to think logically, there was little or no hope of them having anything together, much less a relationship. That thought made Tracy feel a little depressed. She was beginning to realize that after all the years of not even seeing Tom, she still cared for him. She might even love him, even though there was little hope for them.

"Come on girl, get it together. You've got no business even thinking about Tom Norbert," she said softly to herself.

Tracy rose to her feet. She was suddenly feeling very tired. She had no idea how late it was, but she knew it was well past time to get some sleep.

She started back down the hill toward the barn. Tracy walked very slowly. It was not so much that she was tired as it was because of her feeling of being defeated before she ever got started. She wasn't even sure why she felt defeated, but one look at what she was trying to keep together was enough to cause most people to throw their hands up in the air and give up.

Once she was at the barn, she snuck in as quietly as she could. She climbed up into the loft and dropped down on her bedroll. It was not easy for her to fall asleep, but finally exhaustion took over and forced her to sleep.

CHAPTER TEN

The sun had just come up and was starting to shine in the window of Tom's apartment, but it wasn't the sun that woke him. Tom was already up and in the bathroom shaving. He had not slept very well knowing Tracy was out on the range, miles from anyone who might be able to help her, with a man who had served time in prison for murder.

Although their contact with each other was rare, Tom had always treated Will with respect and a healthy dose of caution. For the most part, Tom had gotten along with Will for as long as he had known him. He knew about Will's temper, and he was sure Will was doing very well at keeping it under control. In the small town, news traveled fast so he would have heard if Will had been in any kind of trouble since his release from prison.

Tom was familiar with the circumstance surrounding the killing of the man by Will, but he wasn't sure if that was all there was to it. Everything he had heard was second hand. Tom's real fear was that Tracy might accidentally say something or do something that would set Will off. If that happened, there was no telling what Will might do, or who he would take his temper out on.

After he finished shaving, he got dressed in jeans, a western work shirt and cowboy boots. Tom had reached a decision that he was convinced Tracy would not like. He had decided to go out to the north pasture barn on Atwater's Lazy A Ranch even if Tracy did not want him there. He had a good idea how Tracy would react to his arrival at the barn. He had decided that he would go anyway, even if she told him to leave. He had to know that she was all right.

Tom knew his car would not be able to get him there, but Tracy had said she would leave his pickup at the ranch house if he needed it before she got it back to him. He was going to need it to get out to the north pasture.

As Tom stepped out of his apartment onto the sidewalk, he saw his mother drive up in her new bright yellow Cadillac. He let out a long sigh of disappointment. Tom had hoped that he could get out of town before his mother knew he was gone. The last thing he wanted was to have a confrontation with her. As much as he loved her, he knew she could be rather pushy and very controlling.

Tom stood on the sidewalk and watched her as she got out of her car and came toward him. He made no effort to walk over to meet her. After failing to have dinner with her and his father last night, he knew it was not going to be a pleasant meeting.

"I see you are up early," his mother said with her usual smile as she looked him over.

"Yes, and what are you doing here so early? It's not like you to be up and about at this hour of the day."

"That's not true. I came over to see if there was something wrong."

"Something wrong? Why would you think there is something wrong?"

"You didn't show up for dinner last night. I thought we had an understanding. You would be there to have dinner with your father and me," she said as she looked into his eyes.

"Didn't father tell you that I wouldn't be able to make it?"

"Your father simply said you had other plans and you couldn't make it for dinner."

Tom could tell by the expression on her face and the way she talked that she had not believed his father. But then, she never seemed to pay a great deal of attention to anything he said, anyway.

"Well, mother, that's not entirely true. The truth is I really didn't want to come to dinner last night. I had other things on my mind."

"What things?

"I would rather not discuss them with you."

"I don't understand. You have always been able to talk to me," she said, the look on her face indicating she was hurt by his comment.

"No, mother. We have always been able to discuss what you wanted to talk about. We have never been able to talk about the things that were important to me, and the things I wanted to say."

"Thomas, that just isn't so," she said, her voice showing how shocked she was by his comment and his frankness.

"I'm sorry, mother, but I have something very important to do this morning. I need to get going."

"Well, I think we should go up to your apartment and talk about what it is that you don't seem to be able to talk to me about," she said, then started toward his apartment without waiting for him to comment, or to see if he was going to go with her. She simply expected him to follow along.

Tom shook his head in frustration as he watched his mother walk toward his apartment. He made no effort to follow her. He simply stood on the sidewalk and watched her.

"Mother," he called out.

She stopped, turned around and looked at him as if he had done something she found unforgivable.

"We are not going to discuss it now," Tom said firmly. "I have to go. We can discuss it later if you find it absolutely necessary, but not now."

Tom did not wait for her to respond to him. He simply turned around and walked toward his car.

She stood on the sidewalk in front of Tom's apartment and watched him as he got into his car and started it. She could not believe that he had been so rude to her.

As he drove down the street, she couldn't comprehend what had transpired. He had never been rude to her before. She couldn't understand what had gotten into him. Her first thought was that Atwater girl had gotten her claws into him. She had poisoned him against her, she was sure of it. She would have to figure out a way to get her out of Tom's life, and preferably out of town.

Tom glanced in his rearview mirror as he drove down the street. He could see his mother standing there looking at him as he drove away. The look on her face showed him that she was first of all not very happy with him, and secondly that she wondered what he was doing and where he was going. At this point, Tom had more important things to think about than his mother.

Tom drove out of town and headed down the highway toward the Lazy A Ranch. He was cruising along at a pretty good clip. In fact, he was speeding. When he was coming up on the gravel road that would take him off the paved road toward the Lazy A Ranch, he glanced in his rearview mirror.

Coming up behind him was one of the Sheriff's cars with its lights flashing. Tom pulled his BMW sports sedan off to the side of the road and waited for the Sheriff to walk up to him.

"You're in kind of a hurry, aren't you, Tom?"

"Yes, as a matter of fact."

"You know I'm going to have to give you a ticket. That is unless you can come up with a real good reason for drivin' so darn fast."

Frank and Tom had been friends for a good many years. They had played football together in high school, gone fishing together, and had spent a lot of time camping together as boys. Frank had gotten on the Sheriff's Department after spending several years in the Army as a Military Policeman. He was elected sheriff when the former sheriff retired.

"I've got a good reason, but I don't know if you'll think it's good enough," Tom said.

"Why don't you run it by me and let me decide?"

"You know Tracy Atwater?"

"Yeah, of course. I'm on my way out there to investigate possible rustlers on her place."

"Yeah, I heard about that, but did you know she's out at the old barn in the north pasture with Will Strong?"

"No, I didn't know that," Frank said as his expression turned serious. "You think she's in danger being around him?"

"I don't know. I've not had any problems with him. Have you?"

"No, not since he got out of prison. In fact, I've not seen very much of him. Old man Atwater hired him, and as far as I know he hardly ever leaves the ranch. I've never had a complaint involving him."

"I'm on my way out to the north pasture to make sure Tracy's all right."

"I'll go with you, but you can't take that fancy car of yours out in the pasture," Frank said.

"Yeah, I know. My pickup is at Tracy's. She said it would be parked in the barn if I needed it."

"Follow me. We'll go by and get your pickup, then drive out to the north pasture together. We can talk to her there, and I can check the rustler situation at the same time."

"Okay," Tom said and waited for Frank to get back in his Dodge Durango police vehicle.

As soon as Frank opened the door to the police car, Tom stepped on it. He turned off on the gravel road and sped toward the Lazy A ranch. It didn't take him long to get to the ranch and on up to the ranch house.

As soon as Tom pulled into the ranch yard, he looked down toward the barn. He could see the back of his pickup truck. It was parked inside the barn just as Tracy had said it would be. He turned his car and drove down to the barn. He parked his car off to the side of the barn door and got out.

He ran into the barn, jumped into his pickup and backed it out of the barn. As he turned and headed toward the gate that would let him into the east pasture, he saw Frank was already at the gate and getting out of his vehicle to open it. By the time Tom got to the gate, Frank had it open.

Tom drove through the gate, stopped, got out of his pickup and waited for Frank to drive through. As soon as Frank was clear of the gate, Tom closed it and ran back to his pickup.

Tom followed Frank as he drove across the pasture. The two four-wheel-drive vehicles were kicking up a lot of dust and dirt as they sped across the dry prairie toward the north pasture. It was not an easy ride. The pasture was rough with rolling hills and several ravines that forced them to slow way down as they drove through them.

It had taken them almost two hours to drive from the ranch yard to the hill overlooking the old north pasture barn. As they came over the top of the hill, Tom could see Will riding off in the distance, but there was no sign of Tracy. He rolled down his window and pointed toward Will, then motioned for Frank to go after him.

Frank turned his vehicle and headed off toward Will. Tom continued down the hill toward the barn.

* * * *

The sun was up and the air was cool, but that was a typical morning out on the prairie. Tracy knew that it would be hot before long as there was not a cloud in the sky. She could hear Will moving around below her. She smiled to herself as she thought about how Will would make a little extra noise so she would get up and cook breakfast for him.

Tracy stood up and stretched. The bedroll laid out on the hard floor with only a thin covering of straw for padding. It was not anywhere near as comfortable as her queen-size bed back at the ranch house. She picked up her bedroll and shook off the loose straw. She climbed down and tossed her bedroll over one of the stalls in the barn.

As she stepped outside the barn, she saw Will in the corral. He was putting a saddle on one of the horses. She immediately walked over to where they had been building their fire and started the morning fire. While it was burning down to a useable size, she prepared some dough for biscuits. She knew how much Will liked her biscuits. He needed them in order to have something to take with him while riding the fence line.

As soon as the biscuits were on the fire, she cut and cooked some bacon to go with eggs. She cut a couple of thick slices of ham for Will to use to make sandwiches out of the biscuits for his lunch.

As she looked at what she was making, it became very clear that she had not provided much of a variety of food for Will. The meals at that rate would become not very interesting. It probably didn't matter all that much to Will as long as he didn't have to do his own cooking, but Tracy felt she would have to come up with something more interesting for their evening meal tonight when he returned from riding the fence line.

After they had finished eating, Will put his plate down next to the bucket Tracy was using to wash dishes. He then walked over to his horse, put his foot in the stirrup and swung himself into the saddle.

"Will, you be careful out there. Try to be back before dark. I'm going to fix something different for dinner tonight."

"Yes, Ma'am. What yah got in mind?" he asked a little excited that he might be getting something other than some kind of stew or eggs.

"It's a surprise," she said with a smile.

Will smiled back at her, then turned his horse and rode out of the corral. At least today, Will would have something to think about. He had never had anyone do anything special for him that he could remember, other than Mr. Atwater hiring him when no one else would have anything to do with him. It was that thought that reminded him that he owed the ranch and its owner a lot more than they owed him.

Tracy watched Will as he started up the hill. She turned around and started cleaning up the area when she heard the sounds of vehicles. Her first thought was that she wished Will would turn around and come back. It wasn't until she saw the Sheriff's car that she relaxed a little and felt a bit better.

She was so busy watching the Sheriff's car as it sped off across the side of the hill, she didn't even notice Tom's pickup. It looked to her as if the Sheriff was going after Will. She was puzzled by that thought. Why would the Sheriff be after Will? He had not been to town for weeks. If the Sheriff had wanted him for something, they knew where to find him.

The sounds of a second vehicle caught her attention, and she turned to see Tom's pickup truck coming down the hill toward her. She was certainly surprised to see his truck out there. After all, she had left it in the barn at the ranch house.

Tom pulled to a stop near the corral and got out. He was not looking at her, but was watching the Sheriff catch up with Will. By the time he walked around to the corral, Will was riding back toward the barn with Frank following along behind in the sheriff's car.

"What's going on?" Tracy asked as she walked up to Tom.

"Are you okay?"

"Yes, I'm fine. What's going on? Why is Frank bringing Will back?"

"We just want to have a talk with him."

"Why? He hasn't done anything. He's been out here for the past couple of days and hasn't been off the ranch for several weeks."

Before Tom could respond to her, Will rode up to the corral and stepped out of the saddle. He tied his horse to the fence then walked over to Tracy. The look on his face showed Tracy he was as confused by what was happening as she was.

"What's going on, Boss?"

"I don't know, but it will be okay," Tracy replied as she tried to reassure Will while waiting for Frank to join them.

"You all right, Tracy?" Frank asked as he walked up to her.

"Yes. What's this all about, Frank? Why did you go after Will?"

"Well, it seems Tom was worried about you being out here all alone with him."

Tracy turned and looked at Tom. She didn't know what to think. The first thing that came to her mind was that Tom was sticking his nose into her business where it didn't belong. She wanted to say something to Tom, but she didn't want to say anything in front of Will.

"Will has been here with me for the past couple of days. He has been nothing but a gentleman and a hard working ranch hand. Now if anyone says he's been any place else or done anything he shouldn't, they're wrong. Unless you have some reason to arrest Will, then I suggest you let him go so he can do his work."

Tom could tell by the sound of her voice she was angry. There was no doubt in his mind she was angry with him. In his effort to help and show his concern for Tracy, he had caused more friction between them. That was the last thing he wanted to do.

"I'm out here about the cattle rustlers you called about. I don't want Will for anything, but I would like to ask him a couple of questions about what he saw around the place where your fence was cut," Frank said acting very professional.

Tracy looked at Frank and then at Tom. She had to wonder if it was the real reason he had cut Will off and made him return to the barn. She knew Tom and Frank had been friends most of their lives, and they had even gotten into trouble together a couple times in their younger days. It would be just like them to lie for each other, she thought.

Then again, there was always the possibility they were telling the truth. After all, she had called about rustlers on her place and the dispatcher did tell her they would send someone out to look into it.

She noticed Tom was being very quiet. Tracy was wondering why he was there. She didn't want to ask him until she could do it in private.

"Will, you tell Frank what you found and where. You can go out there with him if he wants you to. Do you understand?"

"Yes, Ma'am," he replied nervously.

Tracy could see Will was a little relieved, but still a bit nervous. She was sure someone had reported him for something. It would not have been the first time someone reported him to the police simply because they were afraid of him. His size alone was rather intimidating.

Frank looked at Will. He could see Will was nervous. He didn't know why he was nervous, but he didn't need to be.

"Let's sit over there in the shade and talk," Frank said to Will.

Will looked at Tracy then followed Frank over to the hay bales near the barn door. Frank sat down and motioned for Will to sit down. Will sat down and looked at Tracy for some kind of reassurance that everything was going to be okay.

Tracy walked over and sat on a hay bale next to Will. She smiled at him before saying anything.

"Will, tell Sheriff Frank everything you told me about the cut fence."

"Yes, Ma'am," he replied, then looked at Frank.

Tom stood a little behind Tracy, leaning back against the barn door as Will told Frank everything he had seen and done. When he finished, he looked at Tracy for her approval. She simply smiled and nodded her head slightly to let him know he had done well.

"Did you see anyone around, anyone at all?" Frank asked.

"I didn't see no one."

"Did you follow the tracks to see where they went?"

"No, sir."

"Why didn't you?"

"It was getting late. Miss Atwater wanted me back here before dark for dinner. As it was I didn't get here 'till after dark. I think that worried her some," Will said.

"That's right. He didn't get back until after dark," Tracy confirmed.

"I drove out in the morning and found the place Will told you about. I followed the tracks over to Spiny Ridge. At one place I found where a hole had been dug behind some rocks. It was about five to six inches in diameter and maybe a foot and a half to two feet deep. Whoever dug the hole didn't bother to fill it in," she explained.

"You got any idea what the hole was for?" Frank asked.

"No, but I think there may be more than just the one."

"What makes you think that?"

"There were a couple of places where the truck had stopped, but I only checked out one. If they dug a hole like the one I found at each place they stopped, there would be at least four more holes out there."

"Tracy, if they dug a hole each time they stopped, would the holes be in a straight line?" Tom asked.

Tracy looked at Tom. She was a little confused by his question, but she took a little time to think about it.

"Yes, I think so. At least they would have been in a fairly straight line. Why? What are you thinking?"

"You said the tire tracks were wider than the tracks made by my truck?" he asked, as his mind was busy trying to put what she had said in some kind of logical order.

"Yes."

"What's on your mind, Tom?" Frank asked.

"Frank, I think we need to go out there and take a look."

"Okay."

"You're not going without me," Tracy insisted.

Tom looked over at Will, then turned and looked at Tracy without saying anything.

"Frank, do you have any more questions for Will?" Tracy asked.

"No, not at the moment."

"Will, you can go ahead and do your job. I'm sure Sheriff Frank is sorry if he worried you."

"Yes, Will. I'm sorry about that, but I did need to talk to you about the cut fence. Thanks for your help," Frank said, then smiled slightly.

Will didn't say anything. He simply nodded his head, stood up and went to his horse. The others watched him as he swung into the saddle, then turned his head to look at them before he spurred his horse on. He started off across the prairie in the same direction he had been going earlier.

CHAPTER ELEVEN

As soon as Will was gone, Tracy turned to Tom. She had no idea why he was there, but if he knew something about the holes along Spiny Ridge. She wanted to know what it was, too.

"I think we best go out there and take a look around," Frank suggested.

"Yeah," Tom replied.

"You want to go with me?" Frank asked.

"We'll follow you," Tracy said, then turned and looked at Tom.

From the look on Tracy's face, Tom was pretty sure she was still a little upset with him for barging in on her without being invited. He had not meant for it to turn out that way, but then things just sort of happened between the two of them that didn't always turn out for the best.

"Well, let's get going," Frank said.

"On second thought, maybe it would be better if you follow us. I can show you where the fence was cut," Tracy suggested, then turned and started toward Tom's truck.

Tom looked at Frank, raised his eyebrows and shrugged his shoulders. Frank smiled, then turned and started off toward his police vehicle. He had known both of them all through school. He was well aware of Tom and Tracy's rather rocky relationship during high school and figured things hadn't changed much since they had returned.

When Tom got to his truck, he found Tracy sitting in the passenger's seat waiting for him. She looked as if she was a bit impatient to get going, but he knew there was more to it than that. He was probably in for a chewing out for sticking his nose into her business. He didn't think he had it coming, but then she would probably see it differently.

He got in the truck and started it. When he looked over at Tracy for directions, he noticed she was sitting up ramrod straight and looking out the windshield.

"Head that way," Tracy said without any expression in her voice as she pointed in the direction she wanted him to go.

Tom noticed she had not turned and looked at him. He thought it might be best if he simply did as he was told and kept his mouth shut, at least until she was ready to start talking to him. He backed away from the corral and started up the hill. He headed north toward the fence line.

A quick glance in the rearview mirror showed Tom that Frank was right behind him. He knew it would take awhile to get to the north fence line, but it would seem like an eternity if Tracy remained silent all the way there. He almost wished they had all gone in Frank's police vehicle. At least, he wouldn't be left with complete silence.

The truck bounced along over the open prairie. Although they were making good time, it didn't seem like it was fast enough for Tracy.

Tom had not bothered to tell her what he was thinking when she asked about the hole in the ground, and he had not bothered to explain it now that they were alone. As long as she didn't ask him about it, he could keep his theory to himself until he had something more to go on than her description of the hole.

Tracy was slowly getting over the feeling that Tom was sticking his nose into her business. He was, she was sure of that, but his reasons might be nothing more than to help her. So far, he had done nothing but try to make things easier for her. That was nice of him, but she still couldn't get rid of the feeling that there would be a price to pay for everything he did; and she was worried about what it might cost her, and when it might come due and payable.

She slowly turned and looked at him. He was looking straight ahead, watching the prairie for ruts. He had strong features and was as handsome as ever. Even in jeans and a work shirt he looked sexy, she thought. Seeing what he was wearing made her realize that maybe he had come out for no other reason than to help her watch over the cattle to protect them from rustlers. After all, he had suggested it to her on the phone. There was also the possibility he was there to watch over her a little, too.

She almost smiled at that thought. She could hardly picture him as her guardian angel. In his youth, he was anything but an angel. Yet, he had been there for her whenever she needed him, and without having to ask for his help. Just like he was now.

"When you get to the fence line, turn east and drive along the fence," she said, the tone of her voice much more pleasant than it had been when he first showed up at the north pasture barn.

Tom didn't reply. He simply nodded his head that he understood and continued north. When he came to the fence, he turned east and drove along the fence line. It wasn't long before he could see where Tracy had driven the day before. The tires of his truck had crushed down the dry brittle grass as they rolled over it.

As he got near where the fence had been cut, he could see the tracks in the dry grass where the mystery truck had come through the fence. He stopped his truck and looked out the window for a minute before he turned his head to look at Tracy. She was looking at him.

"Why are we stopping?" she asked.

"I want Frank to take a look around before we go on. Frank is a hell of a good tracker. He might see something that will give us a clue as to what is going on here."

"Oh," she said as she reached for the door handle.

Frank had pulled up behind Tom's truck and stepped out of his vehicle. He was looking over the area as he walked toward Tom and Tracy.

"Stay here for a minute. I want to look around a little. Is Tom's truck the one you brought out here?" Frank asked Tracy.

"Yes. Once I started following the tracks, I drove beside them so I could see them out the truck's side window and see where they had stopped."

"I'm glad you did that. We might be able to get a good set of tire tracks. Never know, they might come in handy."

Frank started to slowly move closer to where the fence had been cut. He would look at the ground for a bit, then glance up toward the fence, then look back at the ground again. He studied the area in great detail.

When he got to where the fence had been cut, he examined the ends of the bared wire for a minute. He then knelt down and examined the tire tracks closely while Tom and Tracy stayed close to Tom's truck and watched him as he worked.

"What's he looking for?" Tracy asked.

"He's looking for something that will tell him why the truck came onto the ranch. From the tire tracks, he might be able to figure out what kind of a truck it was. That might even help him figure out why they were here."

"Oh," she replied as she continued to watch Frank study the ground.

It wasn't long before Frank stood up, looked off across the prairie on the other side of the fence. He could see that the tire tracks seemed to wander down from the north. Frank knew that there was a gravel road several miles north of there. He took a couple of minutes to think about where the road went before he turned back around and looked at where the tracks came onto the Lazy A Ranch side of the fence.

He looked around a little more while he thought about the tire tracks, then headed back to where Tom and Tracy were waiting. It was obvious Frank was deep in thought as he approached them.

"What do you think, Frank?"

"I seriously doubt it was rustlers who cut the fence."

"Why's that?"

"The type of tires on the truck and the wheel spread would make it a very heavy truck, but a short one. A truck that size wouldn't be able to carry very many cattle, probably no more than two or three."

He then looked at Tracy before he spoke.

"Who owns the land on the north side of the fence?"

"That would be Wilber Blaine's place, the W bar B ranch. Why?"

"That's who I thought owned it. I just wanted to be sure."

"What are you thinking, Frank?" Tom asked.

"Well, I heard a rumor that Blaine was thinking of trying to drill a well somewhere on his property."

"That's right. He had asked the bank for a loan," Tom said as he thought about what that might have to do with the truck coming onto Tracy's ranch.

"These tracks could have been made by a truck used to help them find water. You know, one of those small drilling rigs."

"What would it be doing on my property?" Tracy asked.

"Who knows? It could be something as simple as the driver of the truck thought that Blaine's ranch extended further south than this fence."

"I don't think so," Tom injected. "Wilber was planning on drilling for water closer to his ranch house. Actually, he said he was going to try and get a well sunk just north of the ranch house; that would put it eight, maybe nine miles north of here."

"Could he have changed his mind?"

"I guess so, but if he had told us that he might be drilling for water here, we would not have approved the loan."

"Why not?"

"There have been several test wells in the pasture on Blaine's side of the fence. Nothing ever came of them. I can't see him wasting more money to try again."

"I see," Frank said thoughtfully.

"Frank?"

"Yeah, Tracy?"

"I don't think it was a drilling rig. Where the hole is that I found, you could never get a truck like that in there."

"You might be right," Frank said thoughtfully. "Let's go take a look at the hole. Maybe we can come up with something else. Follow me this time."

Tracy and Tom went to his truck and got in while Frank got in his police vehicle. Frank pulled around in front of Tom and began driving alongside the tire tracks from the mystery truck. He followed them all the way to the edge of the rocky outcropping called Spiny Ridge. From there the tracks turned and ran parallel to the ridge along one of the shorter outer ridges, the one that ran twenty or thirty feet from the bigger and higher ridges that actually formed Spiny Ridge.

Frank hadn't gone very far when he came to a place where he could see signs in the dirt where the mystery truck had stopped. He stopped alongside the tracks and got out of his vehicle.

Tom stopped behind him and got out. By the time Tracy and Tom were alongside Frank, Frank was looking off toward the first and lower ridge.

"What do you think," Tom asked.

"Well, there's no sign that they tried to drive the truck over that ridge. And from the looks of these tracks, the truck would never make it over the ridge anyway."

"I don't think I could get over that ridge with my truck," Tom said as he looked at the ridge.

"Tracy, did you find a hole near here?"

"No. It was down further. I didn't check out the first couple of places that they stopped to see if they had dug any holes."

"How far from the truck would you say it was to where they dug the hole you did see?"

"Twenty-five to thirty feet, maybe a little further."

"In which direction?"

"That way," she said as she pointed to the rather low rocky ridge only fifteen feet from the tracks.

"On the other side of this first ridge?"

"Yeah, but before you get to the bigger ridge beyond."

Frank started toward the ridge with Tom and Tracy right behind him. They climbed to the top of the first ridge. When they got there, they stood and looked down the backside of the ridge. Not more than ten feet in front of them was a hole about five to six inches in diameter.

Frank looked at Tracy and Tom before he started down off the ridge toward the hole. Tom and Tracy were right behind him.

When they got to the hole, Frank knelt down and looked into the hole. He could see that it was about a foot and a half deep, maybe just a little more. It was round as if dug with a gas powered posthole digger, and it looked like the bottom of the hole was flat. He knelt down and examined the hole more closely.

"Tom, look here."

Tom knelt down and looked into the hole.

"Well, I'll be damned."

"What?" Tracy asked impatiently, not being able to see around the two men.

"I get the feeling this is a test hole for natural gas or oil," Tom said as he looked over his shoulder at Tracy.

"You mean there might be oil on the ranch?"

"It's possible, I suppose. Someone must think there's a possibility of something here."

"Wow. That could change everything," Tracy said excitedly.

"I wouldn't get too excited if I were you. They may not have found anything. Sometimes they do hundreds of these test holes before they even get a hint of anything worth drilling for," Tom said. "And that's not all. If they did find something, there's no telling how they will drill for it."

"What do you mean?"

"It's possible that they might try drilling in from Blaine's property."

"You mean drill in at an angle?"

"Yeah. Something like that."

"Is that legal, Frank?"

"I don't know. Do you have the oil and mineral rights to this land?" Frank asked as he thought about the test hole.

"I think so, but I'd have to find out for sure," Tracy said, not sure of what to do next.

"I think we should first of all try to find out who is doing the exploring, find out what they are exploring for, and if they found anything encouraging. It would also be nice to find out who was on your property without permission. I'll do a little checking around and see what I can find out," Frank said.

"There's a drilling outfit over in the next county. I know one of the owners. I'll check around and see if they're doing any exploring and for whom. They might also know of any other companies that are doing some testing in the area."

"I'd appreciate that," Tracy said. "What do we do now?"

"Nothing," Frank said. "Just keep an eye out for anyone on your property that doesn't belong here, and for any other vehicles or tracks from strange vehicles. If you find any or see anyone that doesn't belong here, let me know immediately."

"I will," Tracy said as she turned and looked at Tom.

"You might also let me know if a drilling rig suddenly appears on Blaine's ranch within a couple of miles of your property line," Frank added.

"I understand."

"I want to know, too," Tom said. "If he got his loan under false pretenses, like drilling for oil or natural gas, we can demand he repay the loan immediately and charge him with fraud."

"Right. If we can prove that he told the test people to go ahead and cut the fence and test along Spiny Ridge, you can have him charged with trespassing as well," Frank said.

"I'll keep an eye out," Tracy assured them.

"Tracy, have you or your father had any trouble with Mr. Blaine," Frank asked.

"Nothing serious, at least not recently."

"What do you mean by that? Have you had trouble in the past with him?"

"Yes. About ten years back, he tried to claim that our fence line was on his property and planned to sue us. Dad got a lawyer and had the land surveyed. The survey showed our fence was actually two hundred yards inside where our property line was. My father moved the fence to where the property line really was, where it is now. Blaine was pretty angry about that. He had tried to get more of our land and ended up losing some of what he considered his land."

"It would be my guess that he wasn't a very good neighbor after that?"

"No. It took a judge to really settle it and to get him to stop cutting our fence so his cattle could eat our grass. It got so bad that the judge warned him that if there were any more fences cut by him, he would find himself in jail. Ever since then, he and his family don't talk to us, but we haven't had any more trouble with him."

"I think I remember hearing something about that when we were in high school. That may have been the reason that very few people in town like the Blaines" Frank said. "So, I guess in short, it would be safe to say you don't trust him. Is that correct?"

"Yes. I wouldn't put anything past him."

Frank looked back toward the fence line. He couldn't see it from where he was standing. He was thinking about Blaine. At least he had an idea of who might be involved in trespassing on the Lazy A Ranch. The only question left was why.

"I've got to get back to town and start looking into this. I might be able to help find out who was on your property. By the way, you might want to keep this quiet for now. No sense getting people all worked up when nothing might come of it. We don't know if they had any positive results from the tests."

"I agree," Tom said. "If word gets out someone is looking for natural gas or oil out here, every rancher in the county will be looking for it on his property. I can't really blame them with the way ranching has been these last few years, but until we're sure there is natural gas or oil, it would be better to keep it quiet."

"Right. I've got to go."

"I'll see you back in town," Tom said.

Frank nodded in reply, then turned and headed back toward his vehicle while Tom and Tracy turned around and looked back in the hole. There was no doubt in Tom's mind that the hole and what it meant, was giving Tracy some hope that it might be able to save the ranch. He hoped she wasn't counting on it. He knew it was a little early for that, but it was important enough for Tracy to make sure her father had the oil and mineral rights to the ranch land.

"Tracy?"

"Yeah?" she said as she turned to look at him.

"I think it would be a good idea if you went into town to the court house. You need to find out if your father has the mineral and oil rights here. It may not mean anything; but if push comes to shove, it would be good to know what your options might be."

"What about my cattle? I can't just go off and leave them with only Will to look out for them. It's hard enough for two of us to watch them."

"I'll stay here with Will and keep an eye on your cattle and the ranch while you're gone."

"But who will cook Will's meals?"

"I will."

"You?"

"Yeah. Believe it or not, I'm a pretty darn good cook," Tom said with a smile. "And cooking over an open fire is my favorite way to cook."

"Oh, I can't go. I told Will I would make something special for him tonight. If I disappoint him, he might leave. I can't afford to lose him."

"I'll fix him something special, something I'm sure he will like," Tom assured her.

"I don't know. He's expecting me to cook for him.

"Well, it will be special just having me cook for him.

"That's for sure," Tracy said with a grin. "He's a heavy eater. No light meal will do for him."

"He will get enough to eat, I can assure you of that," Tom said with a grin. "Now let's get back to the barn so you can get into town."

Tracy still wasn't sure it was a good idea to leave Tom out there with Will. She wasn't sure how well Tom could cook for one thing, and she wasn't sure how they would get along for another. She did know Tom could get along with most folks if he wanted to.

As they drove back toward the north pasture barn, Tracy thought about what it would mean to her and her father if oil or natural gas were discovered on the ranch. It would provide the money needed to pay for her father's care at the nursing home. It would also provide the money needed to keep the ranch running by paying the bills and wages of the ranch hands. She might even be able to get Jacob to come back to work for her.

Although she had nothing to go on except speculation, there was no doubt that just the thought of natural gas or oil on the ranch seemed to ease her worries a bit. Even with the thought of riches, she still could not help but hope for enough rain to turn the grass green and add to the water in the watering holes.

The thought of water and grass reminded her of the small valley she had found inside Spiny Ridge. She realized she had not told Tom about it.

She turned her head and looked at him as he drove. For some unknown reason, she felt it might be a good idea to keep it to herself, at least for the time being. If there were oil or natural gas on the ranch, she wouldn't have to tell anyone about it. She could wait and hopefully her father would be able to tell her why he had kept it from her. If there was no natural gas or oil, there might be some way she could use it to keep the ranch from going under until conditions improved.

How that little valley would be of help in keeping the ranch going, she had no idea. Although she was sure it would provide the cattle with food and water for several weeks, maybe months in the driest of times, it would be too difficult to get them in and out of the valley.

Tom glanced over at Tracy and noticed she seemed to be deep in thought. He was sure she was thinking about the possibility of riches, or at least enough money to get the ranch back on a solid footing again. He wanted to say something to her, but he figured it wouldn't hurt for her to dream for a little while. Life on the ranch had been hard for her. She needed a few moments of hope.

"Tom?"

"Yeah?"

"How do I go about finding out if my father has the oil and mineral rights to the ranch without it getting out that something is going on?"

"Good question."

"You know what a blabber mouth Miss Cutchen at the court house is."

"Why don't you sort of hint at the fact that if the weather doesn't change you might have to sell the ranch and want to know if the oil and mineral rights would go with it. You could hint at the fact it might help you to get a little better price. That way you've made no commitment to sell, nor are you saying anything about the possibility of natural gas or oil on the property. You're just looking for anything that might help you get a better price if you should have to sell."

"Yeah. That's a good idea. And if she asks if I'm planning on selling, I can tell her no, but it would be important for me to know these things if I'm forced to sell."

"Right. And besides, if she starts spreading the word you are thinking of selling, I'll hear about it almost immediately. My mother would be the first one she would tell. And you know my mother can't keep her mouth shut for anything," he said with a knowing grin.

Tracy looked at him and laughed. She knew the grapevine in town was faster than the news media. A little story like that would make Mrs. Norbert feel really good. To her it would mean Tracy was likely to leave town, and Tracy knew there was nothing that would make Mrs. Norbert happier than if she left the county.

"I would be able to put a stop to the rumors before they get too serious," Tom added.

Tom dropped over the hill and drove down to the north pasture barn. He stopped over next to the corral and got out. He stood at the door and watched as Tracy moved over to the driver's seat and looked at him.

"There's plenty of food in the coolers. I was planning on cooking a couple of good size steaks tonight. They're in the red cooler. They would make a good meal."

"Don't worry about us. I will make baked potatoes and cook up some carrots to go with the steaks for our dinner."

"Oh, Will likes biscuits."

"No problem, I can make biscuits."

Tom looked into her eyes. She was looking down at him from the truck. She wanted to say something about how much she appreciated his help, and how thankful she was he was there for her, but decided against it. Anything she said right now might be taken as something more than just a thank you.

"I guess I best be going," Tracy said.

"Yeah. Don't try to come back out here tonight. It will be dark by the time you get back to the ranch house from town. Get a good night's sleep and come back out in the morning. I'll be fine, and make sure Will is well fed. Oh, what do you want Will to do tomorrow?"

"He can continue to ride the fence line unless you think he should stay closer to the cattle."

"I'll have him ride the fence line where your property butts up against Blaine's. That way we can keep an eye out to make sure no one cuts the fence again. It will also help us keep watch for any activity on that part of the Blaine place."

"Good idea. Thanks," Tracy said as she smiled at him.

She thought about leaning over and kissing him, but decided she wasn't ready for that, yet. Instead, she closed the door and put the truck in gear.

Tom stood next to the corral and watched as she drove off across the prairie. It wasn't long before she was out of sight.

CHAPTER TWELVE

Tracy glanced in the rearview mirror and saw Tom standing next to the corral watching her as she drove away. He looked so sexy leaning against the fence post. He appeared to be what the perfect cowboy should look like, tall with a narrow waist, broad shoulders and strong features. If he was anything, he was handsome, she thought.

Her thoughts were suddenly interrupted when the truck hit a bump. It caused the truck to shake her back to reality and brought her attention back to what she should have been doing, driving.

The remainder of the trip back to the ranch house went without further incident. She was able to split her thoughts between driving and Tom. As she approached the ranch house, Tracy realized she would have time for a quick shower and still be able to get to the courthouse before it closed, provided she hurried. Tracy pulled up in front of the ranch house and jumped out of the truck. She ran inside and headed straight for the bathroom.

After a quick shower, she put on a sundress that looked nice on her and would be comfortable on such a hot day. It would not only be comfortable, but it would be appropriate for what she was going to do.

On her way out the door, she noticed Tom's BMW parked down by the barn. The car looked a little out of place next to a barn. It was the kind of a car that would look more at home in the big city, but it hadn't surprised her that Tom would own such a car. He had always liked the finer things life had to offer. Yet, he never seemed to flaunt the fact he and his family had money. His best friend, Frank, all through high school hardly had two pennies to rub together and he certainly would not get rich as a sheriff. Yet, they had remained great friends even today.

As she started to get into the truck, Tracy again glanced at the BMW. She then looked at the keys she held in her hand. The keys to Tom's car were on the key ring. It occurred to her that the car would be faster than the truck, and undoubtedly it would be a much nicer ride. The fact that the truck was just as capable of going the speed limit as the car never entered her mind.

Tracy smiled to herself then started across the yard to the car. She got in and started it up. It was the first time she had ever been in such a nice car. It had leather interior and all the up-to-date fancy gadgets that were available on such a car. She slipped the car into gear and backed away from the barn. Putting it in drive, she headed for town.

As she pulled out of the ranch yard onto the gravel road, she found the car handled very nicely even on loose gravel. It wasn't until she got to the paved road that she began to appreciate just how nice a car it really was. The ride was smooth and the car responded quickly to all her commands. It didn't take much for her to understand why Tom liked it.

Tracy went directly to the courthouse, parking in front on the main street. Miss Cutchen, the town's old maid and president of the unofficial local gossip society, greeted her. Tracy had hoped she wouldn't have to deal with Miss Cutchen, but that was not to be.

"Good afternoon, Miss Cutchen."

"Good afternoon, Tracy. I see you are driving Tom Norbert's new car," she said with a silly grin.

"Yes, but it's not all that new. He loaned it to me since, as I'm sure you know, my truck is in the shop for repairs."

"Yes, I did hear something about that."

I'll bet you did, Tracy thought. If she knew anything, she knew Miss Cutchen never let anything going on in the county slip by her. She undoubtedly knew Tracy's truck was not worth fixing, and that Tom had actually loaned her his truck. In fact, she probably knew that Tom had taken care of getting her truck off the street and over to Les's shop for repairs, but she was not there to discuss her personal life.

"The reason I'm here is I would like some information about my father's ranch."

"Certainly, what is it you would like to know?"

"I would like to know if my father has the oil and mineral rights to his property?"

Now that was exciting news to someone like Miss Cutchen. That was better than finding out her neighbor's husband was stepping out on his wife with a woman over in the next county.

It was easy for Tracy to see Miss Cutchen's interest rise. It was written all over her face. Tracy was hoping she would not have to give her much of an explanation on why she wanted the information.

"Well, I don't know for sure, but I'll look it up for you. Why don't you come with me?"

Miss Cutchen led Tracy back into the courthouse vault where the record books were kept. Once in the vault, Miss Cutchen looked around to make sure no one else was in the vault and could hear them talking. She preferred to be the first to know any little juicy tidbits of gossip she could get her hands on. Working in the courthouse had proved to be the perfect place to pick up those little bits of information that would allow her to get rumors started.

The look on Miss Cutchen's face let Tracy know that Miss Cutchen was going to quiz her on why she wanted the information, and there appeared to be no way out of it. She knew Miss Cutchen had to be the first to know everything. Not being the first would be a crushing blow to her status as the number one gossip in the county.

"Do you think there might be oil on your property?" Miss Cutchen almost whispered as she stepped up close to Tracy.

"Oh, no. I don't think so. I don't think anyone has ever found oil in this part of the county, but I'm sure you know that. I just want to know in case I have to sell the ranch," Tracy said with a smile.

"Oh," she said as disappointment washed over her face.

As Miss Cutchen looked at Tracy, the expression of disappointment seemed to fade from her face and was replaced by a friendlier look. Tracy knew she had thought of something else that might provide her with news no one else knew, news she could spread around.

"Are you planning on selling the ranch?"

"No, but times are tough for all the ranchers in the county these days. And with my father in the nursing home, it is getting harder to make ends meet."

"I see."

"I'm just trying to find out everything I can about the ranch in case I do have to sell, that's all. If the oil and mineral rights go with the property it could mean I might be able to get a little better price for it, if I have to sell. Don't you agree?"

"Well, yes. I guess so," she said thoughtfully. "I suppose the more you know about the ranch, the more you could get for it. That is, if you do have to sell."

"I knew you would understand," Tracy said with a smile. "Now, about the oil and mineral rights?"

"Oh, certainly."

Miss Cutchen smiled back, then turned and started looking for the book that would show her if Tracy's father owned the mineral and oil rights to his ranch. It didn't take long before she found them. After all, she knew almost everything about everybody in the county - what their taxes were, how much they owed and to whom. She also knew their family history.

"Let's see," she said as she began flipping though the pages of the record book.

"Here it is. It shows that when your grandfather bought the property, he registered the oil and mineral rights to it as well. It appears you have legal right to the mineral and oil that may lie below your property."

"That's great," Tracy said showing a little more excitement than she had intended.

The look on Miss Cutchen's face quickly brought Tracy's show of excitement back under control.

"Thank you very much. You have been a great help," Tracy said then turned to leave.

Tracy was a little upset with herself since she had not covered up her thrill at finding out what she had only hoped would be the case. There was no doubt in her mind it would be all over town that there might be oil, or something of value, on the Lazy A Ranch. It would probably be all over town before the sun set. She had no idea what problems it might cause, but one thing was for sure. If the rumor got out that there might be oil on the ranch, she might get some serious offers for the ranch if she did have to sell.

Selling the ranch was not in her plans if it could be avoided. Tracy loved the ranch almost as much as her father did. She could never sell the ranch as long as her father was alive.

As Tracy walked out of the courthouse, she saw Tom's mother turn into a parking space next to Tom's BMW. Tracy stopped and watched as she got out of her bright yellow Cadillac, a car that she intended people to notice.

It was the one thing Tracy had not planned on. She was the last person Tracy wanted to see, and certainly the last person she wanted to talk to right now.

Tracy thought about going back inside the courthouse and going out the back door, but it was too late. Tom's mother had already seen her. She noticed that Mrs. Norbert turned her head and looked at Tom's car, then turned back to look at her. Tracy could just about imagine what was going on in her head. Whatever it was, it was not good.

Since it was too late to avoid Mrs. Norbert, Tracy took in a deep breath and started down the sidewalk toward Tom's car. She could see Mrs. Norbert was looking her over. Tracy could also see the look in her eyes. Mrs. Norbert didn't like Tracy, and she especially didn't like her son having anything to do with her.

"Good afternoon, Mrs. Norbert," Tracy said with a pleasant smile.

"Is Tom in the courthouse?" she asked sharply.

It was apparent Mrs. Norbert was not in the mood to give Tracy even a half-hearted greeting, let alone a civil response, but that was nothing new. Mrs. Norbert had always looked down her long narrow nose at the Atwater family, and there was no reason to think she would be any different now.

"No," Tracy said flatly.

"I don't suppose you know where he is?"

"As a matter of fact, I do," Tracy replied without further explanation.

"Would you be so kind as to tell me where he is? I happen to know he is not in his office," she said with a note of anger in her voice.

"You are correct. He is not in his office. He is out at my ranch."

"What in the world is he doing out there?" she asked angrily, her voice getting louder.

"I would think he is looking out for my cattle at the moment. In a little while, however, I suspect he will be fixing dinner for my hired hand and himself since I will not be able to get back in time to fix it for them."

"I don't believe this. First you have his new truck, then his car, and now you have him working for you like a common hired hand. What next?"

"I believe that will be between your son and me, and it's really none of your business," Tracy said without a hint of emotion. "If you will excuse me, I have things I need to do."

Tracy stepped around Mrs. Norbert and walked over to the car. As she opened the door, she looked up at Mrs. Norbert. She could see Mrs. Norbert was very angry, but that was not what bothered her. What bothered her were the nasty rumors Mrs. Norbert would undoubtedly spread around town about her.

Tracy had done nothing to make Tom's mother hate her except to date her son in high school. Up until today, Tracy had always treated her with respect because she was Tom's mother, but that was over. She had no right to look down at the Atwater family and treat them like dirt. It was families like the Atwaters that kept her in things like the ugly yellow Cadillac she was so proud of, her expensive clothes and the fancy large house she lived in on the outskirts of town.

Tracy got into the car and backed out of the parking space. As she pulled away, she could see the irritated look on Mrs. Norbert's face. Tracy thought she could see her mentally working out a way to cause problems between Tom and her.

That last thought began to cause Tracy to think about Tom and herself. If she really didn't want anything to do with Tom, why did it bother her that his mother was trying to drive a wedge between them? It shouldn't make any difference.

The more she thought about it, the more she realized she did have feelings, strong feelings, for Tom. Maybe stronger feelings for him than she should have. She began to think about the kiss he had planted on her lips the other day when he was upset with her. Just the thought of it caused her body to remember how good it had felt.

The long drive back to the ranch gave her time to think. Time to think about Tom, and about how she really felt about him. It also gave her time to think about what she should do about it. Her feelings for him were becoming clear in her head, but she wasn't even sure if she had the ability to do anything about it. How she responded to his touch and his kiss had been out of her control, and that scared her a little.

When she arrived back at the ranch house, she parked his car in the barn. It was still light out, but it was getting on toward time to eat. She spent the next half hour fixing her dinner in sort of a daze. Her mind was too cluttered with thoughts of Tom to concentrate on what she was making.

After she finished her dinner, she decided to spend a little time reading in the hope of finding something else to occupy her mind. She rummaged around in her father's den and found a book she had not read. It was a romance novel, something she was sure had belonged to her mother. She wondered why her father had kept the book.

Opening the cover she saw a short inscription written on the inside cover along with the date. She paused as she read the inscription. The book had been a gift from her father to her mother on their twenty-fifth wedding anniversary. She smiled at the thought of her father actually going into a bookstore to buy a romance novel.

She turned to the first page and began to read. Tracy had not read very much when she heard a knock at the door. She carefully put the book down on the table beside the chair, got up and cautiously walked to the door.

It was dark outside and she had not expected company. When she got to the door, she reached over and turned on the porch light, then looked out the window to see who was there. Tracy was surprised to see a man in a suit standing on her porch, a man she recognized. She reached out, turned the doorknob and opened the door.

"Good evening, Mr. Norbert."

"Good evening, Tracy," he said with a pleasant smile.

Tracy wasn't sure, but she thought she noticed a bit of reluctance in Mr. Norbert's demeanor. It caused her to wonder why he was there.

"Won't you come in?"

"I'm sorry to barge in on you like this, but there is something I would like to discuss with you. I hope this is not too inconvenient for you as I know it is late."

"Not at all. Please come in," Tracy said as she stepped back so he could enter the house.

Franklin Norbert stepped past her, then followed her into the den. She motioned for him to have a seat. He sat down on a sofa and looked up at her.

"Can I get you something?"

"No. Thank you."

"Okay, what is it you wish to talk to me about?" Tracy asked as she sat down in a chair in front of him.

"This is rather difficult for me, but I felt it was important enough for me to talk to you as soon as possible."

Tracy waited for him to speak again. He looked like what he had to say was, in fact, difficult for him. She knew her next payment on the ranch loan was not due for a couple of months, and she was sure he would not have come out so far to talk to her about what would happen if she failed to make the payment. There had to be something else on his mind. Franklin took a deep breath before he spoke.

"I think you know I have always liked you, and I think I have treated you and your father as much as friends as clients of the bank."

"Yes. You have always treated us well, in both our business dealings and socially."

"And I have never interfered with the relationship between you and my son."

Tracy wasn't sure what he was getting at, but if she had to guess he was there because of Mrs. Norbert. She had probably given him an earful of the encounter in front of the courthouse between her and Mrs. Norbert earlier in the day.

"What are you getting at Mr. Norbert?" Tracy said as she crossed her arms in front of her and stiffened.

"Mrs. Norbert told me about how rude you were to her earlier in the afternoon."

"She was rude to me first. She didn't even have the courtesy to offer me a greeting," Tracy said in her own defense.

"Don't get me wrong. I know Mrs. Norbert can be, shall we say, a little upsetting when it comes to Tom. Well, she can be a little upsetting for a lot of other reasons as well. I think it would be helpful if you understood her a little."

"Oh, I think I understand her."

"I don't think you do. You see, Tom is the only child she was ever able to have. She had two miscarriages that were very hard on her. Not to get into all of it, let it suffice to say she quickly became overprotective of Tom."

"But Tom does not need her to protect him. He is a grown man and can take care of himself."

"You are right about that, but over the years she lived her life for him. She has tried to direct his every move. Without much success I might add," he said with a grin. "I am grateful he has led his own life in spite of her. However, her interference has caused a lot of friction between them over the years, especially over the past few years.

"I'm telling you this not so you will not see Tom any more, but so that maybe you can understand his mother a little better. I think you and Tom have something very special. He seems to light up when he talks about you. I've never seen him do that over anyone else," he said with a smile.

Tracy was a little embarrassed by his comment and a little confused. She had thought he was there to tell her not to see Tom. His last comment had showed her that he really did like her.

"I might add his mother is jealous of you. She once got all his attention, but now you seem to have his heart."

"I'm not sure what to say except that what happens between Tom and me is, and will always be, between Tom and me. But I gather from your visit that you want something from me. What is it that you want? Whatever it is, I will not standby and let Mrs. Norbert treat me the way she did in front of the courthouse for the entire world to see. I am not a gold digger, and I am not trying to get my claws into her son."

"I understand that. You two have had something special since high school. I admit you had your problems back then. Going away to school helped both of you to grow and mature.

"I would like it, and take it as a personal favor, if you could see your way to try to, - - I don't know, - - try to get along with Margaret, or at least make every attempt to try to understand her. Believe me, I know how hard that is. What do you say?"

"I don't know what the future holds for Tom and me, if anything. But I will try to get along with Mrs. Norbert. However, I will not allow her to treat me like she did today. If I have to, I will simply avoid her as much as possible."

"I understand. And thank you, Tracy. I appreciate whatever you can do to get along with her. I will talk to her, although I don't expect it to help much," he said, then stood up.

Tracy stood up and walked him to the door. As he stepped out on the porch, he stopped and turned toward her.

"I would appreciate it if you said as little as possible about tonight to Tom. I don't want him getting any more upset with his mother than he already is."

"I will not say anything to him unless he asks me. I will not lie to him."

"That's fair enough. Thank you, Tracy."

"You're welcome," Tracy said with a smile.

She stood on the porch and watched as Franklin Norbert walked to his car and got in. As soon as he had left the ranch yard, Tracy closed the door and shut off the porch light.

Tracy did not return to the den. Instead she went to her bedroom and got ready for bed. She spent the next hour or so lying in her bed thinking about what had happened today.

Tracy had promised Franklin she would try to get along with Mrs. Norbert. She knew it would not be easy. She wondered if it would be easier to make an effort not to see Tom. The more she thought about it, the more she realized that wouldn't be any easier.

It was late when Tracy finally dozed off into a restless sleep.

CHAPTER THIRTEEN

Shortly after Tracy had disappeared over the hill on her way to town, Tom turned and looked around. Will had gone off to ride the fence line. It was time for Tom to saddle up a horse and do a little riding around himself. The cattle needed to be checked on, and it wouldn't hurt if he did a little scouting around to make sure all was quiet.

Tom went inside the barn and took a bridle off one of the stalls where it had been kept. He walked over to the corral at the back of the barn and picked out a chestnut gelding that looked like a good sturdy horse. Tom put the bridle on the horse, walked him out of the corral, then tied him to the corral fence.

He put a saddle blanket on the horse before tossing the only available saddle over its back. One look at the saddle caused Tom to smile. He quickly realized the saddle was Tracy's, and it would take a little adjusting to make it usable for him. After adjusting the stirrups to fit, he untied the horse, swung up into the saddle and rode up the hill behind the barn.

When he got to the top of the hill, he stopped and looked out over the vast prairie. He knew Will had gone north and would be working along the north fence line to the west, since he had gone east the other day. He could see no sense in going the same way. If Will saw anything, he was sure Will would tell him about it at dinner.

Tom turned the horse and headed straight south. It would eventually take him to Spiny Ridge since it ran diagonally from the northeast corner of the ranch almost to the southwest corner over twenty miles away. It would take him a couple of hours before he would get to Spiny Ridge. Tom had a good seven hours before he would have to think about starting dinner, longer if Will didn't return until dark, which seemed to be Will's practice according to Tracy.

Tom had no idea what he expected to find over near the ridge, but it seemed to be the place that was of interest to whoever had come onto the ranch from the north. The long ride to the ridge gave him time to think. The test site he had seen sort of stuck in his mind. What were they looking for? Had they had any positive results in the tests they did? And the most important question to him was why had they come onto private property without the owner's permission?

Tom knew of several companies in the area that did tests for oil and natural gas. Of the ones he knew, all of them seemed to be run by honest people who would not consider trespassing on someone's property. Tom also knew there were companies he didn't know very much about, if anything.

It was at that moment he thought of Mr. Wilber Blaine. He knew why Tracy and her father had not trusted him. Wilber was the type of man who would be dishonest in his business dealings if it suited his purpose. Would he ask for a loan to dig a well for water, then use the money to test for oil or natural gas? That was not a hard question for Tom to answer. If he used his loan for some reason other than what he had requested it for, it could be reason enough for the bank to call in his loan immediately.

What had happened between Blaine and Atwater, played out mostly after he had left for school so Tom knew little of the details. Wilber didn't seem like the type to risk his ranch that way, but some men would do just about anything for money.

All the way to Spiny Ridge Tom had not seen any more tracks he couldn't identify or were not easily explained. He did notice that the cattle had spread out and seemed to be doing well in spite of the conditions. The one water hole he had come across still had a little water in it, but there was plenty of water near the north pasture barn. The further away from the north pasture barn Tom got, the fewer cattle he saw. That seemed to make sense to him as the cattle had more of what they needed closer to the barn.

When Tom finally reached the edge of Spiny Ridge, he reined up and sat there for a minute looking at the rocky formation. The rocky formation sort of reminded him of the backbone of a very large dinosaur. That alone would be enough for some people to believe there had been dinosaurs in the area at one time, therefore, there must be oil down there. The fact that Spiny Ridge was rock, not the remains of a dinosaur, didn't seem to enter into the way some people thought. Even as that thought passed through Tom's mind, he knew it sounded pretty lame and lacked any resemblance to good logic. But sometimes that was all it took to make some people gamble everything they had on a long shot that might make them rich.

Anyone who had lived in the county knew there had been some very extensive testing done in the area looking for oil less than five years ago. There had never been any positive results reported. All the oil in the county had been found on the far end of the county, and not that much.

Tom took a few minutes to look up and down the ridge. He was a long ways from where the drilling had taken place. The test drills were way northeast of where he was. To the southwest of him, the ridge ran several more miles before the rocky ridges seemed to slope down and go underground.

After a few minutes of looking around, he decided he would ride along the ridge back toward where the test holes had been dug. He thought it might be of interest to find out how far along the ridge they had gone before turning back.

He touched the horse in the flanks, reined it around and began to move northeast along the ridge. It was pretty country out there with Spiny Ridge on one side of him and gently rolling prairie on the other. As much as he enjoyed the chance to get out of his office and spend some time on the open range, he still had a job to do.

His job right now was to check on cattle and make sure all was well. As he rode along, he noticed there were three cows standing near a shallow draw with their heads hanging down. They were not eating or moving. Tom turned his horse and started toward them. As he got closer, he noticed they seemed to be having a problem. The only problem he could think they might have was a lack of water.

Tom continued to move closer, being very careful not to spook them. The last thing he wanted was for them to run. When he was close enough, he gently nudged them to get them to start moving. Slowly and patiently, he moved them toward the north pasture barn where they could get plenty of water. It took him most of the afternoon to get them back to the barn. When they got there, they went directly to the watering trough. He was pleased with himself. It had been several years since he had done anything with cattle, and he liked the way it made him feel. He turned his horse and walked it back to the corral.

The evening shadows were getting long. It was time to build a fire and start fixing dinner. It would not be long before Will would be returning. He had a special dinner to fix for Will, and it had better be good.

After seeing to his horse, he gathered what he needed. He built a fire in the same place Tracy had been using then began to prepare biscuits and the potatoes. Dinner was well under way when he heard Will riding down off the hill.

Will rode up to the corral and saw Tom kneeling down next to the fire. He wondered where Tracy was, but since it was none of his business, he swung out of the saddle.

"Hi, Will."

"Hi, Mr. Norbert," Will replied cautiously.

"You hungry?"

"Yes, sir."

"Okay. Dinner will be ready in a few minutes. You have time to take care of your horse and wash up a little," Tom said.

The expression on Will's face caused Tom to smile. He knew Will had expected Tracy to be there. She was going to fix him a special meal tonight. Will looked around as he led his horse to the corral. Tom was sure that Will was looking to see if Tracy was around.

"Tracy won't be here tonight," Tom said when he saw the confused look on Will's face. "She had to take care of some business in town. I'm fixing your special dinner tonight."

"Oh," he said as he walked by to the corral.

When Will returned with his saddle in his hands, Tom looked up and asked, "How do you like your steak?"

Will stopped and looked at Tom. He hesitated a moment before he spoke, "A little better then medium."

"Medium-well it is," Tom said with a nod and a smile. "Be ready in five minutes."

Will stood there and looked at Tom for a moment before he went into the barn and tossed his saddle on a stall railing. He then went back out and washed a little of the dust and dirt off his hands and face.

He walked over to the corral where Tom was cooking. Will stood there for a couple of minutes watching Tom as he turned the steaks on a grill over the fire. After watching him for a little while, he began to think Tom might not be all that bad a cook. He had watched others at the ranch fix steaks and they did it much the same way.

Tom turned and saw Will watching him. He smiled then asked, "You ready to eat?"

Will just nodded and walked over next to the fire. Tom placed one of the large steaks on a plate then added a large potato, a couple of scoops of cooked carrots and a golden brown biscuit.

"Sink your teeth into that," Tom said as he held the plate out to Will.

Will reached out and took the plate, then stood there waiting for Tom to hand him a cup of coffee. Once he had the coffee, he walked over to the bale of hay he was used to sitting on while he ate.

By the time Tom got his dinner served up and went over to one of the bales to sit down and eat, Will was well into his meal. It was obvious he found the meal very much to his liking.

"Well, how's the food?"

"Pretty good," Will said as he took another bit.

Tom couldn't help but smile. The way Will was putting away his dinner was compliment enough.

As Tom continued to eat, he began to wonder how things were going with Tracy. He knew he would have to wait until she got back to find out.

As soon as dinner was finished, Tom went to work cleaning up. When he started to wash the dishes, Will came over and stood next to him. Tom looked up at him wondering what he wanted.

"You need some help?" Will asked.

"Nah, I can get it."

"I don't mind helpin'. I helped the boss with the dishes sometimes."

"Well, in that case. If you want, you can dry."

"Okay."

As Tom washed the dishes, he would rinse them off and hand them to Will. Will dried them and stacked them on the dish chest. They worked well together and were done in short order.

When they were done, Tom poured himself a cup of coffee. He looked up and saw Will looking as if he hoped there was a cup of coffee left for him.

"There's a bit left," Tom said as he held up the pot. "Would you like it?"

"Sure," Will said with a smile.

Tom filled Will's cup, then walked over to sit on the hay bale. Will followed along behind.

"How did it go today?"

"Pretty good."

"Any problems on the fence line?"

"Nope."

"Did you see any tracks or cuts in the fence?"

"No, but there was a place where a couple of strands of fence were down. I fixed it."

"Good. Did you see anyone around out there?"

"Yeah. I saw Mr. Blaine."

"Where was he?"

"He was on a horse out in his pasture, but there weren't no cows around."

"Did you talk to him?"

"No. He was too far away. Besides, he was talking to someone in a pickup."

"Do you know who was in the pickup?"

"No, but it was white, and looked fairly new."

"Did it have a sign or any kind of logo on it?"

"No. Not that I could see. But - - ," Will said, then took another sip of his coffee.

"But what?" Tom asked impatiently.

"I don't know. Maybe it was nothing."

"Tell me, Will."

"It seemed that as soon as they saw me ridin' along the fence line, they turned and went off ta the north over the hill in kind of a hurry. I didn't see them again."

"I wonder what they were up to?" Tom said more to himself than to Will.

"Got no idea. You thinkin' they're up ta no good?"

"Don't know, Will."

"You want me ta do anything?" Will asked, setting his jaw firmly as if waiting for orders.

Tom looked at Will. He was sure Will was from the old school, the one that says if you ride for the brand, you do whatever is necessary to protect the brand.

"No, but I'm going to find out what's going on over there."

"If you need me ta help, you just let me know. Miss Tracy has been good to me. I owe her and her father a lot."

"Thanks, Will. I'm sure Tracy will be pleased to hear that. Right now there's nothing we can do, so we might as will get some shuteye."

"Okay, Boss," Will said as he stood up.

Tom watched Will as he walked over to the fire. It had already burned down some. Will tossed the remains of his coffee on the fire, put his cup on the dish chest then returned to the barn. When he got to the barn, he stopped and looked at Tom.

"Miss Tracy always sleeps up in the loft. I sleep down here in that stall," he said as he pointed at the first stall on the right. "Where you plannin' on sleepin'?"

"I'll sleep over there," Tom said as he pointed at the first stall on the left.

"Okay. Goodnight, Boss."

"Goodnight, Will."

"By the way, that was a fine dinner you fixed."

"I'm glad you liked it, and thanks for helping clean up. I'll have breakfast for you before you head out tomorrow," Tom said with a smile.

Will smiled a little and nodded his head before he headed into the barn. Tom got the feeling Will was not only a good worker, but was probably a loyal employee and would be loyal to anyone he liked, and he liked Tracy.

Tom sat in the darkness for a while thinking about what Will had said. He wished that Will had gotten a better look at the side of the pickup. If there had been a sign or logo on the side, it might have proved helpful in finding out what was going on, but what was done was done.

Tom tipped his head back and looked up at the sky. He wasn't very tired right now and he certainly wasn't sleepy. He decided a little walk might help him feel sleepy, and it wouldn't disturb Will.

He walked up to the top of the hill and looked out over the prairie. It was dark and there was only a little light from the moon. The sky was clear and full of stars. Tom took a few minutes to scan the area, but saw nothing except for the yard lights of a couple of ranches that were actually several miles away.

Tom sat down and looked off toward the north. He wondered if Mr. Blaine was planning to drill for something other than water. He got to thinking about his friend, Frank, and what he might have found out about the truck that had come onto the Lazy A Ranch.

After a few minutes, Tom's mind began to think about Tracy. The first thing that crossed his mind was Tracy's visit to the court house for information on mineral and oil rights. He wondered how that had come out for Tracy. He was hoping that her inquiry into mineral and oil rights wouldn't get people's hopes up. It often seemed that people had short memories. They would soon forget about all the testing that had gone on in the county when the only place that oil had been found was over on the other end of the county, and very little at that.

Tom also wondered what Tracy was doing now. He felt that she was probably either getting ready for bed, or was already in bed. He yawned then looked up at the sky again. It was time for him to get some sleep.

Tom stood up and looked once again off toward Mr. Blaine's ranch before he returned to the barn. When he got to the barn, he spread out a bedroll in the stall and laid down on it. It took him only a few minutes before he drifted off to sleep.

CHAPTER FOURTEEN

When morning came, Tom was up fixing breakfast when Will came out of the barn. He handed Will a plate of bacon, pancakes, eggs and a large biscuit.

"I've fixed you a steak sandwich to take with you. Where are you going today?"

"I guess I'm supposed ta ride fence again. Miss Tracy didn't give me no other orders," Will said, as he looked to Tom to see if he wanted him to do something different.

Tom was sure Will would ride fence until he was told to do something else.

"I'd like you to go back up north. When you get to the fence line, I want you to ride east toward Spiny Ridge. When you get to the ridge, turn around and come back the same way. That should take most of the day."

"But I already checked that part of the fence."

"I know. I want you to do it again."

"Okay. You want me ta back track back ta here?" Will asked a little confused about what Tom wanted.

"Yes. What I really want you to do is keep an eye out for anything happening on either side of the fence. Be alert, pay close attention to anything you see. If you see anyone on Mr. Blaine's side of the fence, we want to know about it. If you see anyone or any new tracks on this side of the fence, I want to know about that, too."

"Oh. You want me ta see if anyone comes trespassin' on Miss Tracy's ranch."

"Right. But I also want you to see if there is anything happening on Mr. Blaine's side of the fence. I don't want you to do anything but observe and report it to me or Miss

Tracy. And do not cross the fence line onto Blaine's place. Do you understand?"

"Yes, sir. I understand."

"One other thing. If you see something, you get back here as quickly as you can and let us know what you saw. I don't want you to do anything about it except to report it to Miss Tracy or to me. Whoever is on Miss Tracy's ranch might be dangerous. I don't want you to take any chances. Okay?"

"Okay. I get it," he said with a smile. "I'll get started.

Tom simply nodded and smiled, then watched as Will got a horse ready to go. He watched as Will headed the horse north while he cleaned up the morning dishes. When Will was out of sight, Tom began to think about what was going on. He also began to wonder when Tracy might return. Tom had things he knew had to be done to make sure that the cattle were doing well. He would need to ride out and check on them. Tom didn't want to be too far from the barn in case Tracy returned early, or in case Will returned with something important to report.

After he had finished cleaning up from breakfast, he put out the fire and stored away everything, then he saddled a horse. The horse he picked out was a gray gelding that looked like he could run, and looked to be a strong and sturdy horse.

His idea was to spend a little time checking out the cattle to make sure that they were doing well. He felt that it would take Will the better part of two hours just to get to the north fence line from the barn, and close to five hours to get to Spiny Ridge from the barn.

He wasn't sure how long it would be before Tracy would get back. He took a look at his watch. Since she had probably spent the night at the ranch house, she would not get out to the barn for at least three or four more hours. That would give Tom time to check out most of the herd if he checked them from some of the surrounding hills.

Tom mounted up and rode off to the west until he came to the top of a hill. From the top of the hill, he could see for a long way toward the west. There was nothing much to see. The rolling hills and grass lands of the Montana plains allowed a person to see a long way from the top of almost any rise. There were a lot of cattle in that area. At the base of the hill was a large watering hole. Even from the distance Tom was from the watering hole, he could see that there was adequate water in the hole. Most of the cattle were in the area that he could see and were not very far from the watering hole, which was understandable. With the hot dry weather, they tended to stay fairly close to water.

After slowly looking over the area, Tom rode down the hill and headed south toward another hill that would give him a good vantage point to see a large part of the ranch to the south. From yesterday, he knew that there were cattle in that area. Although he had seen a good number of them, he still wanted to check to make sure that they had an adequate supply of good water, and were not in any kind of distress.

Again, he rode to the top of another hill, stopped and looked out over the surrounding area. The cattle seemed to be doing well. Tom continued his circling of the area at a reasonable distance from the barn. He went from one hilltop to the next, stopping at the top of each hill to check on the cattle in the area.

Tom made it a point to pay close attention to what was going on around the pasture. Since he had not gone much more than a couple of miles from the barn at any given time, he could return to the barn before or shortly after Tracy returned.

A quick look at his watch told him that there was a good chance that Tracy would be getting back to the barn at almost any time. He took one quick look around then turned his horse and headed back toward the barn. A quick glance at his watch told him that he had been gone for little more than three hours. It crossed his mind that Will would be riding along the north fence by now.

Tom hadn't gone very far on his way back to the barn when he noticed a white SUV moving across the pasture. It was headed in the general direction of the barn. As the SUV turned a little, he could see the side of it. It was one of the Sheriff's vehicles.

Tom started waving his hat in the air as he rode toward the SUV. Suddenly, the Sheriff's vehicle turned toward him. He could see Frank wave at him and point toward the barn. Tom waved that he understood and headed for the barn.

It wasn't very long before Frank and Tom met at the barn. Frank was parked near the back of the barn when Tom rode into the corral at the side of the barn. Tom turned the horse loose inside the corral then walked over to Frank. Frank was standing at the door to the barn.

"What's up? Did you find out anything about the trespasser?"

"No, not yet. I'm here because of a complaint we received from Mr. Blaine. He claims that Will took a shot at him while he was on his own property. He claims that Will was on his property when he shot at him."

"I can't believe Will would cross the fence to Blaine's property. I am sure that Will would not go onto Blaine's ranch without instruction to do so. I gave him clear instructions not to make any contact with Blaine. And I certainly can't believe that Will would shoot at him. What reason would he have to do that?"

"I don't know, and it doesn't make any difference. Blaine filed a formal written complaint. I have to find Will and question him about it."

"I'm sure you do. When was this supposed to have happened?

"Yesterday, about six in the evening."

"Where was Mr. Blaine when Will was supposed to have shot at him?"

"He claimed that he was a good two hundred yards from the fence line."

"I'll bet," Tom said sarcastically. "Did he say what kind of gun Will used to shoot at him?"

"Yeah. He said that Will shot at him with a rifle," Frank said. "What are you getting at?"

"Will wasn't carrying a rifle yesterday, and he isn't carrying one today."

"Are you sure?"

"Yeah, I'm sure. He didn't have a rifle on his saddle when he returned from riding fence line last night. And he wasn't carrying a side arm, either. I think Blaine is trying to discredit Will because Will saw him with someone else in his pasture. Will said that Blaine was on a horse and was talking to someone in a white pickup. When they saw Will, they took off in the direction of Blaine's ranch house in a hurry."

"When did Will tell you that?"

"Last evening when he returned from riding the fence line."

Frank looked at Tom as he thought about what had been happening the past few days. He also knew that Blaine had it in for the Atwaters. He wondered if Blaine might have a pretty good idea of the problems it would cause Tracy if she didn't have Will to help her. Something was going on here, and Frank didn't know what it was.

"Could Will identify the pickup if he saw it again?"

"I'm not sure," Tom said. "He said it was just a white pickup, a fairly new one."

"Where is Will now?"

"He's riding the fence line from straight north of here, then east to Spiny Ridge. I gave him clear instructions to watch both sides of the fence for anyone. If he saw anyone, he was to return here immediately. I told him not to confront anyone, just report to me or Tracy what he saw," Tom said.

"You think he would do what you told him?" Frank asked.

"Yeah. He's like the old cowboys. He rides for the brand and does what he's told. As you well know, there are a lot of people that don't trust him. With his record, people will believe anything bad about him, but he's a good worker and does what he's told."

"When do you think he'll be back?"

"Unless he comes back early because he saw something, he won't be back until almost dark. I made him a sandwich so he had something to eat. He comes back for his evening meals here, and spends the night here. And before you ask, yes, he was here all night."

Frank walked over to a hay bale and sat down. He was sure that Tom, of all people, would not lie to him. He also knew that Will had not been in any sort of trouble since he got out of jail and moved back to the county. In fact, he had not seen him in town more than a couple of times since Sam Atwater had hired him over four years ago.

"I don't know what is going on, but it sounds to me like Blaine is looking for something that he doesn't want anyone to know about," Frank said."

"I agree, but what?"

"I don't know."

"I wish Will was here to talk to," Frank said as he looked out over the grassland.

"Like I said, he won't be back until dark unless he sees something strange going on."

"When's Tracy due back?" Frank asked as he turned and looked at Tom.

"I expect her any time now. She went into town yesterday to check to see if Sam has the oil and mineral rights to this land. I'm hoping that he does."

"I got to thinking about that last night. If I remember right, the old Sheriff told me that he knew that Sam had the oil and mineral rights to the ranch. I was told that Sam told the Sheriff he had the rights about the time that they were testing for oil and natural gas in this part of the county a few years back."

"I'm sure if you know that, then with that old busy body at the court house, everyone in the county knows it."

"I'm sure you're right. But what are you getting at, Tom?"

"With the new technology in the oil industry, it would be possible for Blaine to drill for oil from his property to under Tracy's property without anyone knowing about it."

"You think that is what he is planning on doing?"

"I wouldn't put it past him. When I get back to town, I'm going to find out what he is using the money for that was loaned to him to drill a well for water."

"Even if he is drilling for oil, what can you do about it?"

"For one thing, I can call in the loan and foreclose on him if he can't pay it back."

"It would take months to foreclose on him. What good would that do if he has already started drilling?"

"Not much, I'm afraid, but it will prevent him from getting any other loans. I might be able to get the courts to stop his drilling if I can prove he's using the loan money improperly."

Just then, they could hear the sound of a truck coming over the hill behind the barn. Frank and Tom got up and walked around the corner of the barn to see who was coming. It was Tom's truck coming down off the top of the hill toward the barn.

* * * *

Tracy came over the hill behind the barn. She was hoping that Tom was there. It came as a surprise to see a Sheriff's vehicle parked near the back of the barn. As she came close to the barn, she saw Frank and Tom step around the corner. She had expected to see Tom, but not Frank. She wondered what he was doing there.

As she pulled to a stop next to the Sheriff's vehicle, she looked out the windshield at Tom and Frank. From the look on their faces, she just knew that there was something wrong. She got out of the truck and walked toward them.

"What brings you all the way out here?" she asked Frank as she walked toward them.

"I'm here to have a talk with Will. It seems that Blaine has filed a complaint stating that Will shot at him while he was on his own property."

"That's ridiculous. Will wouldn't shoot at anyone unless they shot at him first."

"Tracy, does Will have a gun?" Frank asked.

"He might have a pistol in his saddlebag. Most of the ranch hands in this county carry at least a pistol. You know that as well as I do," she said as she looked at him.

"Does he have a rifle?"

"He might, but he doesn't have it out here. If he has one, it would be in the bunkhouse."

"Are you sure?"

"Yes, I'm sure," she said then looked around. "Where is Will?"

"I sent him up to ride along the north fence line from straight north of here to Spiny Ridge," Tom said.

"Why there? He checked out that part of the fence line the other day," Tracy asked.

"I wanted him to see if anything was going on along the section of the fence where the truck had come through the fence. I also wanted him to look around and report back to you or me if he saw any activity in the area. If he did, he was to come right back here," Tom said.

"I remember," Tracy said as she nodded her head in agreement. "We talked about that yesterday."

She then turned and looked off in the direction that Will would have gone. She was thinking about what was going on. What was Blaine up to? What was he trying to do? She then turned back and looked at Tom.

"How long has he been gone?"

"About four hours, maybe a little longer. What's on your mind?" Tom asked.

"I was thinking that maybe we should take one of the vehicles and see if we can catch up with him."

"Are you worried about him?" Frank asked.

"Yeah, I guess I am," Tracy said thoughtfully."

Frank looked at Tom, then shrugged. He could see no reason not to go looking for Will. After all, he had a formal complaint that he needed to investigate.

"Okay," Frank said. "We can take my vehicle. That way if we run into any trouble, it will be more official," he said with a grin.

"Okay," Tom agreed, then looked at Tracy to see if she agreed.

Tracy nodded, then turned and started toward Frank's patrol vehicle.

Tom held the door for Tracy so that she could get in the front seat. Tom got in the back seat directly behind Tracy while Frank got in behind the wheel. Once they were all in Frank's patrol vehicle, he started it up and headed north toward the fence line.

The patrol vehicle moved along the rough ground with a certain amount of ease. It could not travel much faster than a horse could run on the same ground. However, it was much more comfortable and cooler than riding a horse. The vehicle was well equipped for traveling across the open prairie and made pretty good time. It could also travel at a fairly high rate of speed on a paved road, if it was necessary.

Tracy kept an eye out for Will. If he had shot at Mr. Blaine, he must have had a very good reason. If he did shoot at Mr. Blaine, it was probably because Blaine shot at him first. Tracy was also pretty sure that Will would have mentioned that he had been shot at to Tom.

Once they reached the north fence line, Frank turned east and drove alongside the fence. While they were still several miles from Spiny Ridge, they could see it off in the distance. Frank steered around rough spots in the ground while Tracy and Tom continued looking around in an effort to see Will.

"Stop! Stop!" Tracy yelled as she looked off toward the south.

Frank quickly pulled to a stop and looked in the direction that Tracy was looking.

"What is it?" Tom asked, not seeing anything unusual.

"I'm not sure. I thought I saw a horse down in the ravine."

"Let's check it out," Frank said as he backed up then turned his patrol vehicle down the hill toward the ravine.

They had not gone very far down the hill when Tom saw a chestnut colored horse with a saddle, but no rider.

"Over there," Tom said as he pointed at the horse.

"That's one of my horses," Tracy said. "Is that the one Will took out this morning?"

"I think so," Tom said.

"We better catch it. Stop here and let me out," Tracy said.

Frank stopped and waited for Tracy to get out. Tom remained in the back seat. He didn't think that it would be a good idea to get out, too. He was afraid that it might cause the horse to spook and run off, making it harder for Tracy to catch it.

Tracy slowly moved closer to the horse. She talked to it in low soft tones so as not to scare the animal. As she approached the horse, it backed away from her a few steps but did not run away. Tracy continued to talk to the horse. It finally allowed her to get close enough that she could take hold of the reins.

When she got hold of the reins, Tracy slowly moved closer to the horse. She reached out and gently touched the horse. The horse didn't seem to mind. Tracy gently led the horse back toward the patrol vehicle.

Tracy continued to rub the horse's neck while Frank and Tom got out of the patrol vehicle and walked slowly up to the horse. While Tom walked up next to Tracy, Frank started walking around the horse. He was looking the horse over for any sign of something that might have caused the horse to lose its rider. The brand on his flank was the Lazy A brand.

"It's one of your horses," Frank said.

Frank continued to look over the horse. He found a couple of dark spots on one side of the saddle and on one of the saddlebags. He reached up and touched one of the dark spots, then looked at his finger. The dark liquid was sticky. There was little doubt in his mind that it was blood.

"I think we have a problem. There are some bloody spots on the saddle and saddlebag. If this was the horse that Will rode out on this morning, we need to find him quickly."

"Can you track the horse?" Tracy asked Frank.

"Yeah. Tom, you drive. I'll ride the horse. I should be able to see his tracks better from the back of the horse."

Without any hesitation, Tracy and Tom got in the patrol vehicle while Frank mounted the horse. Once in the saddle, Frank could see where the horse had been. He nudged the horse in its side. The horse started off in the direction that Frank was guiding it. The horse's tracks seemed to be taking Frank back toward the fence.

After a short time, the tracks showed where the horse had been running. It made them easier to follow. It wasn't long before Frank saw something on the ground. The closer he got, the clearer it became that they had found Will. Frank rode up to Will then pulled up and got off the horse. He immediately went to Will and knelt down beside him.

Tom and Tracy had stopped the patrol vehicle and ran up to Will. Frank turned and looked at Tracy.

"He's alive, but in real trouble. It looks like he was shot," Frank said. "Stay with him. Tom, come with me."

Frank took what vital signs he could, before he returned to his patrol vehicle. Tracy knelt down next to Will while Tom and Frank went to the patrol vehicle.

When Frank and Tom got to the patrol vehicle, Frank handed Tom a first aid kit.

"See what you can do to get the bleeding stopped. I'm calling for an Air-Vac chopper."

Tom nodded as he took the first aid kit, then ran over to Will. He immediately began to take a dressing from the kit, put it over the wound and applied pressure with his hand. Tracy and Tom could hear Frank on the radio telling the dispatcher where they were located and that the victim had been shot and was unconscious.

As soon as Frank had given all the information he could to the dispatcher, he ran back over to where Will was lying. He again took Will's vital signs. From Frank's experience, he knew that Will was in real trouble. If the chopper didn't get there soon, they might lose him.

"Tracy, we need to get that horse away from here. When the chopper gets here, it will scare the horse," Frank said.

"I'll take it," Tom said, knowing that Tracy would want to stay with Will for as long as possible.

Tom took the reins of the horse and led it away. He took the horse around on the other side of the patrol vehicle.

He stood with it, holding its reins and gently stroking its neck.

It wasn't long before they could hear the sound of a chopper. It was flying a bit south of their location. Frank first looked at the chopper, then at his patrol vehicle. He got up and ran to his patrol vehicle and turned on the bright flashing lights on the light bar.

Almost as soon as he turned on the light bar, the chopper made a sharp turn toward them. It was coming fast to where Will lay on the ground. In just a few minutes, the chopper was on the ground and two EMTs were running to Will's aid.

Frank and Tracy moved back out of the way so that the EMTs could do their job. While the EMTs worked on Will to get him ready for transport to a hospital, Frank and Tracy stood by and watched.

It was not long before Will was put on a stretcher, strapped down then loaded into the chopper. A lot of dust and dirt was stirred up when the chopper's big blades began to turn faster so it could lift off. The three of them watched as the chopper rose up, tilted its nose down and rapidly began to move up and off in the direction of the nearest hospital.

As soon as the chopper was out of sight, Frank and Tracy walked over to the patrol vehicle where Tom was standing with the horse. Tom could see the look on Tracy's face. He could see that she didn't know what she was going to do now that her last ranch hand was in no condition to work.

Tracy looked up at Tom. He was looking at her while still holding the reins to the horse.

"I don't know what I'm going to do now. Without Will to help out, I don't see how I will be able to keep things going," Tracy said with a look of defeat on her face.

"I'll help you," Tom said.

"What can you do? You have a job in town. I can't expect you to drop everything and become a ranch hand."

"Excuse me, but I have a lot of work to do right now," Frank said. "I have to collect any evidence that I can find. Hopefully it will help us find out who shot Will."

"Frank, do you still carry that Winchester 30-30 in the back of you patrol vehicle?

"Yeah. What's on your mind?"

"I'm going to be filling in for Will for a few days. I would prefer not to be out here without some kind of fire power."

"You're not planning on going after Blaine for this, are you?"

"Of course not. That's your job. I don't know who shot him any more than you do. If I'm going to be out here looking after Tracy's cattle, I want some protection."

"Okay. It's in the back of the patrol car. There's a box of ammo in the gun case, too."

Tom went around to the back of the patrol vehicle and opened the back. As he reached in and pulled the gun case to the rear of the vehicle, Tracy walked up beside him. She watched him as he took the rifle out of the gun case and started to load it. He glanced at Tracy as he loaded the gun.

"Here's how I see it. We have one vehicle out here that will be returning to town before long. We have another vehicle at the barn. We have one horse and no trailer to put him in, so someone has to ride him back to the barn.

"I know that you want to make sure Will is doing okay, and I know it is not very safe out here right now. That being the case, I think you should go back to the barn with Frank when he is done looking around."

"But I should be - - - - ."

"I'm not finished," Tom interrupted.

Tracy looked at him for a second or two before she nodded that he should continue.

"I think you should go back to the barn and get my truck, then go to the house. From there you can take my truck, or my car, and go into town and make sure that Will is being cared for. I know a lot of people don't like him, mostly because they are afraid of him. Take a couple of days if that's what it takes to be sure he is doing okay and is getting good care.

"In the meantime, I will stay out here and keep an eye on your livestock and your land. There is plenty of food back at the barn so there's no problem there. What do you think?"

"I think you are crazy, but I don't have a better idea."

"Good. When Frank gets done here, you go back to the barn with him. By the way, in a locked compartment under the backseat of my truck is a pistol in a holster and a box of ammunition. Leave it under your bedroll in the loft of the barn. The key to the compartment is on my key ring for the truck."

"Okay," she said as she leaned close to him and kissed him lightly on the lips. "Thank you."

He looked at her for a moment, smiled, then said, "You are very welcome."

Tom thought about reaching out and taking her in his arms, but was interrupted by Frank.

"Tom, could you come over here?"

Tom handed the reins to Tracy, then walked over to see what Frank wanted.

"What's up?"

"I don't think that Will was shot here. He was shot somewhere else. My guess is that he was able to hang onto the saddle to this point. He was probably trying to get back to the barn to let you know what happened."

"If that's the case, he could have been shot almost anywhere," Tom said.

"I'm going to have to try and back track the horse to see if I can find out where he was shot. If he was shot while he was in the saddle, it could be almost impossible to find out where he was shot. If he was shot while he was on the ground, there would be a better chance of finding the place. Either way, it could be very difficult to figure out where the shooter was when Will was shot. There is a lot of ground to cover and little chance of finding it."

"What do you want me to do?"

"I'm going to need some help."

"You want me to try to find the place where he was shot?" Tom asked.

"No. I want you to be very careful out here," Frank said. "I don't want to have to come out here looking for you. I think it would be best if I got over to the hospital in the hope that Will might be able to tell me something that will help. If not, I'll have to bring out some of the guys to look for where Will was shot."

"Okay. I'm going to ride the horse back to the barn. Tracy is going to take my truck and go on to the hospital. I'm going to stay out here and keep an eye on her cattle."

"See to it that's all you do," Frank said. "I don't want to find you lying in some ravine."

Tom didn't respond to Frank's comment. He simply turned and headed back to where Tracy was standing with the horse. Frank followed Tom toward his patrol vehicle. When Tom walked up to Tracy, he reached out and took the reins from her.

"I'll see you in a couple of days. I really hope that Will pulls through this. He really is a good ranch hand," Tom said.

"Will you be okay out here by yourself?"

"Sure. I have no plans to do anything foolish or stupid. Just do what I told you when you get back to the barn."

"I will," she said as she leaned close to him and kissed him again on the lips.

"That makes this all worth it," he said with a grin.

"Hey, Tracy. We best get going," Frank called out to her, then turned and got into his patrol vehicle.

"I better go before we both have to ride the horse back to the barn."

"I might not mind that," Tom said.

"I'm sure you wouldn't," Tracy said then turned and walked over to the patrol vehicle.

Tom watched her as she walked away from him. He couldn't help but think how nicely she filled out her jeans, and how good it felt when she kissed him.

When Frank pulled away and started across the prairie in the general direction of the barn, Tom swung up in the saddle. He nudged the horse in the ribs and headed toward the barn. It was going to take him a while longer to get back to the barn, but it would give him time to think.

* * * *

Tom arrived back at the barn when the sun was just starting to get low in the western sky. After he took the saddle off, he rubbed down the horse. He then fed the horse and put it in a stall for the night. He climbed up into the loft and found the gun and holster under Tracy's bedroll with a box of ammunition. Tom loaded the gun then strapped it on. He had no idea what to expect over the next few days, but he was not going to be caught unprepared.

As the sun was going down behind the mountains to the west, he built a small fire and prepared his dinner. When he had finished eating, he cleaned up his dishes and pans, then sat down to have a cup of coffee. He looked out over the rolling hills that made up a large part of the Lazy A Ranch.

His thoughts turned to Blaine and the truck that had come onto the ranch. It was clear that something was going on, but he was not sure what it was. The holes that they had found on the edge of Spiny Ridge were not the same as those used to search for oil. It was obvious that whoever had trespassed on the ranch was looking for something. The fact that they had come from Blaine's side of the fence, and that Blaine had filed charges against Will, led Tom to think that Blaine was up to something. There was also the fact that Blaine had been seen talking to a man in a pickup from apparently an unknown company. By Blaine's actions, he had indicated that he didn't want to be seen talking to the man in the truck which simply added to the suspicions in Tom's mind.

It was starting to get dark and Tom was beginning to feel the stress of the day. It was time for him to put out the fire and get some sleep.

As soon as the fire was completely out, he climbed up into the loft to get some sleep. He took off the gun belt and laid it close to the bedroll, then laid down. He found it hard to get to sleep as he had a lot on his mind. The shooting of Will was one of them. It made him think about the old days when range wars were started over things not so much different than what was going on now, right there.

Tom's thoughts turned to Tracy and the kisses she had given him before she left him to ride the horse back to the barn. He began to think that maybe he would have a chance to show her that he was the kind of man that she wanted. He already knew that she was the kind of woman he wanted.

With pleasant thoughts of Tracy running through his mind, Tom finally fell asleep.

CHAPTER FIFTEEN

It was still very early when Tom woke. The sun had not yet come up over the horizon. He stretched then sat up. It was very still and quiet. He stood up and started for the ladder to go down from the loft when he thought of something and stopped. Tom looked back toward the bedroll and saw the gun lying beside it. He returned to the bedroll and picked up the gun. After strapping the holster around his waist, he checked the gun to make sure it was ready to use before going down the ladder.

As he stepped out of the barn, he noticed that there were several cows looking off toward the hill behind the barn. Very carefully, he moved to the corner of the barn. He then peeked around the corner. It was just barely getting light enough to see anything. It wasn't until it moved that he saw what had gotten the cows attention. It was a lone coyote. It was walking slowly along the top of the hill looking at the cows as if they were some sort of strange creature.

Tom had to smile, but the smile soon faded away as his thoughts turned to what could have been on the top of the hill. The thought that Will had been shot while riding along the fence line was enough to keep Tom watchful. With all the ravines and gullies that could hide an enemy on the prairie, he knew that he would have to stay alert to any possible danger.

Tom looked around, then decided that he would make himself a good breakfast before going out to check on the herd. He built a fire, cooked himself some eggs and a slab of ham. When he was finished, he put out the fire and went around to the corral behind the barn where the extra horses were kept. He picked out one that looked like a good mount then led the horse into the barn where he saddled it. After taking the horse he had ridden yesterday out of the stall and into the corral, he made sure that there was plenty of water and feed for all the horses, enough to last them for the entire day.

As soon as he was satisfied that he had taken care of the horses and had done everything that needed to be done, he mounted up and rode up the hill behind the barn toward the north fence. He knew that it would take him close to two hours to get to the fence, but that was where Will had gone yesterday. He was going to follow Will's tracks until he found where Will had been shot. The only difference was that he was going to be watchful of what was around him, and he was armed so that he could fight back.

* * * *

When Tracy had finally arrived at the hospital, Will was already in surgery. In talking to the nurse, she found out that there was little hope that he would survive the shooting. Tracy had decided that she would wait for as long as it took to find out if he would survive or not.

Last night had been a long night for Tracy. She had spent the entire night sleeping off and on in a chair in the surgery waiting room, waiting for word on how Will was doing. She had told the nurse to wake her if there was any news about his condition. When she woke, the sun was just starting to come up over the horizon. She was feeling a little stiff, and stretched as she sat up.

Once she was sitting up, she took a look around the waiting room. There was one other woman in the waiting room. The woman was tall and slender. Tracy could not remember ever having seen the woman before. The woman had not been in the waiting room last night before Tracy had fallen asleep.

The woman looked over at Tracy and smiled. Tracy wondered why the woman was smiling at her and decided to find out. She got up and walked across the room to the woman. When she was in front of the woman, she stood for a moment looking down at her before speaking.

"Excuse me, but do I know you?"

"No. I don't think so. But I know you. I'm Helen Baker. I'm Will Strong's sister," she said with a smile.

"I didn't know Will had a sister."

"I'm not surprised. Will didn't talk much about his family. As you probably know, he doesn't talk much about anything."

"Yes, I have noticed that about him," Tracy said as she sat down next to Helen. "I'm sorry that we have to meet under these circumstances. How did you find out that Will was here in the hospital?"

"The sheriff's deputy found my name and address in his wallet. They called me and I came as soon as possible. Can you tell me what happened to him? I understand that he was working for you when the accident occurred."

"Yes, he does work for me. We don't know what happened, but we know it was not an accident. All we know is that he was shot while riding the fence line on my property."

"It was not an accident? The deputy said that he was accidentally shot while working on your ranch," she said with a surprised and confused look on her face.

"He was working on my ranch, but it was no accident. He was alone on my property doing his job. He was shot while riding the fence line," Tracy said, her anger in what had been done to Will showing in her voice. "He didn't have a gun with him."

"Have you been having trouble on your ranch?"

"We have had someone trespassing on the ranch in the area where Will was shot."

"Were they rustlers?"

"It doesn't look like it."

"Then why was he shot?"

"We don't know."

Helen turned her head and looked out the window. There was no question that she was a little confused. She once again turned and looked at Tracy.

"Why would the deputy tell me that he was shot by accident?"

"I don't know. Maybe it was because they don't yet know what happened."

"Thank you for letting me know what really happened to Will."

"You're welcome," Tracy said, then stood up and returned to where she had spent the night.

Tracy was sure that Helen wanted a little time to herself to think about her brother, and maybe to say a prayer for him.

As Helen watched Tracy return to her chair, her thoughts turned to Will. She began to think about the hard life that Will had had. He was not very bright and had a difficult time around people. She was thankful that Sam Atwater had hired him to work on his ranch, especially since he had been in jail for killing a man.

The hiring of Will had proven to be not only good for the Atwaters, but it was good for Will. Helen was glad that Will had found a place to live where he could work and be looked after. She knew that he could not live with her and her husband in the same small town where he had killed the man. As it was, they were having a hard time as the kin of a killer. It didn't seem to matter to the small minded town's people that the killing was ruled as manslaughter only because the man killed was the son of one of the wealthiest people in town.

If it had been anyone else that Will had killed under the same circumstances, it would have been ruled as justifiable homicide. Will had accidentally killed the man while trying to protect a woman the man was trying to rape. It didn't help him any that the woman had a reputation for being a flirt. That made it easier for some of the people who lived in the town to think she was asking for it.

* * * *

Time passed slowly while the two women sat waiting for news of Will's condition. It was almost noon when a nurse came into the waiting room and walked up to Tracy.

"I have some news about Will Strong."

"Just a moment," Tracy said. "The woman sitting over there is Helen Baker. She is Will's sister. I'm sure she would like to hear what you have to say."

The nurse looked over at the woman, then started across the room toward her. Tracy followed along then sat down next to Helen. The nurse sat down in a chair across from Helen then looked at Tracy. The nurse then looked at Helen again before she spoke.

"Will is in very critical condition at this time. Surgery was done to remove the bullet from his chest and to repair the damage done by it. At this time he is in a coma and is on life support to help his breathing. He can breathe on his own, but not well enough to get enough oxygen into his system. He has tubes in his chest to keep his lungs from collapsing.

"It will be touch and go for at least the next twenty-four to thirty-six hours. If he makes it that long, he will stand a good chance of recovering."

"Can I see him," Helen asked.

"In a few minutes, but only for a few minutes. He will not be able to talk to you, or even know that you are in the room."

"Thank you," Tracy said.

As the nurse left the waiting room, Tracy looked at Will's sister. She could see a tear slowly slide down the woman's face. Helen looked at Tracy.

"Would you go in with me to see him?" her eyes pleading for Tracy to go with her.

"Sure."

It was just a few minutes before the nurse returned and told Tracy and Helen that they could see Will. They walked into the recovery room where Will lay in a bed. Tracy had never seen him look so frail and weak. To her, he had always been the mountain of strength. Just seeing him like that made Tracy angry. She wanted the person who had shot him to pay, and pay dearly for what he had done to Will.

After a few minutes, Tracy and Helen left the room and returned to the waiting room. They sat down together but didn't say anything for some time. Finally, Tracy looked over at Helen.

"Are you all right?" Tracy asked.

"Yes. I only wish I could stay. I have two young children at home with their grandmother. She has a hard time with them."

"What about your husband?"

"He won't get home from out of town until late tonight. I have to meet him at the airport. I do wish I could stay here with Will."

"Would it help if I keep you informed on how he is doing?"

"That would be great. Here is my phone number. Would you be so kind as to call me if there are any changes in his condition?"

"I'd be glad to," Tracy said with a smile.

"Call me any time there's a change in his condition. I don't know when I will be able to get back here. I really have to go," she said almost apologetically.

"I'll keep in touch with you," Tracy promised as she took the piece of paper that had Helen's phone number on it.

Helen thanked Tracy again, then left the waiting room. Tracy sat in the chair and watched the woman leave. Tracy had no idea what kind of a relationship Will had with his sister, but it seemed clear to her that his sister was really concerned about him.

Tracy looked around the waiting room. She was beginning to feel hungry. She left the waiting room and walked down the hall to the nurse's station. As she walked up to the desk, the nurse looked up at her and smiled.

"I need to get something to eat. I'll be gone for a little while."

"That will be fine. I don't really expect anything to change in Mr. Strong's condition for some time."

"I'll be back in a little while," Tracy said.

The nurse smiled and nodded. Tracy turned and left the hospital. She could have gone to the cafeteria in the hospital, but she had eaten there a good many times when her father was in the hospital. She never liked the food that was served there. Instead, she walked down the street to a small café that had good homemade style food.

* * * *

Tom followed the tracks made by Will's horse the previous day. It was clear that Will had done what he had been told. He had gone north to the fence, then turned and headed east toward Spiny Ridge.

It was also clear by the tracks that Will's horse had not been running, but Tom had not expected Will to run the horse. Will knew how to treat a horse and how to get the most out of a horse without killing it. In the hot dry weather they had been experiencing, no one ran a horse hard unless it was an emergency of some kind. To run a horse in that kind of weather would lead to only one thing. The horse would give out and the rider would soon be walking, and no cowboy liked to walk if he could ride. And no real cowboy would treat his horse like that in the first place.

Tom made it a point to keep his eyes open and moving. He looked for anything that moved and for anything that might be out there that could cause him harm.

One thing that Tom noticed was that Will had been riding some distance from the fence. He never seemed to be so far away from the fence that he couldn't see it, but far enough away from it that it would be fairly easy for him to take cover if he thought it necessary. There was no doubt in Tom's mind that Will had been being very careful, and that he was trying to make it hard for anyone to see him before he saw them.

Off in the distance, Tom noticed a dust devil. It seemed to be moving rather slowly, but it was kicking up a lot of dust. To him, it was just another sign of the extremely dry conditions that had been the norm for the past several months.

As Tom came up on a little rise, he stopped and took a minute to look around. He could see a long way from where he sat. Off to the north was Mr. Blaine's ranch. He could not see a single cow anywhere on the north side of the fence. The pasture land had little grass on it, indicating that it had been overgrazed. Even with several good rains it would take a year or two for it to recover and be a good pasture again.

Tom's eyes caught something that looked like it was moving slowly across the north pasture in the general direction of Spiny Ridge. He might never have seen it if it wasn't for the dust kicked up by it. At first he couldn't tell what it was. He wished that he had brought his binoculars with him, but he had left them in his truck. As best he could tell from where he was, it was a white pickup truck. There was nothing special about it that he could see.

He watched it for several minutes before he took a quick glance at the ground. Tom could still see where Will had been riding. The tracks continued toward Spiny Ridge. He nudged the horse in its sides and began moving toward the ridge again. He continued to watch, splitting his time between watching the white pickup and watching the tracks that Will's horse had made yesterday. The one thing that crossed through Tom's mind was that if the pickup continued on the course it was taking, it would cross onto Tracy's ranch near Spiny Ridge. And if he continued on his present course, he would cross paths with the pickup very close to Spiny Ridge on Tracy's side of the fence.

As Tom moved along the tracks left by Will's horse, he began to wonder what was going on. The only thing he could think of was that whatever was going on, it had to be worth a lot of money. What other reason would there be to shoot Will? Shooting Will would only bring the Sheriff out here to investigate. Tom had a feeling that whoever was crossing onto Tracy's ranch wouldn't like the Sheriff nosing around and maybe discover them. It also might delay whatever it was they were trying to do.

That being the case, why was Will shot at? Had he discovered what was going on? Had he caught someone on the ranch that didn't belong there? Maybe he had caught someone by surprise? There were a lot of questions that would not be answered until Will could talk to them.

Tom was well aware of the trouble there had been between Sam Atwater and Wilber Blaine. He also knew that Wilber had lost his fight in a court of law to get control of some of Sam's land. As a result, Blaine had bitter feelings about it. Blaine had threatened Sam a couple of times saying things like, "You put one foot on my land and I'll shoot you."

Now he claimed that Will had crossed onto Blaine's land and had shot at him. Within a short time after that, Will was shot. But as far as Tom knew, Blaine was not claiming that Will had trespassed on his land a second time. In fact, as far as he knew Blaine had not said anything about the shooting of Will. That caused Tom to wonder who it was that had shot Will. Was it Blaine or someone else?

Time slipped by as Tom continued to move toward Spiny Ridge. It seemed to take forever to get any closer to the ridge. He was still riding beside the tracks left by Will's horse on his way toward the ridge when he came upon a place on the ground where the tracks of the horse seemed to take a sudden turn. The tracks seemed to show that the horse might have been spooked, or was suddenly frightened.

Tom pulled up and got out of the saddle. Holding the reins of the horse in one hand, he knelt down to examine the ground.

On the ground he could see where it looked like someone had fallen, probably from a horse. There were also tracks that looked like someone might have crawled a little ways, plus there was blood on the ground. It all led to Tom being sure that it was the place where Will had been shot. Tom was not as good a tracker as Frank, but he was sure that he could figure out what had happened there.

Based on the tracks, apparently Will had been riding along watching the fence line for any breaks in it and looking for anything going on across the fence. Up to that point, Will's horse had been pretty much walking along. It was at that place a bullet hit Will in the chest knocking him off his horse. The horse jumped around nervously and ran off a little ways. Will was apparently still conscious and able to drag himself over to his horse. He was able to get back on the horse. Very close to where the drag marks left by Will in the dirt stopped, he could see where the horse took off at a run. That was a clear indication showing how Will got to where he had been found.

Set in his mind what had happened, Tom took a minute to look around. What he was looking for was a place where the shooter might have been when Will was shot. With all the signs pointing to Will being very alert, the shot had to have come from somewhere Will would not have seen the shooter.

Since Tom was sure that Will had been spending most of his time looking to the north and east, Tom began to look to the south. Will had not been shot in the back, but that didn't rule out someone being behind him. If Will had heard something, he might have turned around before he was shot.

Off to the south, Tom could see what looked like a narrow ravine. There was a fairly small cottonwood tree growing in the ravine. A tree out there was rather rare. But that tree indicated to Tom there was a place in that ravine where water would collect whenever it rained.

Since the ravine was rather crooked, it was likely that the place where the water would gather got very little sun. That would account for the tree being able to survive in times of little or no rain. There was also the slight possibility that there was a small seeping spring near the tree. A spring that was seeping just enough water to keep the tree alive in times when there was little or no rain.

Tom decided that the only way he was going to find out was to check it out. After mounting his horse, Tom drew his rifle from the saddle scabbard, levered a cartridge into the chamber then turned his horse toward the ravine. He slowly moved closer to the ravine while keeping an eye out for any trouble.

When he got to the edge of the ravine, he rode along it until he was at a place where his horse could get down into the ravine without much difficulty. Looking into the ravine, he decided against riding down into it for now.

Sitting on his horse at the edge of the ravine, he could see that there was grass in the bottom. The tree was growing out of the grass. With green grass after months of drought, there had to be a seeping spring in the bottom of the ravine.

Tom stepped down from his horse and walked closer to edge of the ravine. It wasn't very deep at that point. From the edge, he could see where someone had been walking around in the bottom of the ravine. He turned and looked back up the hill toward where Will had been shot. The place where Tom was standing made the perfect place to shoot someone if they were about where Will had been shot. Since Will had been shot in the chest, he must have turned sideways just before he was hit. Will had probably seen the shooter just before he was shot.

With the tracks of someone walking around in the ravine, Tom decided that he would not go down into the ravine at that location. He did not want to disturb what evidence might be there for Frank to check out. Maybe Frank could get some castings of the footprints as evidence.

Tom walked back over to his horse and slipped the rifle back into the scabbard, then looked back up the hill again. There was no doubt in Tom's mind that Will had been intentionally ambushed. He was probably shot to stop him from going any farther, but why? What did they not want Will to see?

It was time for Tom to make a decision. Should he go back to the barn and get in contact with the Sheriff's office, or should he try to find out why Will was shot? He was not a law enforcement officer. He knew and understood that. But he really wanted to know why Will had been shot.

Tom looked off in the direction of Spiny Ridge. He quickly discovered that if he stayed down off the top of the rise he could get almost all the way to Spiny Ridge without being seen by anyone on Blaine's property. And if he went down into the ravine and followed it, he could get very close to the Spiny Ridge without anyone seeing him. That pretty much answered the question on how someone was able to get behind Will without him seeing them.

It occurred to Tom that the one piece of information that they didn't have was who the white pickup belonged to. That piece of information could lead them to who was trespassing on Lazy A Ranch. It also might lead to what was going on.

Tom looked again at the ravine. He felt that he could go up the ravine toward the Spiny Ridge without anyone seeing him. If he could get a look at that white pickup, he might be able to find who it belonged to and what was going on.

He walked back to his horse then swung into the saddle. He rode the horse slowly along the edge of the ravine until he came to a place where he could ride on down into the ravine easily and not disturb any evidence that Frank might need. Once in the ravine, he rode along the bottom toward Spiny Ridge. It was a lot longer and took more time to ride along the crooked bottom of the ravine, but it kept him out of sight.

Tom moved along slowly, being very mindful of his surroundings. He wanted no surprises. The ravine provided him with some protection from being seen. But like everything else, it had another side to it. The ravine also could trap him in a confined area if he was not very careful.

As he came around a corner in the ravine, he could see almost a hundred yards in front of him. It was the place where the ravine started. If he were to ride out of the ravine at the end, it would put him out in the open. A quick look at the ground showed him that someone else had walked in the bottom of the ravine.

Tom swung out of the saddle and studied the tracks that had been left in the dirt of the ravine. It showed two sets of tracks. One showed the tracks of someone going down the ravine toward the little tree, while the other showed someone walking up the ravine. It was clear to Tom that the tracks were made by the same person. In Tom's mind, there was little doubt that the tracks were made by the person that had shot Will.

The question that crossed Tom's mind was how did the shooter know that Will would be riding close enough to the ravine to get a good shot at him? If Will had been closer to the fence, it would have been much harder for the shooter hit him. There had to be someone else involved in the shooting besides the shooter. He wondered if the other person was Blaine.

Tom had to decide if he was going on, or turning back. He now had what he believed to be evidence that Will was intentionally shot. It was clear that someone had ambushed him, but why? Since Will had been shot so far away from Spiny Ridge, Tom was sure that it was done to keep the Sheriff from nosing around the ridge. He had found enough evidence to get the Sheriff to send out enough men to find out what was going on and who was involved.

Tom took one last look toward Spiny Ridge as he thought about what he should do. The wise thing for him to do was to return to the barn for tonight. Since it would be almost dark by the time he would get back, he would spend the night at the barn. First thing in the morning, he would get a fresh horse and ride back to the ranch house. From there he would take his truck or car, whichever one Tracy had left there, and go into town to talk to the Sheriff.

Just as Tom turned around, his horse's head came up and his ears perked up. Tom looked off in the direction the horse was looking. Up on the ridge to the south was a white pickup just pulling to a stop. There was a man getting out of the white pickup truck with a rifle in his hand.

Tom reached down and grabbed the rifle from the scabbard on his saddle and ducked into the ravine. He had no more than hit the dirt when a bullet slammed into the side of the ravine just a foot or so from him. Tom crawled to the edge of the ravine and returned fire. His first shot hit the white pickup on the passenger's side just behind the door. It caused the man to duck down. His second shot kicked up some dirt under the truck causing the man to fall to the ground.

He wasn't sure if he had hit the man or just scared him, but it gave Tom a chance to get out of there. He ran to his horse and jumped into the saddle. The horse took off at a run along the bottom of the ravine. Tom leaned over the horse's neck and let the horse run.

After he figured he was out of range, Tom glanced over his shoulder to see if he was being followed. The white pickup was starting to move. If his shot had hit the man, it had not put him out of action. Tom was pretty sure that he couldn't outrun the pickup, but he could keep the man far enough away to prevent him from getting a good shot off.

Suddenly, Tom felt a sharp pain, then everything went blank. He bounced around in the saddle for several yards before he fell off the horse. The horse continued to run on down the ravine.

* * * *

While Tom lay in the ravine, the man in the white pickup stopped and looked down toward Tom. Tom was not moving. The man leaned his rifle up against the pickup, then retrieved his binoculars from the front seat. Looking through the binoculars, he could see the blood on the side of Tom's head. He could also see that Tom was not moving. He smiled to himself, then looked around to see if there was anyone else in the area. The only thing he saw was the horse still running in the bottom of the ravine. Satisfied that he had done what he had been paid to do, he got back in the pickup and turned around. He headed back toward Spiny Ridge.

CHAPTER SIXTEEN

Tracy walked into Betty's Café and sat down at a table in the corner. She was tired and hungry, and she had a lot on her mind. What was she going to do without Will to help her? How long would Tom be around to help her before he got tired of working a ranch, or had to get back to his job at the bank?

It seemed as if everything that could go wrong had gone wrong, that was until she looked out the window. She was not happy to see who was coming toward the cafe. Tracy had no interest in talking to anyone, but it looked as if that was not to be.

Tracy hadn't been there for more than a couple of minutes when the door to the café swung open. She looked over toward the door and watched the person who came into the cafe. She shook her head in disgust at the sight of Tom's mother. Tracy was hoping that she was not going to have to talk to her; but from the look on Mrs. Norbert's face, that was not going to happen. She had the look of someone who was on a mission. It looked as if her mission was to talk to Tracy, and make her day just that much harder to cope with.

"Hello, Mrs. Norbert," Tracy said politely as the woman approached her table.

"Where is my son?" Mrs. Norbert demanded sharply.

"Please sit down and have a cup of coffee," Tracy said in an effort to be as nice as she could.

"I don't want a cup of coffee. I want to know where my son is. Do I have to call the police? I know you have his car. Did you steal it?" she asked loud enough so those sitting anywhere near Tracy could hear her.

"No, I didn't steal it. He loaned it to me so I could be with my ranch hand. He was shot and is in the hospital," Tracy said trying very hard to keep her temper under control.

"I don't care about your stupid ranch hand. You will tell me where my son is right now, or I will have you arrested for stealing his car," Mrs. Norbert said sharply as she stomped her foot on the floor much like a small child that wasn't getting her way might do.

Tracy looked around the café. It seemed that everyone in the café was looking at them. She wasn't sure if the patrons of the café were wondering what Tracy had done with Mrs. Norbert's son, or if they were just looking at Mrs. Norbert as a woman who had totally lost it and was having a mental meltdown. Either way, it was a little embarrassing to Tracy to have some woman yelling at her in front of half the town.

Tracy just looked up at her without saying a word. She was fuming inside and could think of several things she would like to say to Mrs. Norbert and a couple of other things she would like to do, but none that would make the situation any better. It was at that moment that she came up with a great idea.

"I'll tell you what. I will call the sheriff for you," Tracy said as she reached in her pocket for her cell phone.

Tracy punched in the number of the local Sheriff's Office. The phone rang several times before it was answered.

"Sheriff's Office," the voice on the phone said.

"Hi, Maggie. This is Tracy Atwater."

"Hi, Tracy. What can I do for you?"

"You can send an officer over to Betty's Café and have me arrested for kidnapping Tom Norbert. Oh, and for stealing his car. His mother is over her ranting and raving at me and I'm a little tired of listening to her. If you don't get someone over here fast, I won't be responsible for what I do," Tracy said as she glanced up at Mrs. Norbert to make sure that she had heard her, at least the last part of the conversation.

"You're kidding?"

"No. Not one little bit."

"I'll have Frank over there in a minute."

"Thanks," Tracy said then hung up.

She looked up at Mrs. Norbert and smiled.

"I hope you're happy. I called the sheriff for you."

Just then Betty came out of the back and walked over to where Tracy was sitting. She looked at Mrs. Norbert, then looked at Tracy.

"What the hell is going on out here?"

"Mrs. Norbert thinks that I kidnapped Tom's car and stole him, or stole Tom's car and kidnapped him. I'm not sure which."

"You think you're being funny. Well, we'll see about that when the Sheriff gets here."

"No. I don't think I'm funny. It's pathetic. What I do think is that you have lost it. I told - - -."

Tracy was interrupted by Frank and Mr. Norbert coming into the café. The look on Mr. Norbert's face showed that he was mad as hell. The look on Mrs. Norbert's face was one of shock when she saw her husband show up with Frank.

"What is going on here," Mr. Norbert demanded as he looked at his wife.

"She won't tell me where our son is," Mrs. Norbert said.

"Our son is out at her ranch. He was kind enough to help her while her hired hand is in the hospital. It was his idea, and his choice. Our son is an adult, and not everything he does is any of our business. You owe Miss Atwater an apology, and I suggest that you give her one now before she charges you with slander, and God knows what else."

"But - - ." Mrs. Norbert started to say.

"Now, Margaret," Mr. Norbert insisted sharply.

She looked at her husband as if she was going to defy him, but thought better of it. She had pushed her luck with him about as far as she dared.

"Now, Margaret," Mr. Norbert demanded.

Mrs. Norbert slowly turned and looked at Tracy. She took a deep breath before she spoke, then straighten up and pulled her shoulders back.

"I'm sorry," she said, but there was no true meaning in her voice.

Tracy did not respond. Instead she looked at Mr. Norbert. She could tell that he was very disgusted with his wife at that moment, and very embarrassed by her actions in front of everyone. Tracy felt a little sorry for him. He nodded slightly to Tracy, then took his wife by the arm and forcefully led her out of the café. Tracy turned and looked up at Frank. Frank smiled, reached out and pulled out a chair then sat down.

"Not the best of days?"

"No," Tracy said.

"How's Will doing?"

"Not well. He's in a coma."

"Sorry to hear that," Frank said then turned and looked out the window. "You want to tell me what this was all about?"

Frank turned back and looked at Tracy. He patiently waited for her to answer his question.

"She's just overprotective of her son."

"It sounded like there was more to it than that."

"I don't think that Tom told her that he was going out to the ranch to help me. She's just afraid that Tom and I will get back together again. She has always looked down her nose at us. By us, I mean the entire Atwater family. It seems that she thinks the Atwaters are too common for her son."

"Are you sure that's all there is?"

"No, but that's most of it. She has always been against Tom and me dating, even in high school."

"Yeah. I kind of remember something about that. Well, try to avoid her as much as you can. I'll have a talk with Mr. Norbert and advise him to keep his wife away from you."

"Thanks."

"Enjoy your lunch," he said as he stood up.

"I'm not very hungry now."

"You better eat something. You have a long day ahead of you."

"You're probably right. I'll get something to eat before I go back to the hospital."

"See you later," Frank said, then turned and left the café.

Betty came over to Tracy and took her order. It wasn't long before her lunch arrived. Tracy ate it, but didn't really enjoy it after all that had happened. When she was finished she paid the bill and returned to the hospital.

* * * *

The sun was low in the sky when Tom first opened his eyes and tried to move. At first he had no idea where he was, what time it was, or what had happened to him. As the fog of unconsciousness started to clear from his head, he began to feel the pain. His whole head seemed to ache. It was the worst headache he had ever had.

His head began to throb as he tried to sit up. The pain was so severe that he laid back down and closed his eyes in the hope that the pain would go away.

After a short time, Tom opened his eyes again and forced himself to sit up. It took a few minutes before the pain subsided enough that he could start to think. He slowly began to look around.

Tom began to put together what had happened. He had been shot and was lying in a ravine. He reached to his hip and found that his gun was still in his holster. He remembered that he had had a rifle with him and began to look for it. He found it just a few feet from where he had been laying. Tom started to stand up, but found that it made him dizzy. He sat back down to rest for a few more minutes.

After taking a few deep breaths and waiting for his head to clear a little more, he tried to stand again. Although he still felt dizzy, he managed to stand. It didn't take but a couple of minutes before the dizziness went away.

Tom walked over to his rifle and carefully bent down and picked it up. He looked around for the horse he had been riding, but it was nowhere in sight. There was only one thing for him to do, and that was to begin the long walk back to the barn. He knew that he was a long way from the barn, but he had no choice but to walk back.

As he slowly began to walk, he began to think about what had happened to him. Everything began to become clearer as his head cleared. Tom began to get angry. Someone had the nerve to shoot him, and that person was going to pay for it.

Tom's first thought was that it was Blaine who had shot at him. But the more he thought about it as he walked along the bottom of the ravine, the more he decided that it probably was not Blaine who had done the shooting. He didn't think Blaine would want to be a part of killing someone, although he wasn't all that sure.

If he remembered correctly, Blaine had a temper. Tom believed that Blaine might be smart enough to figure out that to kill someone on the Lazy A Ranch, especially someone who actually belonged on the ranch, would point a finger directly at him. Tom doubted that he would want that. Blaine would want no connection to the shooting. If that were the case, then who shot him, Tom wondered.

It occurred to Tom that someone hired by Blaine might be responsible for shooting him. In fact, that was the most likely scenario. At least if Blaine hired someone to shoot him, or anyone else that might interfere in what they were doing, Blaine could be somewhere he would be seen by a lot of people, giving him an airtight alibi. It would make it easier for him to deny any involvement.

The shooter would have to be someone who was not known in the area, or in the county. The shooter would have to be someone who would come in, shoot him, and then leave the county. If Blaine was smart, the person he hired would not be staying in town or on his ranch. He would probably not be staying anywhere near Blaine's ranch. Maybe not even in the county.

The only thing going for Tom was the white pickup truck. He knew that pickup trucks were as common as grass in that part of the country. So was the kind of rifle that the shooter had used. As far as Tom knew, Blaine didn't own a white pickup truck. The white pickup he had seen had no markings on it to help identify it, but it was a new model.

Was it possible that the person who shot him had purchased the pickup to make him look more like one of the locals, to make him blend in? It was certainly possible. There was also the possibility that the pickup truck was rented, but probably not from any place close or even in the county.

Another thought came to Tom. From what he knew, Blaine didn't have a lot of money. He had seen the application Blaine had made to get money to drill a well. Blaine didn't appear to have much cash money. That brought up the question of where would he get the money to hire a shooter? It would certainly take a lot of money to get someone to shoot a person. Did Blaine have outside help with finances? That could be the case. Was someone else backing him in an effort to find whatever it was they were looking for? They were all good questions, but Tom had no answers.

There was another thought that suddenly ran through Tom's mind. Was it a tactic to force Tracy to sell the ranch?

If it was, who had the money to buy it? Certainly not Blaine in his present financial condition.

All Tom had were speculations and questions. He had no proof of anything except that someone had shot him and Will. Speculations would not go very far in putting the blame for what was happening on any one person. He needed proof.

Tom took a deep breath and let it out slowly, then looked up at the sky. It was clear that it wouldn't be long and he would be surrounded by darkness. He wasn't sure how far he was from the barn, but he knew he still had a long way to go. He thought about finding a place to bed down for the night rather than risk getting lost wandering around all night. He knew that it would probably be cold, and without a bedroll could be very uncomfortable for him. Building a fire, even in the ravine, was not a good idea, either. Besides, there was very little firewood out on the prairie.

Tom had been following the ravine that had provided him cover while working his way toward Spiny Ridge. Now the ravine provided him with a path, of sorts, that would take him at least part way back toward the barn.

As he came around a curve in the ravine, he suddenly found himself almost face to face with the horse he had been riding earlier. The horse was just standing there looking at him with his ears pointed toward him and his head up. It was obvious that the horse recognized him because he didn't move away.

"It was nice of you to wait for me," Tom said softly as he slowly approached the horse.

As soon as he was close enough to the horse, he reached out and took hold of the reins. Tom put his rifle in the saddle scabbard, then put his foot in the stirrup. He swung into the saddle, but not without his head letting him know that it was not easy and that he shouldn't move too quickly. He sat in the saddle for a moment or two to allow his head to stop throbbing.

As soon as he was ready, he nudged the horse in the sides and started the horse walking along the bottom of the ravine. When he came to the place where he had ridden into the ravine, he turned the horse and rode out. He then let the horse walk along. He thought about trotting, but the jarring would not help the way his head felt.

It was dark and very late by the time Tom arrived back at the barn. He stepped down out of the saddle and took a minute to take a breath. Tom wasn't feeling very hungry. All he wanted to do was to lie down and rest. But before he could do that, he had to take care of the horse. He walked the horse into the barn and into a stall. He stripped the bridle and saddle off the horse and rubbed the horse down. He then fed the horse a well deserved helping of oats and hay. As soon as he was finished taking care of the horse, he went to the stall where he had been sleeping. He laid down on his bedroll and almost immediately went to sleep.

CHAPTER SEVENTEEN

The sun came up and shone into the large windows of the waiting room of the hospital. It woke Tracy where she had been sleeping in a chair all night and was feeling the stiffness in her muscles. Stretching in order to relieve some of the stiffness only seemed to make her muscles react to the stiffness even more, causing Tracy more discomfort.

Tracy was also feeling hungry. She thought about going across the street to Betty's Café, but remembered what had happened yesterday. She had no desire to have another confrontation with Mrs. Norbert. Rather than risk a public war of words with her, Tracy decided that she would go to the hospital cafeteria. The food was not all that good, but it would fill her stomach and hopefully give her the energy she would need to face another day of sitting around and worrying about Will.

Just as she stood up and stretched again, she saw one of the nurses coming into the waiting room. Tracy looked around to see if there might be anyone else in the room that the nurse was coming to see. When she saw no one else in the room, she looked back at the nurse. The nurse was smiling. Tracy wondered if she might have a little good news.

"Tracy, Will is still in a coma, but his vital signs have improved slightly. If he continues to improve, he might be able to breathe without any assistance in the next day or two," the nurse said.

"Does that mean he's going to be all right?"

"It's still a little too early to know, but it is a good sign. He is still not out of the woods, yet. Will is very strong. We still won't know for sure for some time. I just thought you would like to be kept up-to-date on how he is doing."

"I most certainly do. And thank you. I think I will go down to the cafeteria and get a bite to eat," Tracy said.

"Might I make a suggestion?" the nurse asked.

"Certainly," Tracy said, wondering what kind of a suggestion she might have.

"It won't do Will, or you, any good for you to sit around here and wait for him to come around so you can talk to him. He will most likely be in a coma for several days. Do you have a cell phone?"

"Yes."

"If you would like, I'll take down your number and call you if there is any change in his condition. You could also call us if you like."

"Okay, but I'm not a relative. I didn't think you could give out information on a patient to anyone but a relative."

"You signed him in and signed a form that says you are responsible for him. That gives us permission to call you about his condition and for you to call us," she said with a slight grin.

"What about his sister? I'm sure she would want to know of any change in his condition."

"We will notify her, as well."

Tracy could see no reason to argue with her. It would also give her the opportunity to get some things done that needed to be taken care of. She smiled at the nurse and then gave her both her home phone and her cell phone numbers. Tracy also told the nurse that in some locations on the ranch her cell phone would not work, but they should leave a message. After that, Tracy left the waiting room and went to the hospital cafeteria.

After going through the cafeteria line and getting a good breakfast on her tray, she went to a table in the corner to eat.

She had just sat down when Mr. Norbert came into the cafeteria.

Mr. Norbert stood near the door and looked around the room. As soon as he spotted Tracy, he headed toward her table. He wasn't sure that she wanted to talk to him, but as long as his wife was not around he didn't think she would mind.

"I'm sorry to disturb your breakfast, but I felt that I needed to talk to you."

"It's all right. Please, sit down. Can I get you a cup of coffee?"

"No, thank you," he said as he pulled out a chair and sat down. "How is Will doing?"

"He is showing a little improvement, but he is still in critical condition."

"I hope that he gets well soon. I think I have a pretty good idea how difficult it must be for you, especially at a time when you are having problems at the ranch."

"Thank you. It helps that Tom is helping me by watching over my cattle."

"I'm very proud of him. He has turned out to be a good man."

"Yes, he has, but you didn't come over here for their fantastic breakfast, or to talk about how proud you are of Tom," Tracy said as she looked him in the eye. "What's on your mind, Mr. Norbert?"

"You're right," he said as he looked at her. "I came to apologize for any stress that my wife may have caused you. She is very concerned about Tom and his happiness."

"I'm sorry, Mr. Norbert, but she is only concerned about Tom marrying the 'right woman'. The 'right woman' in your wife's eyes is almost anyone but me. She has always looked down her nose at my family and me."

Mr. Norbert just sat there looking across the table at Tracy. He knew that she was right as much as it hurt him to admit it, even to himself.

Tracy could see the hurt on Mr. Norbert's face. She felt the need to say something that would make him feel better.

"I'm sorry. You have always treated us with respect, and you have always been friendly toward us. You have been nothing but helpful when we needed a little help. I hold nothing against you. You have always been fair."

"Thank you. I will continue to treat you and your father with respect. I will always be as fair as I can and as helpful as I can. I just - - - I just wish my wife could see what I see between you and Tom. I don't think I will ever understand why she can't see that Tom is happiest when he's with you. He loves you, and I think you love him."

Tracy looked at Mr. Norbert. She had no idea what she should say to him. All she could do was think about what he had said. Tracy knew that Tom loved her. She knew that from the first time he kissed her since her return to the ranch. It was almost a shock to hear someone else tell her what she already knew.

"I'm sorry that I disturbed your breakfast. I'll be on my way," he said as he pushed back the chair and stood up.

"Mr. Norbert, I will try to get along with Mrs. Norbert."

"I'm sure you will," he said with a smile. "I know she is sometimes very hard to get along with. If she gives you any more trouble, please let me know."

"I will," Tracy said.

"Thank you," Mr. Norbert said as he slid the chair back under the table, then turned and left the cafeteria.

Tracy finished her breakfast and then left the cafeteria. As she stepped out on the sidewalk, she looked both ways. She thought about going back to the hospital, but what could she do there? All there was to do was to sit and wait. Since they had her phone numbers and had told her they would call her if there was any change in Will's condition, she figured that she might as well get something done.

She decided to go to the grocery store and pick up a few supplies for out at the barn. Tracy was sure that Tom would be running short of a few things. She would pick them up and go out to the barn so that he could return to town and get some of his own work done.

After picking up what she thought was needed at the barn, she loaded the supplies into Tom's car and headed for the ranch. Once at the ranch, she transferred the supplies into Tom's pickup truck, then went into the house. She took a shower and got into some clean clothes.

Tracy returned to the truck. She started out across the prairie for the long and bumpy trip to the barn.

* * * *

The sun was already up and a gentle breeze was blowing in from the west when Tom woke up. He still wasn't feeling his best, but he did feel better. Tom had only a slight amount of discomfort where he had been struck by the bullet. He still had a bit of a headache, too, but it was bearable. He was feeling hungry, which was a good sign.

Tom got up and let his horse out into the corral behind the barn with the other horses, then went to where he had had his fire for cooking. He got the fire going then put on the coffee pot. He cut a slice of ham from a large piece and cooked it along with several eggs.

After he had finished his breakfast and cleaned up the area, he sat down on a bale of hay with a cup of coffee to think. As he was thinking about what he should do next, he reached up and touched the wound on his head. It hurt when he touched it. Even though it hurt, he knew that it would be a good idea if he tried to clean it. He set down his coffee and pulled his handkerchief out of his pocket. It looked clean. He wet the cloth with water from one of the coolers and began dabbing at the wound. Not being able to see it, made it difficult to see if it was clean.

When he finished cleaning the wound as best he could, he sat back down with his coffee. His thoughts turned to what he should do now. He wanted to call the Sheriff's Office and talk to Frank, but his cell phone didn't work very well out at the barn. Tom knew that he could ride a horse back to the ranch house and get his truck, then drive into town to talk to the Sheriff.

It was a plan, but he had told Tracy that he would keep an eye on her cattle. Tom had made a promise, and he would keep his promise. He went out to the corral in back of the barn and picked out another horse, one that was fresh and had not been ridden in several days. He led the horse into the barn, took the halter off it and put on a bridle. He then saddled the horse and took it outside where he tied it to the corral fence.

Tom went back into the barn and picked up his rifle. Just as he was about to come out of the barn, he stopped and backed up. A white pickup truck had just come over the top of a hill off to the east and stopped. He couldn't be sure if it was the same white pickup he had seen when he was shot, but he wasn't about to take any chances. He quickly set the rifle down while he strapped on his pistol. He then picked up the rifle and levered a cartridge into the chamber as he walked to the door of the barn.

Staying inside the barn out of sight, he watched the pickup. It had stopped near the top of the hill and just stayed there. He could see that there was someone inside the truck, but he could not make out who it might be.

It seemed to take forever, but it was just a couple of minutes before Tom saw someone get out of the truck. Whoever it was, he had gotten out on the far side of the truck and was leaning on the hood. It was too far for Tom to see just what the man was doing, but it looked as if the guy at the truck was looking toward him using binoculars to see if anyone was around. Once again Tom wished that he had not left his binoculars in his truck.

Tom took a quick look around. It was clear to him that whoever was up on the hill by the white pickup would know that there was someone around. The fact that there was a horse saddled and tied to the corral fence, and that the horse was ready to ride, would be a dead give away. Tom doubted that the person next to the pickup had seen him, however. He had been inside the barn when the truck came over the hill.

Being careful not to be seen, Tom continued to watch the person at the pickup from inside the barn. Tom wondered if he was trying to decide if he should come closer or not.

Tom looked around for a second. He thought about seeing if there was some way he could get closer to the man at the pickup without being seen. Sitting on the top of the hill gave the man at the pickup a definite advantage. If it was the same man who had shot at him yesterday, Tom would like very much to get closer to him.

Suddenly, the man straightened up and looked off toward the south. He quickly turned, got into the truck and sped off in the general direction of the way he had come.

At first, Tom wasn't sure what it was that made the man take off in such a hurry. It became clear when he looked off to the south.

Tom could see a black pickup truck coming toward the barn. He was sure that it was his pickup. That could only mean that Tracy was returning. It didn't look like she was in any big hurry.

He was glad to see her, but his thoughts turned to Will. Tom wondered if she was coming back because Will had not made it. If he had died, it would be murder instead of attempted murder. After glancing back at the hill to the east, he stepped out of the barn and watched as his truck came closer.

Tracy drove up in front of the barn, stopped and got out of the truck. She looked at Tom and saw him with a rifle in his hands. When she looked up at his face, she saw the wound on the side of his head. The wound on Tom's head caused her to be concerned, and she hurried to him.

"What happened to you? Have you had some trouble here?" she asked as her worry for him showed in her voice.

"Whoa. Not so fast," Tom said with a smile, pleased that she was worried about him. "I'm okay."

"You don't look okay. What happened? And why the rifle?"

"Yesterday I trailed Will's horse from here and along the fence line until I found the place where he had been shot. I also found the place where he had been shot from. I got into a gun fight with some guy in a white pickup. The guy got away, but not before clipping me alongside the head."

"Let me look at it," Tracy said as she moved closer and looked at the wound on his head.

Tom turned his head and allowed her to look at the wound. He flinched a little when she touched it.

"Careful, it's a little tender."

"It looks clean. I don't think it needs stitches, but I should put a dressing on it to keep it clean. Sit down over here," she said as she pointed at a bale of hay.

While Tom sat down on the bale, Tracy retrieved the first aid kit from the barn. She took it over and set it in Tom's lap, then opened it. She put some antiseptic on the wound then covered it with a dressing to keep it clean.

As she was finishing up, she asked him, "Why the rifle in your hands this morning?"

"I had some company that I wasn't sure I wanted to see without a little fire power."

"What do you mean?" she asked as she looked up at him.

"There was a white pickup truck on top of the hill just to the east of here. It looked like the same truck the guy that shot me had been driving yesterday, but I wasn't sure. I didn't want to meet him again without a gun."

"You mean he had the nerve to come all the way over here."

"I don't know if it was the same pickup or not. But I was not about to take any chances. He left in a hurry when he saw you coming."

"Oh. How are you feeling now?"

"Much better," he said as he smiled at her.

"I think we need to get Frank out here. He needs to know what is going on."

"I agree. Someone wants your land and is willing to do anything to get it," Tom said.

"I understand that, but this is not the old west any more. They can't just go around shooting people," Tracy said.

"It may not be the old west to you and me, but it still is to someone."

"I don't understand what they could want. The tests they did several years ago showed that there is no oil or natural gas on any of the land around here. The drought has almost ruined the land for cattle. Even some of the wells and stock ponds are drying up. It makes no sense."

"It makes sense to somebody. Are you sure there isn't something on this land that someone might know about that would make someone want it?" Tom asked.

Tracy sat down on a bale of hay and began to think. At first, she could think of nothing that anyone would want other than the desire for more land. Then suddenly, like a bolt of lightening, she sat up straight up as she remembered the thick green grass and the spring inside Spiny Ridge. It occurred to her that someone, besides her father and her, could know about the little valley. It didn't seem likely as her father had not even told her about it. She was pretty sure that he would not have told anyone else. But then there was the possibility that someone could have been nosing around in Spiny Ridge and discovered it.

Tom was watching her. He noticed a sudden change in the look on her face. He wondered what it was that she was thinking.

"What's on your mind?"

"I was just thinking about something," she said without looking at him, but didn't say anything for a moment or two.

"You want to let me in on it?"

Tracy turned her head and looked at Tom. He had been there for her when she needed someone to help. Deep down in her heart she knew that he was the only one she could really trust with what she was thinking.

"My father would sometimes ride across Spiny Ridge to get to here from the ranch house."

Tom just looked at her for a moment before he spoke.

"There is no way to ride across Spiny Ridge."

"I think there is. Dad told me once that he had saved almost three hours getting to this barn from the ranch house on horseback by crossing Spiny Ridge."

"Do you think that he might have been kidding you?"

"No. I think he was serious."

"If what you're saying is true, I don't see what difference it would make in someone wanting this land," Tom said as he looked at her while thinking about it.

"Do you promise not to tell a soul what I'm about to tell you?"

"Of course," Tom said as he listened to her every word.

"I found a way into the center of Spiny Ridge. I didn't find a way out the other side, but what I did find was beautiful."

"What did you find," Tom asked with a hint of excitement in his voice.

"I found that the ridge is really two ridges, actually more than two, but two major ridges. In between the two major ridges, there is the most beautiful little valley that you ever saw. It has moist green grass that is almost belly deep on the horses. There is a small grove of five or six oak trees, big oak trees. Yes, I said oak trees," she said when she saw the look on Tom's face.

"Are you sure?" he asked. "You don't find oak trees in this part of the country."

"You do in that valley. I know what an oak tree looks like. There has to be a spring in the valley somewhere."

Tom looked at her. He had grown up out on the prairie just as Tracy had. He had never seen an oak anywhere in the entire county. Cottonwood trees, yes, but not oak trees.

"Are you sure they were oak and not cottonwood trees?"

"Yes. They were oak, big oak trees."

"Do you think you could find your way into that valley again?"

"I think so."

"That valley could be what they're after."

"Do you think that Blaine knows about it?" Tracy asked.

"I don't know, but I guess it's possible."

"What do we do now?"

"We need to find out what is in that valley that someone would want. We know there's water there. Right?"

"Right. There has to be to grow oak trees and grass like that in a place that hasn't had any rain for months. And to grow oak trees like the ones in the valley would take a lot of water and a good many years. I would think that most of the trees have to be close to a hundred years old, if not older," she said with a hint of excitement.

"If there is water there, then why would they be drilling test holes at the outside edge of the ridge?" Tom said more to himself than to Tracy.

"Do you think they might think there is something else like - - oil or, maybe natural gas under the ridge?" Tracy asked.

"It's possible," Tom said thoughtfully.

Tracy watched Tom as he thought about the valley and the test holes that he had seen on the outside edge of the ridge. She wasn't sure what he was thinking, but she didn't want to disturb his thoughts until he was done. Suddenly, Tom looked at her and smiled.

"First of all, we can't say anything to anyone about the valley," Tom said.

"I think that goes without saying," Tracy said with a smile.

"Secondly, we need to find out what is in that valley besides grass, oak trees and water."

"What will that prove?"

"It might help us understand why someone wants to drill under the ridge. If someone thinks that there is oil or natural gas under the ridge, they could drill under the ridge at an angle so it would look like they're drilling on Blaine's property, when they are actually drilling under the ridge on your property. It's been known to happen before."

"But I have the mineral and oil rights to anything found under my property."

"Do you think that anyone who would shoot Will, and shoot at me, gives a damn about rights?"

"No. I guess you're right. They wouldn't give a damn who they hurt or kill to make a bunch of money. Okay. What do we do?" Tracy asked as she looked to Tom for answers.

"I don't think your cattle are in any immediate danger of being killed or stolen. They don't seem to care much about your cattle. That's not what they want. And your cattle have been doing pretty well by themselves. They should be all right if we were to disappear for a day or two. Do you agree?"

"Yes," she replied as she looked at him for some idea of what he was thinking.

"I don't think it's safe around here right now. I'll unsaddle the horse and put him in the corral. After we make sure that the horses have plenty of food and water to keep them for a couple of days, we are going to leave."

"Where are we going?" Tracy asked.

"We're going to the ranch house and call Frank. Then in the morning, you and I are going to look for your valley. From there we are going to see if we can find out why someone has such an interest in your land."

"And maybe find a way out on this side of the ridge?" Tracy asked.

"And maybe find a way out on this side of the ridge," he said with a smile. "But right now we have work to do."

Tom took the horse he had saddled into the barn and unsaddled it. He then turned the horse loose in the corral behind the barn. Tracy and Tom worked hard to get the horses set up for a couple of days without anyone around to care for them. When they were finished, they got in the truck and headed back toward the ranch house.

Tom was not worried about someone seeing them leave. He figured that if they saw them leave, it would mean that they would have at least a day or two before anyone would come out to investigate the shooting of Tom. That would give them time to clear out and leave no trace of them being there.

As they drove across the prairie toward the ranch house, Tom remembered the lone tree that was growing in the ravine. He also remembered the thick green grass around the bottom of the tree. He was sure that there was a seeping spring near the base of the tree. If there was a seeping spring there, why couldn't there be one in Spiny Ridge?

"I found a seeping spring in a ravine that ran from Spiny Ridge out into the pasture," Tom said. "It wasn't big enough to use for watering cattle, but it was there."

"You think the water might be coming from Spiny Ridge?"

"From what you tell me about the interior of Spiny Ridge, it certainly seems like a possibility."

Nothing more was said on the drive back to the ranch house. Both of them were deep in thought.

CHAPTER EIGHTEEN

It was late in the afternoon when Tom and Tracy arrived at the ranch house. They had not hurried to get there as they would not be able to start looking for the way into Spiny Ridge until morning. As soon as they arrived at the ranch house, Tracy went into the kitchen and began fixing something for dinner.

While she was making dinner, Tom was on the phone to Frank. She could hear only Tom's side of the conversation, but it was clear that he was telling Frank about the shooter and the white pickup truck.

Tracy was peeling potatoes for their dinner when Tom walked up next to her. She looked over at him and waited for him to tell her what was going on.

"Frank is on his way out here to talk to us. Will there be enough for three for dinner? I sort of invited him for dinner," Tom said sheepishly. "I'm sorry that I didn't ask you first."

"There should be plenty," she said with a forgiving smile. "What's he think about all this shooting?"

"He more or less agrees with us. He thinks that whoever is doing all the shooting thinks that there is something of value under Spiny Ridge."

"Did you tell him about the valley and the grass and oak trees out there?"

"No. You didn't want me to tell anyone," he said as he looked into her eyes.

Tracy smiled at him, then turned her head and continued peeling the potatoes. She smiled to herself as she thought about Tom. She couldn't help but believe that he was trying very hard to get her to believe in him, and to trust him to say what he means and be honest with her. She couldn't help but think about what his father had said about them. There was no doubt that Tom was in love with her. And her doubts about Tom were rapidly fading away. She was beginning to feel that his father was right. Deep down in the recesses of her mind, she knew that she loved Tom. Her only question was why was she afraid to let him know that she loved him?

"Are you going to just stand there with that potato in your hand, or are you going to put it in the pot and cook it?" Tom asked as he looked at her face.

Tracy suddenly turned and looked at him. She then looked at the potato as if she was wondering how it got in her hand. Then she began to smile as she again turned her head and looked back at Tom.

"I was thinking," she said softly.

"About what, if I may ask?"

"I'm not sure I want to tell you just yet. Maybe later," she said with a sexy smile.

"I can hardly wait," he smiled as he leaned close to her.

Tracy leaned toward him until their lips met in a light and loving kiss. Neither of them wanted the kiss to end; but Tracy knew that if it didn't end soon, she might not let it end at all. She leaned back away from him and smiled.

"If we keep this up, we won't eat until mid-night. I'm not sure how Frank will feel about that."

"He would understand," Tom said jokingly.

"Maybe, but we didn't have any lunch. I don't know about you, but I'm hungry."

"Okay. I surrender. I'll leave you to your cooking. Is there anything that I can do to help?"

"Yes. You can set the table."

While Tracy returned to preparing dinner, Tom set the table. He then sat down at the table and leaned back in a chair. For a few minutes, he simply watched Tracy as she worked to prepare their dinner. But it wasn't long and his mind drifted off to what had been happening around the ranch.

There was something on the Lazy A Ranch that someone wanted, and they were willing to do anything to get it. The only thing Tom could think of was that it had to be something of great value. No one would go to the extent they had without expecting a pretty big return for their efforts at the end. The white pickup truck, the shooting of Will, the test holes along the edge of Spiny Ridge, and the shooting of himself, filled Tom's mind with a lot to think about while he waited for Frank.

Suddenly, Tom's thoughts were disturbed by the sound of a vehicle pulling into the ranch yard. He sat up and looked over at Tracy. She was looking out the window, then turned and looked at Tom.

"Frank's here," she said.

Tom stood up and went to the door. He pushed open the door just as Frank stepped up on the porch. Frank walked into the house and Tom followed him. Tracy came out of the kitchen to greet Frank.

"Hi, Frank."

"Hi, Tracy. I want to thank you for inviting me to dinner."

"You're welcome. Dinner will be ready in just a few minutes. If you would like, you and Tom can sit down at the table. I'm assuming that you will be discussing what has been going on, and I would like to hear it."

"Sure," Frank said.

They all went to the kitchen. While Tracy was getting the dinner ready to put on the table, Tom and Frank sat down. Frank made a couple of comments about the wound on the side of Tom's head, but said little else until the food was on the table. As the dishes were passed around the table, Frank began talking about what he had been able to find out so far.

"It seems that Energy Testing entered your property and were planning to drill twelve test sites for a new kind of testing system they have. They were going to test along the edge of Spiny Ridge," Frank said. "They got six test sites prepared for the tests before the foremen got there and told them to get off the property immediately, that they were trespassing.

"So they knew they were trespassing," Tracy said.

"Sort of. The owner of the company said that his men on the site were told by Blaine that it was his property. Of course, we know that it was not his property.

"As soon as the foreman found out where they were digging the test sites, they left your property. Blaine was told that if there were any problems as a result of his lying to the foreman's crew, he would sue him in a heartbeat."

"So Energy Testing never actually did any tests, is that right?" Tom asked.

"That's right."

"So, no one knows if there is anything of value under the ridge?" Tracy asked.

"Well, that may not be the case."

"What do you mean, Frank," Tom asked.

"According to the owner of Energy Testing, he heard rumors that another company came out and did some tests."

"Did he know who the other company was?" Tracy asked.

"No. Like I said, 'he heard rumors'."

"Does the other company have the same new testing technology?" Tom asked.

"We don't know since we don't know who it is. We have to assume it does."

"Before my father had his stroke, he said that they never tested on our land five years ago," Tracy said. "Is it possible that if they had, they would have found something then?"

"Since they didn't do any tests on your land, there's no way of knowing," Frank said.

"What color are Energy Testing's trucks, especially their pickup trucks?" Tom asked.

"They are white, but every one of their trucks has a very large black logo on the doors with the name of the company in large red letters," Frank said.

"Did you see any of their trucks?" Tracy asked.

"Yes. And every one of them has a logo on the side. Energy Testing has never had a complaint signed against them. Everything I can find out about them says they operate legally. And I found the owner to be straight forward with his answers to my questions. He answered my questions without a moment's hesitation, even when they were not in his favor."

"Then who is it that owns the white pickup truck that was driven by the guy that shot me, and probably shot Will?"

"We don't know. We are looking for that white pickup. No luck in finding it, so far. But we don't have anything to distinguish it from the hundreds of other white pickup trucks in the county."

Tom took a few bites of his dinner while he thought about what Frank had said. That white pickup had to belong to someone. The one thing he knew for sure was that the white pickup had a bullet hole in the passenger's side just behind the door.

"Frank, can you put out the word around the state to be on the lookout for a late model white pickup truck with a bullet hole in the passenger's side just back of the door?"

"Sure. Are you sure you hit the truck?"

"Very sure."

"Do you think that the pickup might belong to Blaine?" Tracy asked.

"I doubt it. I checked the records at the state office. There is only one pickup registered to Blaine. It is an old model dark blue Ford three-quarter-ton pickup," Frank said.

As the three of them continued to eat their dinner, they continued to talk about what was happening. Frank was able to give them an update on Will's condition, which had not changed since Tracy had last talked to the nurse at the hospital.

They did a lot of brain storming while eating dinner. When dinner was over and the table was cleared, they went into the living room where they continued to talk. They all had their own ideas as to what was going on, but unfortunately no one had any proof.

There were two things that they all seemed to be able to agree on, and that was Blaine was behind it in some way. Everything seemed to point to Blaine, but there was no proof that he was responsible for the shootings. His claim that Will had taken a shot at him while he was on Blaine's property was probably a ploy to cause confusion.

It was well after dark when Frank decided that it was time for him to leave. He stood up and started for the door. When he got to the door, he turned around and looked at Tom and Tracy who had followed him to the door.

"Tom, I don't think it's a good idea for you to go any further east than the barn, at least until we get a better handle on who is doing the shooting and who hired the shooter."

"I have some cattle that have wandered off that way," Tracy said.

"I will be going over to have a talk with Blaine in the morning. Then I'm going to take a look at where you were shot and see what evidence I can find. I'll be checking out that ravine you told me about," Frank said to Tom.

"While I'm looking around, I'll keep an eye out to see how your cattle are doing," he said to Tracy.

"Okay. I'll do as you say, but I can't wait too long. I have to check on the cattle. I'm sure that you are aware of the fact that I can't afford to lose any cattle," Tracy said.

"I know, Tracy. I'll do everything I can to make it safe out there for both of you."

"Thanks for coming by," Tom said.

"Thank you for dinner, Tracy. It was really good. And Tom, you keep your head down," Frank said with a grin. "I don't have that many friends that I can afford to lose one."

"Drive safe," Tom said as Frank turned and stepped off the porch.

Tom and Tracy stood inside the door and watched as Frank walked to his car, got in and left. As soon as he was gone, they turned and went back inside. Tracy went right to the kitchen and began cleaning up. Tom followed her and helped with the dishes.

They didn't do much talking while cleaning up the kitchen. Tom kept looking at Tracy out of the corner of his eye. He also noticed she was glancing at him from time to time.

* * * *

Tom and Tracy sat in the living room after they had finished in the kitchen. They talked about Spiny Ridge and where the entrance on the ranch house side of the ridge might be. It seemed as if neither one of them was willing to open the subject of going to bed.

Tracy had finally figured out that she was in love with Tom, but she wasn't sure what would happen if she told him about her feelings. The two times he had kissed her since her return to the ranch had shown her that she really wanted to be with him, but she was still afraid of what would come of it.

The way he had helped her without asking for anything in return had shown her that he had changed a great deal since high school. He had matured. He had become the kind of a man that she wanted to share her life.

Tom was using the time they had together to show her that he was concerned about her and the ranch. He had tried not to make any of his suggestions sound like orders to her. He had been holding back on telling her how he felt about her for fear that it would drive her away from him. Tom wasn't sure how long he could find things to talk about to avoid the subject of going to bed.

"Tom, don't you think it would be a good idea if we went to bed? It is getting late."

"Yes. It could very well turn out to be a long day tomorrow."

"Where would you like to sleep?" she asked, hoping he would say with her.

Tom looked around the room before he answered.

"I guess I could sleep on the sofa."

Tracy looked at the sofa. The look on her face showed that she might be just a little disappointed. She turned back and looked at Tom, but didn't say anything.

"Now, if you're really asking me where I would like to sleep, and really mean it, I would like to sleep with you," he said hoping that she would not shut him out because he told the truth.

"Would we get any sleep?" she asked with a coy smile.

"Oh, I'm sure we would, but it might take awhile," he answered again hoping that what he was hearing was true.

"Okay. But I need a shower."

"So do I," he said with a smile. "If you don't mind, we could shower together. That way we wouldn't waste a lot of hot water."

"I wouldn't count on that," she said playfully.

"Count on what?"

"I wouldn't count on saving any water. It could take just as long to shower together, maybe longer."

"Oh, I hope so," he said as he stood up and reached out a hand to her.

Tracy stood up and took his hand. Together they walked into her bedroom. Once in the bedroom, Tom pulled Tracy around to face him, then drew her close to him. She reached out and put her hands on his shoulders as she looked into his eyes.

As he looked into her eyes, he slid his hand around her and drew her up against him. Tom leaned down as he pulled her body up against him. He could feel the firmness of her breasts as she pressed her body against him. Their lips met in a strong, passionate kiss. Tom let his hands slide down over her firm behind which caused her to moan softly and press harder against him. It was a long hard kiss that had been waiting years for them to share. When they broke off the kiss, they were both breathing hard.

"I want you," Tracy said breathlessly.

"I want you, too," Tom replied.

After looking into each other's eyes for a moment or two, they stepped back from each other. They quickly undressed, scattering their clothes on the floor. As soon as they were both naked, Tom took Tracy's hand and led her into the bathroom.

Tracy stood next to the shower while Tom leaned in and turned on the water. As soon as the water was warm enough, but not too warm, he stepped into the shower and held out his hand to her. She took his hand and stepped into the shower with him.

Tom pulled her up against him as he backed into the spray of the shower. Wrapped in each other's arms, they let the warm water flow over them while they kissed.

After several minutes of passionate kissing and caressing under the shower, they broke off the kiss and began washing each other. Their touching and fondling caused their desire for each other to grow. It wasn't long before their desire for each other had turned into passion. They quickly rinsed off, then dried each other.

Tom reached out and picked Tracy up in his arms and carried her to the bed. He laid her down on the bed, then slipped in beside her. He wrapped his arms around her beautiful body and pulled her close. She pressed her body to his and whispered in his ear.

"Make love to me," she said softly.

Tom rolled over her and he made passionate love to the woman he had loved for so many years. When their excitement and need for each other had subsided, Tracy rolled up against Tom's side and held him close. Snuggled up against the man she loved, she drifted off to sleep, content and happy in her love for him, and his love for her.

CHAPTER NINETEEN

Morning came with the bright sun shining through the window on the lovers. Tracy woke with Tom rolled up against her back. He had his arm wrapped around her, and was holding her against him as if to protect her from the cold cruel world. It had been a long time since she had felt so secure and safe. Having the responsibility of running a ranch without anyone to lean on or to help make decisions had taken a toll on her. She had the help of a ranch hand to do the hard, heavy work, but he was not someone she could lean on when she felt like crying.

That thought made her smile. Tom had been there when she needed him. He had been there to help by loaning her his new truck, when she needed someone to help keep an eye on the herd, and now when she needed someone to hold her and make her feel safe. Tom was there for her in the true meaning of the words. She was beginning to realize that she not only needed him, but she wanted him and loved him.

Tracy reached out and slid her hand over his hand, then guided it to her breast and held it there. She smiled as she remembered the love for each other that they had shared last night. She wanted it to be like that always.

Tracy closed her eyes and thought about the two of them. She tried to think of what it would be like living on the ranch and raising not only cattle, but a few kids as well. She was sure that he would make a wonderful father.

Her thoughts turned to Tom and what he might like. She realized that she had no idea if he would like to have children, or if he would like to live on a ranch.

Tracy began to wonder if they really did have a future together. It occurred to her that he might like to continue to work in his father's bank and live in town. Could they work it out? Could the two of them make a go of it, each wanting something different?

Suddenly her thoughts were disturbed by Tom moving his hand lightly over her breast. It felt so good. He was so gentle with her. She knew that there would be things that they could work out if they really tried. She loved him too much not to try.

"Hey, beautiful. Are you ready to get up?" he asked as he continued to gently run the palm of his hand over her firm breast.

"You are making it very hard for me to want to get up," she said in a soft whisper.

"I don't know about you, but I am very hungry."

"I'm starving," she said.

"Roll over here."

Tracy turned over so she was facing him. As he wrapped his arms around her, she slid her arms around his neck. Tom rolled her over on top of him, then slid his hand down the smooth lines of her back, from her shoulders to the small of her back and on over her firm behind.

"You are so sexy," he whispered. "I could stay right here all day."

"I would like that, but we have things to do before we can spend a whole day in bed."

"Does that mean that there is hope of spending a whole day in bed with you," he said with a slight grin.

"You're not the only one who enjoyed last night," she said as she laid on top of him and looked down into his eyes.

Tom squeezed her butt, then slid his hands up her back. He pulled her head down until their lips met in a long passionate kiss. They were both breathing hard when the kiss ended. Tracy rose up and looked down at him and smiled.

"I think we better get out of bed before we end up staying in it all day. I'd like a shower first, then I'll fix some breakfast."

"Can I take a shower with you?" he asked playfully.

"I don't think we will get out of the house if we do that," she said. "But I'm pretty sure that there will be another time."

"In that case, you take a shower, then I'll take one."

Tracy smiled, then rolled off him. She sat up on the side of the bed and looked over her shoulder at Tom. He was a handsome man, and he loved her. She smiled at him then stood up and walked into the bathroom.

While she was taking a quick shower, Tom laid on the bed with his hands behind his head. He was looking up at the ceiling. He had started thinking about Tracy and how much he loved her. But it didn't take long for him to begin to think about what had been going on around the ranch. He couldn't help thinking that it might not be safe for her on the ranch.

Tom knew that Frank would be talking to Blaine today. He also knew that Frank would be roaming around the pasture near Spiny Ridge looking for clues concerning who might have shot Will, and who was responsible for shooting him. There was something in or around Spiny Ridge that someone wanted very much. What was it?

It wasn't long before Tracy came out of the bathroom. She was wearing a short robe that came down to just above her knees. Tom couldn't help but think how sexy she looked.

"Are you sure you don't want to come back to bed?" Tom asked.

"If you want something to eat you will get out of that bed and get yourself ready for the day. We have a lot to do. Besides, I want you to see the valley in Spiny Ridge."

"Okay. You win. I'll be out as soon as I get a shower."

Tom rolled out of bed and went into the bathroom. Tracy could hear the water running as she took off her robe and got dressed in jeans and a woman's western style shirt. Tracy put her long hair in a ponytail since they would be riding horses into the ridge. As soon as she was ready, she went to the kitchen and began fixing breakfast.

It wasn't very long before Tom showed up in the kitchen. Tracy was just putting breakfast on the table. They sat down to eat, neither of them saying very much. They were both thinking about the day. What was going to happen today? What would they find once they were inside the valley? Would they find the way across Spiny Ridge to the other side? Would they even be able to find the entrance to the valley?

As soon as breakfast was over, Tom went out to saddle a couple of horses while Tracy packed some food for them. She had just finished packing the food in the saddle bags when Tom walked up to the house leading two saddled horses. After tying the saddle bags on the saddles and putting rifles in the saddle scabbards, they mounted up and headed toward the ridge.

* * * *

Tom and Tracy rode toward the ridge. When they got to the ridge, they turned and headed in a northeasterly direction along the steep face of the ridge. They moved along at a walk, both of them scanning the rock formation for an opening. They had been riding for some distance when Tracy spotted the opening she had taken a few days ago.

"Here," she said. "This is it."

"It doesn't look like much of a trail back in there, but if you say so," Tom said as he shrugged his shoulders. "Lead on."

Tracy turned her horse and coaxed the mare into the very narrow canyon. It was so narrow that her stirrups rubbed against the rocks on both sides from time to time. The horse was reluctant to move along in such a narrow canyon, but with a little prodding by Tracy the mare went along with it.

Moving through the canyon was slow. Each twist and turn seemed to be a new adventure. As before, when Tracy broke out of the narrow canyon, she was suddenly in deep, rich green grass. It was as exciting and as breathtaking as it had been the first time.

"Wow," was all Tom could say as he rode his horse into the valley. "This is beautiful."

"I told you it was beautiful," she said as she turned in the saddle to look back at Tom.

"Yeah, I know. But I never expected anything like this."

"Come on. I'll show you that the trees I told you about are oaks, not cottonwoods."

"I believe you," he said as he followed her off across the valley.

Tom didn't say anything for a long time. He was too busy looking around. He couldn't help but think that he had suddenly been magically transported to a completely different world. Tom had never seen anything like it before. The horses walked across the valley in thick green grass that came up above the knees of the horses.

As they approached the other side of the valley, Tom could see the small grove of large oak trees. Some of them were as tall as sixty feet with a spread to match. For as hot as it had been before they started into the ridge, it was cool and very pleasant in the valley. He saw several birds flying in and out of the trees. When they got to the oak trees, they rode into the shadow of the trees and stepped out of the saddle.

For several minutes, Tracy stood by her horse and smiled as she watched Tom as he looked around. She couldn't help smiling at him. He was so taken in by the beauty and the quiet of the place. Tom looked over at Tracy and smiled.

"I have to admit that this is the most beautiful place in the world. It's almost as if you and I are the only people in the world."

"I felt the same way the first time I saw it. At least, now I understand why my father never told anyone about it. It would be a shame if everyone knew it was here. They would want to make a park or something like that out of it. People would come from all over to see it, and that would ruin it."

"It sure would," Tom agreed.

"I still haven't found the way out of here that leads to the north pasture and the barn."

"Well, that way is north," he said as he pointed in the direction that was generally north. "I think we should start here behind the oak trees and work our way along the ridge toward the northeast. With all the twists and turns getting in here, I'm not sure how far we are from the north fence line."

"Okay," Tracy said. "If we don't find any way out of here going that way, we can come back here and go the other way."

Tracy put her foot in the stirrup and swung into the saddle. Tom swung into the saddle on his horse, then turned him around and headed along the ridge. They walked the horses along so as not to miss any narrow canyon that might take them out of the valley and into the north pasture.

They had gone some distance when Tom noticed a narrow opening in the almost solid rock wall. It looked like it was almost too narrow for them to get through if they tried to ride the horses. Tom looked at it for a couple of minutes before he stepped down off his horse. He looked up at Tracy as he handed her his horse's reins.

"I have my doubts that this is the way out of here. It looks almost too narrow, but I think we should check it out."

"Okay," Tracy said. "Are we going to walk the horses?"

"Not yet. I think I'll walk back in a ways and see where it goes. I'd hate to get in there with the horses and not be able to turn around."

"Good idea. Be careful," Tracy said.

Tom nodded and smiled up at her, then turned around and started into the narrow canyon. He had not gone very far when the canyon made a sharp turn. He was sure that a horse could make the turn. He continued on for another sixty to seventy yards when the canyon made another sharp turn. Again, he believed that a horse could make the turn. Almost immediately he noticed that the floor of the canyon went up a fairly steep slope for a short distance, but he was sure that the horses could manage it. As he got closer to the top, it widened out. When he got to the top, he found himself on the very top of Spiny ridge.

Tom also discovered that Spiny Ridge had several smaller ridges that ran almost parallel to the main ridge. From his vantage point he could see at least three ridges that ran almost parallel to each other, but looked as if they might come together at some point southwest of his location. If they did, that might be why it was generally thought that it was one ridge when it was actually several ridges that converged down to one point that went underground near the southwest corner of the Lazy A Ranch. Tom knew that all of Spiny Ridge that was above ground was on the Lazy A Ranch, and almost cut the ranch in two at an angle.

Tom had seen enough. There was no doubt that it was the way out of the valley. All they had to do now was to work their way across the smaller less challenging ridges to the north pasture and then on across the prairie to the barn.

Tom turned and walked back into the narrow canyon. It didn't take him very long to get back to the valley where Tracy was waiting for him.

When he got there he found Tracy near the entrance to the narrow canyon. She was sitting on a large rock with the reins of their horses in her hand. She stood up when he stepped out into the valley.

"I think we found it. We'll have to walk the horses through the canyon, but it takes us up on top of the main ridge. It's very pretty from up there, in a rugged sort of way."

"Well, let's go," Tracy said as she handed Tom the reins of the horse he had been riding.

Tom immediately led the way into the canyon. Tracy followed along behind. As they moved through the narrow canyon, Tracy was beginning to think that it was not the way. But she immediately changed her mind when she stepped out of the narrow canyon into the open.

"It is beautiful in a rough rugged sort of way," she said as she looked around. "It is funny, but you don't realize how wide the ridge becomes from down below. It takes up a lot of the ranch."

"It sure does," Tom said as he stood beside her. "I'm sure your father knew that, too."

"I wonder why he kept it such a secret."

"Maybe because he didn't want the world to know about the valley."

"You could be right, but I think he knew something else about this place that we still don't know about."

"That's possible, too. Shall we get going? We still haven't found our way all the way across Spiny Ridge." Tom suggested.

"Yes," she replied.

Tom and Tracy mounted up then started riding along the closest ridge. It wasn't long before they found a place where they could easily cross the ridge to the next one. They were then able to cross the next smaller ridge without difficulty.

When they came to the next ridge, they began riding along the edge of it looking for a place where they could get across. Tom suddenly stopped. Tracy moved up close to him. He turned and motioned for her to be very quiet. She wondered what it was that he had heard.

"There's someone just on the other side of the ridge," Tom said in a whisper.

"Any idea who it might be?"

"No, but there isn't supposed to be anyone on your property."

"What about Frank? He said that he was going to come out here to look around."

"Yeah, but I didn't think he was going to be out here with anyone. There are at least two people over that way," he said as he pointed toward the other side of the ridge. "I'm going to find out who is over there, just to be on the safe side."

Tom stepped out of the saddle. As he did, Tracy stepped down, too. She took hold of the reins of both horses and held them while Tom slid the rifle out of the saddle scabbard and levered a cartridge into the chamber.

"Be careful," Tracy said as she looked into his eyes.

"I'll be right back," Tom said then smiled at her.

Tom took a look at the rocks that formed the ridge and decided which way he was going to go. He moved slowly among the large rocks in an effort to be as quiet as possible. He picked his way along until he found a place where he could see across to the other side of the ridge, and he could see what was going on. His position put him slightly above and directly behind two men with rifles. The rifles were hunting rifles with scopes.

Tom was close enough to the men to hear them talking. They were looking out over the prairie in a westerly direction, in the same direction that he had come from when he was shot in the ravine.

Meanwhile, Tracy found a bush and tied the horses to the bush. She removed her rifle from the saddle scabbard and moved over next to the rocks where she could cover Tom's retreat if he had to get out of there in a hurry.

CHAPTER TWENTY

"I saw some cop over in that ravine where you shot that guy yesterday. It looks like he's doing a little nosing around," the younger of the two men said.

"He's just some cow town sheriff's deputy. He wouldn't know a clue if it hit him alongside the head. All we have to do is stay here, be quiet and he'll never see us."

"What about the truck?"

"What about it?"

"He'll sure find that."

"I doubt it. It's pretty well hidden. Besides, even if he does find it, by the time he finds out that it's a rented truck, we'll have ditched it."

"Yeah, but I signed for it. He'll know who we are."

"You used the phony driver's license and insurance papers I gave you, didn't you?"

"Sure."

"Then there's no problem. He'll be chasing a man that doesn't exist."

"But, - - - -," the younger man started to say when he was cut off by the older of the two.

"Will you just shut up. We've got nothing to worry about if you keep your mouth shut."

Tom was listening and watching the two men. He didn't know either of them. They didn't look like anyone he had seen around the county before, and he didn't think they looked like cowboys to him. They were wearing jeans and western style shirts, but they had on boots more like hunters would wear. Their hats were camouflaged colored baseball caps, not that it would help them much here. They were green camouflaged and the rocks were a dusty gray. The rifles they had were hunting rifles with scopes, not the usual saddle rifle most cowboys in the area used.

Tom watched the two for several minutes as he thought about what they had said. The only "cop" he could think of that would be in the area nosing around was Frank.

Slowly, and very carefully, Tom raised his rifle and laid it over the rock. He was not about to let them shoot his best friend if he could stop it.

From his position, he could not see Frank. The only clue he had that Frank was in the area was based on what the two men directly in front of him had said. He would watch them; and if it looked like they might be getting ready to shoot at someone, he would certainly let them know he was behind them.

Tom had the advantage. He knew the men were there, and he had the drop on them. He also had the advantage in the fact that they were trespassing on private property.

Tom wasn't sure if there were others in the area. He would have to be ready for anything, just in case. He raised his head up and looked around as carefully as he could without making himself a target. Just then his attention was drawn back to the two men in front of him.

"Look there," the younger man said as he pointed down in front of them. "It's that deputy we saw the other day. Looks like he's nosing around again."

"Yeah. It looks like he might be a pretty good tracker."

"Maybe too good a tracker. If he's a good tracker, he could probably follow us right back in here."

"I don't think so. He can't track us on rock," the older man said. "He'll lose our tracks on those rocks. He'll play hell following us up here."

"What do we do?"

"We wait and see if he's alone. If he gets too close, we shoot him and dump his body well away from here. We don't want anyone snooping around here and delaying us any."

Tom could now see Frank. He was obviously following some tracks. He was trying to figure out how to warn Frank.

Since it would be very difficult to warn Frank without giving his position away, Tom turned his attention to the two men below him. It was clear what they intended to do. He got himself ready to stop the two men from shooting at Frank if they decided to try.

Tom aimed his rifle toward the two men and watched the men carefully over the sights of his rifle. If either of them looked like he was going to shoot at Frank, Tom would let them know he was behind them in a way that would convince them that it was not in their best interest to shoot an officer of the law.

Time seemed to pass slowly as Tom watched the two men. They had made no move that would indicate that they were ready to shoot.

Suddenly, the older of the two men raised his rifle to his shoulder. Tom did not hesitate one second. He drew a bead on the man's rifle and pulled the trigger. There was the sudden loud sound of a rifle shot. The bullet from Tom's rifle hit the scope on the man's rifle and shattered it to pieces.

Tom quickly levered another round in the chamber and pointed the rifle at the other man.

"One move and you get it. You'll be dead before you know what happened," Tom yelled out. "Toss your gun away, and it better be far enough that you can't reach it."

Tom waited to see if there was going to be the need to fire again. The man tossed his gun about ten feet away then turned around sat with his back against the rocks. He sat there without moving.

"You with the shot-up rifle, slowly push the rifle over the top of the rock in front of you then turn around," Tom said.

Tom waited and watched. The man raised his head a little then pushed the rifle over the rock. He then turned around and leaned his back against the rock. Tom could see that when his scope exploded in front of his face from Tom's shot, it kicked up several pieces; and some of them kicked back and hit the man in the face. He had a deep cut on his nose and several smaller cuts above his right eye.

"Now just sit there and don't even think about moving," Tom said.

Tom glanced back when he heard the sound of someone coming up behind him. He quickly turned back around when he saw that it was Tracy. She ran up and knelt down beside him.

"Are you all right?"

"Yeah, I'm fine."

"This is Sheriff Frank Garring. Who's up there?"

Frank was down behind some large rocks with his gun in his hand. He was looking up toward where the shot had come from.

"It's me, Tom. You better come up here."

Tom watched as Frank moved out from behind the rocks and began working his way up to the ridge in front of the two men. As he approached the rocks, he came across the gun with the smashed scope. He picked it up and climbed over the rocks. Frank quickly found the two men sitting with their backs against the rock.

"You might want to search them for any other weapons," Tom called down.

Tom kept an eye, and his rifle, on the two men while Frank searched them for weapons. He came up with two pistols. Frank stepped back and held a gun on them while Tom and Tracy came down from up above. Once Tom and

Tracy were next to Frank, Tom held a gun on the two men while Frank cuffed them.

"Thanks for the fine shooting, Tom."

"You're welcome. I couldn't let my best friend walk into a trap as long as I could do something about it."

"I'm glad to hear that. What have we got here besides a couple of bushwhackers?" Frank said.

"Well, I'm sure you can come up with more than I can."

"You can't prove anything. All you got us for is trespassing. A fine and we walk."

"We have the bullet from Will Strong, the cowboy you shot, and your guns to compare it to. And standing right there is the cowboy you shot the other day," Frank said as he pointed at Tom.

"We have two witnesses that you were going to ambush a law enforcement officer with intent to kill him. And I wouldn't doubt that we could get you on several other charges. By the way, who are you working for? I know you're not from around here."

"We ain't talking without our lawyer," the older of the two men said.

"Tom, if I was to leave these two with you while I go get my patrol car, do you think that they might talk to you," Frank said with a grin."

"I don't know if they will or not, but not being a law enforcement officer what do I do if they try to escape?"

"That's up to you. But since they are trespassing on Miss Tracy's ranch, and they have guns; and since you want to protect Miss Tracy from harm, I guess you could just shoot them. I know I'd have little problem with that, and I'm sure the judge wouldn't have a problem with it, either. After all, there's a good chance that one of them shot you."

"That sounds good to me. I would love to get even with the SOB that shot me," Tom said as he looked directly at the older of the two men.

"I'll be back in a few minutes. I left my patrol car some distance from here."

"Take your time," Tom said as he looked at the two men.

Tracy just stood there and listened to what Frank and Tom had said. She wasn't sure what was going on, but she figured that they might have a plan to get these two to talk. She quickly decided that she would play along.

Frank turned and walked away. He had left their pistols with Tom.

As soon as Frank was gone, Tom walked up close to the younger of the two men. He stood looking down at him for several minutes without saying anything. It was clear that it was making the young man very nervous, which was just what Tom wanted it to do. Tom could see the sweat start to form on the young man's forehead.

"I want to know just one thing. I want to know which one of you shot me."

Tom was looking directly at the younger of the two men. Tom believed that he was the one who would break first. He thought that because of the conversation he had heard when they were planning to shoot Frank. It was clear that the younger of the two was scared of getting caught.

"I want to know who shot my ranch hand and left him out here to die. One thing is for sure; if he does die, I will see whoever shot him put to death," Tracy said.

"I wonder which one will confess first. It is like that old game. The first to answer the question wins," Tom said. "Isn't that the way it goes?"

"Yeah, I think so," Tracy said.

"We ain't talkin'. So you might as well stop acting as if you would hurt us. If you do, you will be the ones that end up in jail," the older one said with a note of confidence.

"Now who's going to be around to tell anyone what happened. If I shoot both of you, there will be a hearing.

With no witnesses, and both of us being well known and upstanding members of the community, what do you think will happen?

"Jake, what do I do?" the younger one said, a strong note of fear in his voice.

"Don't say nothing. They can't prove anything."

"You are right. We can't prove anything, yet. However, if the ballistic tests of the bullet they took out of Will Strong comes back a match to either of these rifles, I think the saying is, 'Got yah'. And I think one of those rifles did the shooting. It's only a matter of who pulled the trigger," Tom said.

"I've got a better idea. I've seen it work in the movies," Tracy said.

"What's that?"

"All you do is put a gun to the crook's knee and ask him what you want to know. If he tells you, you've got him. If he doesn't, you blow his knee off," Tracy said. "Who's going to know that he didn't get shot trying to escape?"

"Jake?" the young man pleaded.

"Keep your damn mouth shut."

"I think that's a good idea, but it's so messy. It's not really going to matter if they talk or not. I think the bullet from Will is going to be enough to hang them," Tom said.

"By the way, you will probably both hang; and it won't matter to me which one of you shot him. In this state, the accomplice to a crime is held to the same standards as the one who actually committed the crime. In short, you are both equally guilty. But if one of you should talk and tell what happened, and who did the shooting, it might go a little easier on him."

"Jake?" he pleaded again

"I said to keep your damn mouth shut."

Just then, Frank returned. He took a quick look at the two men and then at Tom and Tracy. He wondered what had been going on while he was gone. It was obvious that Tom didn't want to say anything, at least for now.

"Okay, you two. Let's get moving. Get up."

"What about my face?" Jake asked.

"What about it. Your cuts are not life threatening. You can wait until I get you to the hospital."

"I'm in pain. You have to air-vac me out of here."

"Like hell I do. Your cuts are not life threatening; so you go in the patrol car with me. Now shut up and start moving."

Reluctantly, the two men moved slowly down through the rocks toward the patrol car. Tom turned to Tracy.

"I'm going to go with Frank to his patrol car just in case they decide to give him any trouble. Would you mind bringing the horses down to his car?"

"No. You go ahead."

Tom followed Frank to his patrol car. By the time Frank had the two men secured in the car, Tracy was coming along with the horses.

"You need any help with them?" Tom asked.

"No. They're not going anywhere. They're cuffed to the floor of the patrol car. I'll get some help before I release them from the car. I would like you in my office as soon as possible to make a statement."

"Sure."

"I'll see you in town," Frank said as he got into his patrol car.

Tom watched as Frank drove off. He then turned and walked over to where Tracy was sitting in the saddle waiting for him. Tom took the reins from Tracy, then swung into the saddle.

"Where to now?" Tracy asked.

"I think we should go to the barn and spend the night there. It's too long a ride back to the ranch house."

"Okay," Tracy said, then nudged her horse in the ribs.

Tom and Tracy rode side by side all the way back to the barn. Neither of them had much to say. It had been a long day and it was starting to wear on them.

* * * *

Tom and Tracy rode up to the barn and into the corral. They stepped down from their horses and tied them to the corral fence.

"Are you hungry?" Tracy asked.

"Yeah," Tom answered.

"Would you like a hot meal, or the sandwiches I brought?" Tracy asked.

"I would prefer a hot meal."

"I'll fix something to eat if you will take care of the horses."

"Sounds good. I don't know what is left to eat, but I'm sure you can find something to make a hot meal."

Tracy went over to the place where they had been building fires to cook on and began by starting a fire. As soon as the fire was going good, she put on the coffee pot. She then started searching through the supplies for something to eat.

Meanwhile, Tom took the horses into the barn one at a time. He stripped them of their saddles, rubbed them down, then turned them out into the larger corral at the back of the barn with the other horses. When he was finished taking care of the horses, he went to the water pump and washed up a little.

Tracy was cooking some stew she made out of what was in the supplies when Tom came up behind her. He could see her stirring it. It smelled good.

"What are you making? It sure smells good."

"It's a stew made from what I could find. It might not be the best stew you ever had, but it will fill our stomachs."

"It really doesn't matter. I could eat hay with the horses I'm so hungry."

"The horses may not want to share their hay with you. But I will share the stew with you."

"Thanks a lot. When will it be ready?"

"In a few minutes. The coffee is ready now."

Tom got a cup and poured himself a cup of coffee. He sat down on a bale of hay and watched Tracy as she cooked the stew. He couldn't help but think about how beautiful she was, even in jeans and a work shirt.

He looked up at the sky and could see the first hint of a star. The sky was clear and the sun had set over the western hills, but it was still light enough to see what was around them. Tom had spent many nights out on the prairie in his youth. The past few years had kept him from enjoying times like those where he would sleep out under the stars.

Tom's thoughts were suddenly disturbed by Tracy calling him to dinner. He looked at her and smiled, then got up and walked over to the fire. Tracy dished up a large serving of the stew and handed it to him. He took it and returned to the bale where he sat down. It was just a minute or two before Tracy sat down beside him. Without any more conversation, they began to eat. After a while, Tom spoke.

"I really like it out here. I remember when Frank and I would go camping. We would lay on top of a hill and watch the stars until we fell asleep."

"I used to sleep in the loft of the barn and look at the stars out the loft door," Tracy said with kind of a dreamy tone in her voice.

"It will be dark soon. How would you like to take our bed rolls, go up on the hill and sleep up there tonight? It sure doesn't look like it will rain."

"Are you sure that sleeping is what you have in mind?"

"Eventually we would get some sleep," he said with a grin.

"As long as we will get some sleep," she said as she smiled at him. "But first we have to clean up here and put the fire out."

As soon as they finished eating, they washed the dishes. While Tracy put the dishes away, Tom put out the fire, then went into the barn and gathered their bedrolls. When all was secure at the barn, they walked hand in hand up the hill behind the barn.

Once they were at the top of the hill, Tom rolled out the bedrolls side by side. They then laid down on them. The sky was now full of stars that seemed to be endless in their numbers.

"It is a beautiful night," Tracy said.

"Yes, but not as beautiful as you."

"You're pretty good looking, yourself. I'll bet you turned the heads of a lot of girls in college."

"Are you jealous?" he said playfully.

"No. Well, maybe a little."

"You have nothing to be jealous about. You have my undivided attention."

"Of course I have, there's no one else out here," she said with a chuckle.

"If I tell you something, do you promise not to laugh?" he asked.

She looked at him and quickly realized that he was being very serious. She wondered what he might say that was so important to him that he would not want her to laugh. Tracy knew that he loved her, and that she loved him. If what he had to tell her was that important to him, she would promise not to laugh.

"I promise," she said as she looked him in the eyes.

"I've loved you since high school. All the years that we were away at different colleges, I could think of no one but you. Oh, I dated a few other girls in college, but none of them made me feel the way you do."

Tracy just looked at him. She found what he had told her hard to believe. It was certainly nothing to laugh about.

"I've always wanted you," he said when she didn't say anything for several minutes.

"Tom, you have me forever. If you still want me after the way I treated you, then I am yours."

Tom didn't say anything. He just moved closer to her and put his arms around her. He gently pulled her close to him until their lips met. It was a long hard passionate kiss that sent waves of desire through both of them.

Tracy returned his kiss with the same passion that he had shown. It wasn't long before they were wrapped up in their love for each other. Their passion grew as did their desire for each other, and their need for each other. Tracy pulled back a little and looked into Tom's eyes. They were both breathing hard.

"Make love to me," she whispered.

It wasn't long before they were both out of their clothes. Tom took his time with her. Their passion for each other grew quickly, and their love for each other was shown in their passion.

CHAPTER TWENTY-ONE

When morning came to the hill behind the barn, the sun found the two lovers wrapped in each other's arms. A blanket covered them as they slept.

Tracy was the first to wake. She could feel Tom's breath on the back of her neck, and his hand gently resting over one of her bare breasts. She smiled as she thought of last night and how good it felt to be really loved.

"Are you awake?" Tom whispered.

"Yes. Are you ready to get up?"

"I think we better. We are expected in Frank's office this morning."

"I almost forgot that, but then I wanted to forget it."

"Can I have a kiss before we get up?" Tom asked.

"Just a kiss?"

"Well, maybe a little more than a kiss."

"Okay," she said as she rolled over to face him.

Tracy wrapped her arms around his neck as she pulled him down over her. Their lips met in a long and passionate kiss. When she released her hold on him, he drew back a little and looked into her eyes.

"You know what I would like to do?" he asked in almost a whisper.

Tracy smiled up at him and said, "I think we did it last night."

"Not that, well, yeah that," he said with a silly grin. "What I would really like to do is spend a few days in the little valley with you. Just the two of us camping, making love and sleeping under those big oak trees."

"I think that could be arranged. I know the owner," she said as she looked up at his face. "But I think we better get dressed and head for town."

"Can we take a shower at the ranch house before we go into town?"

"I would like that."

Tom kissed her again then rolled away from her. They got dressed, gathered the bedrolls then walked back to the barn. Tracy fixed breakfast while Tom fed and watered the horses. After breakfast, they cleaned up the dishes and put them away. When everything was done, Tom saddled two horses for the ride back to the ranch house.

While crossing the pasture, they looked at the cattle. They seemed to be getting enough to eat and enough water. None of the cattle looked like they were stressed, which pleased Tracy.

When they arrived at the ranch house, Tom and Tracy took care of the horses. They went to the house arm in arm. Once in the house, they went directly to the bathroom where they stripped out of their clothes and got into the shower together. It turned out to last a lot longer than they had planned, but neither of them seemed to object.

As soon as they were dressed, they went out to Tom's car and drove into town. They went directly to the Sheriff's Office.

* * * *

It was almost noon when Tom and Tracy walked into the Sheriff's Office. Maggie was sitting at the dispatcher's desk. She looked up and Tracy smiled at her. Maggie didn't say anything as she seemed to be busy, but Tracy could not see what she was doing. After a few minutes, Maggie looked up at Tracy again.

"Hi. Frank is in the interrogation room at the moment. He should be out before long. You want to wait for him?"

Tom glanced at Tracy before he replied.

"I think we'll go over to the café and get a bite to eat. We haven't had lunch, yet."

"I'll tell him where you are. He might come over. He hasn't had lunch, either."

"Thanks, Maggie," Tom said.

Maggie just nodded that she understood. Tom and Tracy left the Sheriff's Office and headed across the street to Betty's Café. Once inside, they found a booth back in a corner and sat down. It was only a minute or so before Betty came over to the booth and slipped in next to Tracy.

"How is Will doing?" Betty asked.

"The last word I had was that he was holding his own. He was stable, but critical," Tracy said. "I'm afraid that he will be laid up for a long time."

"I know he doesn't have a very good reputation around here, but he is a good man. He doesn't bother anyone, and he works hard."

"I know. I'm not sure what is going to happen to him if he can't work on the ranch any more. It was his life," Tracy said. "How is it that you know so much about him?"

"We grew up in the same small town. He was always picked on by some of the other kids because he wasn't as smart as most of them. He was a little slow, but he was strong. When he grew up, he was bigger and stronger than most of the kids he had gone to school with. People became afraid of him after he killed a man."

"I heard about that. He went to jail for manslaughter, I believe."

"Yes. He never should have been convicted of it. The man he killed was a prominent member of a small town over in Clark County. Will didn't get a fair trial."

"What did he do? I don't know any of the details."

"He killed a man who was slapping a woman around. The man was hitting the woman pretty hard. In fact, the man almost killed the woman, and would have if Will had not stopped him. When the man wouldn't stop hitting the woman, Will hit the man with those big strong hands of his. The man went flying and cracked his head on a steel post. He died as a result of hitting his head on the post. The woman spent three weeks in the hospital and was in physical rehab for six more months before she could even walk without a walker."

"So, Will got five years in jail for protecting a woman from an abusive man?"

"Yeah. Isn't justice grand," Betty said sarcastically. "I would have hired him to work here, but even people around here were afraid of him. Your dad was kind enough to give him a job."

"I'm glad he did. Will has been a God send to the ranch. I'm hoping that he will be able to return to work; but if he can't, I'll still try to find something for him to do around the ranch."

"That would be great. He might need a little rehab time before he can do very much."

"He will be welcome at my place for as long as he wants to stay," Tracy said.

"Thanks," Betty said as she glanced out the window and saw Frank coming across the street toward the cafe. "Looks like Frank is here to see you guys. I'll talk with you later."

Tom and Tracy looked toward the door and saw Frank coming across the room toward them. The look on his face showed that he did not look very happy.

"You look like it's been a hard day," Tom said to Frank as he slid into the booth beside Tom.

"The two thugs I've got in jail seem to think that their lawyer is going to get them out on bail, so they're not talking."

"Will their lawyer be able to do that?" Tracy asked.

"He might, but I'm not going to let them out without a fight. I've talked to the judge and our county attorney about them. They've agreed to make the bail very high since two people were shot, and one is in critical condition and might not survive. The judge said that they won't get out on bail at all if I can come up with any solid evidence that would connect them to either shooting."

"That's good, isn't it?" Tracy asked.

"Yeah, but I can't hold them very long if we can't match up the slug from Will to at least one of the rifles, I'm afraid. I'm hoping to get the ballistics report back from the state crime lab soon."

"Have you been able to find out who they are working for?" Tom asked.

"Not yet. Like I said, they're not talking. I have a feeling who they are working for, but I can't prove it. I don't even know who they are, yet. I have sent off their fingerprints to the FBI and the state crime lab to see if we can find out who they really are. At this point they have not said a word, not even their names."

"The younger guy called the older one Jake. That's the only name I heard either of them use."

"Not much help without a last name. We did find the white pickup with a bullet hole on the passenger's side. I have the state forensic team going over it. I know they found several sets of prints, but they don't know whose they are, yet. They are also doing the ballistic tests on the bullet taken from Will's chest and the rifles they had. All we know so far is they are all .30 caliber, both rifles and the slug from Will's chest. We can't find the slug that hit you."

"Have you had a talk with Blaine?"

"I would like to, but according to his wife, he isn't on the ranch. I've got a feeling that he is there, probably hiding somewhere in the house. She told me that she didn't know when he would be back. She also told me that since I was a friend of yours, and would believe anything you said over her husband, I would have to have a warrant if I wanted to come on their property to talk to him."

"It sounds like they are not going to cooperate with you. I have to wonder why that is," Tom said. "You think Blaine is involved in all this?"

"I think he is involved up to his neck, but I can't prove it. If I could, I would get a warrant and search that ranch from one end to the other," Frank said. "I would also put out an APB for him.

"We all know that Blaine was not a man with any savings in the bank, and had to borrow money to drill a well. If he used the money to get that truck for test drilling on the Lazy A Ranch, there would most likely be a record of it somewhere. I, for one, would like to know what the test holes showed," Tom said.

"I sure would like to know," Tracy said.

"We know that one company drilled six holes before they found out they were on Tracy's ranch. They didn't do any actual testing," Frank said. "The thing is that we found a total of twelve holes when we were searching the area for evidence where we caught the two we have in jail. What I would like to know is who drilled the other six holes we found yesterday, and what they discovered, if anything."

"I know of six companies that do that kind of work in the county," Tom said. "There are three more in Clark County and two over in Battle County that I know of."

"How is it that you know of those companies?" Frank asked.

"We make loans for people that want to drill for water, oil or natural gas. We have to know if someone wants a loan to drill a well, that there is some evidence that what they want to drill for might actually be there. Blaine got his loan for a well for water. I want to know if he spent it on those test holes along the ridge."

"I could have Maggie call every one of the companies and see if they have done any testing for Blaine," Frank said. "Can you get me the phone numbers of those companies?"

"Sure, but I think it would be a better idea if I made those calls. They wouldn't think twice about me calling to see what they might have found, since we are the ones who make loans for drilling," Tom said with a grin.

"Good idea. Can you get right on it?" Frank asked.

"I will, after I have something to eat. I'm starving."

"Okay. I'll see you later. Let me know what you find out."

"We will," Tracy said with a smile.

As Frank left the café, Tom waved to a waitress. The waitress came over to the table and took Tom and Tracy's orders. It wasn't long before Tom and Tracy had their lunch. They ate it without much conversation. Both of them were deep in thought. After they finished their lunch, they went over to the bank to make the calls.

Tom went directly to his office and sat down at his desk. Tracy followed him and sat down in front of his desk and waited for him to find the list of companies that did test drilling. She waited patiently while he began making the calls.

Tom began calling each company. He asked the same question of each company representative who answered the phone. What he asked was had Blaine hired them to do any testing for him?

It wasn't until he got to the seventh company on his list that he was told that they had recently done some work for Blaine. It was one of the two companies in Battle County that did the type of testing they found at the edge of the ridge. It was also a company that was the farthest away from Blaine's ranch.

"What kind of work did you do for him?" Tom asked.

"We did several test sites on his land."

"Did he say what the tests were for?"

"Yes. He said he was planning on drilling a well for water in one of his pastures."

"Where was the testing done?"

"It was done along Spiny Ridge."

"Why there? Did he tell you?"

"Yes. He said that he felt there was water in that area, but he needed proof so he could get a loan to pay for the drilling of a well."

"Did your test show anything?" Tom asked, hoping that it might prove important to Tracy.

"Yes. It showed that there might be some natural gas deposits under the ridge."

"Really?"

"Yeah."

"What was Blaine's reaction?"

"I didn't see his reaction. He had called in for the results after my men were finished. He acted as if he was disappointed. He said that he was looking for water. I told him that if there was natural gas there, he wouldn't have to worry about water. He would be able to truck in all the water he wanted."

"What did he say about that?"

"He said that he wasn't interested in natural gas. That didn't make a lot of sense to me. If he found a well that produced natural gas, he would have the money to do anything he wanted with his ranch."

"So I take it he didn't call you back to do the drilling for the natural gas?"

"No. In fact, I haven't heard from him again, but it has been less than a week since we finished the testing."

"Are any of the men who did the test holes available for me to talk to?"

"Yes. The lead driller is here. Let me find him for you. Hold please," he said, then music began to come over the phone.

Tom looked at Tracy and smiled. It was clear that he had found something that might be helpful. He could see that she was very impatient to know what was found. Tom put his hand over the phone.

"I think we've got something. It looks like, - - -," he was interrupted by someone on the phone.

"This is Bill Martin. What can I do for you?"

"I need a little information, Mr. Martin" Tom said. "Are you the one who was in charge of drilling the test holes at Spiny Ridge for Mr. Blaine?"

"Yes," he answered. "We dug six. There were already six when we got there. Why? Is there a problem?"

"Did you cross a fence line to get to Spiny Ridge?" Tom asked, ignoring his question.

"Yes, we did. Mr. Blaine was with us. He told us that we could run over the fence as it was to come out soon anyway. He pointed out to us where his property line ran. Why? What's going on?"

"So I take it you drove over the fence," Tom asked, again ignoring Bill's question.

"No, sir. We cut the fence before crossing it. What's this all about?"

"When you crossed over the fence line to get to Spiny Ridge, you trespassed onto the Lazy A Ranch."

"We didn't know that," Bill said with a tone of excitement in his voice. "Mr. Blaine was right there. He told us that we were on his property."

"Would you be willing to swear to that in court?"

"You bet. I have two other crewmen that were with me on that day. They'll swear to it as well."

"I'm hoping it won't come to that, but if it should I'll want you in court. For now, I want you and the other crewmen that were with you on the day you crossed onto Lazy A Ranch land to come over here and make a statement to the Sheriff about what happened, where you went and what you did. Include in your statement that Mr. Blaine told you to drive over the fence, and that he told you it was his property."

"Yes, sir. I'll get the guys together and we'll be right over. Ah - - Are we in trouble?" Bill asked with a hint of concern in his voice.

"I don't know for sure. If you make the statement just like what you told me, I can probably get the owner of Lazy A Ranch not to press charges for destruction of property and trespassing. I would suggest that in the future you might want to check property lines before you cut fence lines," Tom said.

"You can be sure of that. We'll be over there as soon as we can get there."

"By the way, was there anyone else with Mr. Blaine when you crossed onto the Lazy A Ranch, or maybe someone hanging around the area while you did the tests?"

"Yes. There were two men, one young and the other one a little older. Blaine never introduced us to them. In fact, they spent most of the time sitting in a pickup truck just watching us, more or less."

"What color was the pickup?"

"White. It was plain white."

"Can you describe the men?"

"Sure."

"When you and your men get over to the Sheriff's office, tell the Sheriff about them. He might have you look at a couple of guys he has in jail that might be the men you mentioned."

"I will do that."

"Thank you for your help," Tom said, then hung up.

Tom looked over at Tracy. He was grinning from ear to ear.

"We've got Blaine," Tom said. "He told the test crew to drive over the fence, and that the area where they were to do the testing was his land. Also, they found evidence that there might be natural gas under Spiny Ridge."

"That means that - - - that means that if there is natural gas under the ridge, it could be enough to make my payments and save the ranch?" Tracy asked almost afraid that it was some kind of a cruel joke.

"If there is natural gas under the ridge, you could end up being one very rich ranch owner," Tom said with a grin.

"I don't know what to say," she said then took a deep breath. "I'm afraid to believe it."

Tom couldn't help but smile. He had never seen her so excited before.

"What do we do now?"

"We go have a talk with Frank and tell him what we found out. The one thing we don't do is say anything to anyone else about this, at least for now."

Tom waited and watched Tracy as she tried to catch her breath. Finding natural gas under the ridge could be the thing that saved the ranch and paid for her father's stay in the nursing home.

As soon as she had settled down a little, Tom and Tracy went across the street to the Sheriff's Office to tell Frank what they had found out.

When they walked into the Sheriff's Office, they found Frank leaning against a desk talking to a man in an expensive suit. Tom knew right away that it was probably the lawyer for the two men Frank had in custody.

"I'm sorry, Mr. Wilson, but there isn't going to be a hearing with regard to bail until the judge gets back from fishing. He might be back tomorrow afternoon, then he might not."

"You better not be lying to me. If you are, I'll have your badge," the lawyer threatened sharply.

Frank took a deep breath and let out a sigh of frustration before he spoke. He then looked the lawyer in the eyes and spoke very clearly so that there would be no misunderstanding.

"You won't like it if you get my badge because you would have to deal with people just like you. Good day, sir," Frank said then turned his back to the lawyer and walked back in his office, shutting the door behind him.

Mr. Wilson watched Frank until the door closed. It was easy to see that he didn't believe the judge was fishing. It was also easy to see that it would not do him any good to try to pressure the Sheriff any more. It was pretty clear that the Sheriff wasn't going to put up with him if he tried.

Tom and Tracy smiled at each other as they watched the lawyer leave the office. As soon as he was gone, they walked into Frank's office. They weren't a hundred percent sure about the discussion that Frank had had with Mr. Wilson, but it was good to see that Frank was not going to be pushed around by some big city lawyer.

"Not your best day, hey, Frank?" Tom said with a grin.

"No. And if you don't have something to make it better, I suggest you leave now. I'm not in a very good mood."

"I think we just might be able to make your day. First of all, we have three men from the company that drilled some of the test sites and did the tests on their way over here. They're coming to sign sworn statements that Blaine had hired them to do testing for water where they had drilled the test sites.

"Secondly, they will include in their statements that Blaine told them to 'drive over the fence' as it was going to come down anyway, and that they would still be on his property."

"At least that ties Blaine in on all this. But all we can get him for is trespassing."

"It does more than that," Tom said. "The tests didn't show that there might be water below the ridge, but that there is a strong possibility that there is natural gas there. I would think that would give motive for Blaine to want to make it so difficult for Tracy to keep the ranch that she would have to sell it."

"That's all good in theory, but theory is not proof. What's the connection between the two men I have in jail and Blaine?"

"I don't know, but it should provide enough evidence to arrest Blaine and get a search warrant for his property."

"You're right about that. I think I'll go fishing," Frank said with a grin.

Tom looked at Tracy as if he didn't understand what Frank had said. From the look on Tracy's face, she didn't understand it either.

Frank smiled at them, then said, "I just happen to know where the judge is fishing. I'm sure he would be more than happy to sign a warrant for Blaine's arrest and for a search of his property."

Tom and Tracy began to laugh.

"I'll get a warrant for Blaine's arrest and a search warrant. Then I'll head out to Blaine's place and put him under arrest. When the two in jail see him, I wonder who will talk first," Frank said.

"Oh. One more thing. The men coming to your office to sign statements saw two men with Blaine. Bill Martin said that they had not been introduced to the men, but the men hung around and watched them work. You might want to show them the two you have in jail."

"I'll do that."

"Tracy and I will be at my apartment if you need anything."

"Okay."

Frank went to the judge's home where he found the judge working in his garden. He obtained a warrant for Blaine's arrest as well as a search warrant. He took a couple of deputies out to the Blaine ranch where they found Mr. Blaine hiding in the basement of his house. Blaine was taken to jail while his ranch was searched from top to bottom. The deputies found enough evidence to connect Blaine to the two men Frank had in jail.

Blaine began to talk in the hope of getting a lighter sentence. He told how he had hired the two men, Jake Sutton and Jimmy Bob Roberts. Frank discovered rather quickly that they were both wanted in Mississippi for shooting a man in a robbery, and for extortion. They had come west to avoid being caught, and to avoid being sent back to Mississippi to stand trial.

Blaine told Frank that he had found them camping out in a northern part of his ranch. They were hungry and needed money. He promised to pay them a lot of money if they would keep anyone from nosing around Spiny Ridge, and he didn't care how they did it. He had been making arrangements to start drilling for the natural gas on the Lazy A Ranch, but the shooting of Will and Tom had caused him to delay it for fear of getting caught.

CHAPTER TWENTY-TWO

Tom and Tracy went to Tom's apartment. Once they were inside and Tom had closed the door, he took Tracy in his arms. He held her tightly as he kissed her. After the kiss, Tom looked into her eyes.

"Tracy, will you marry me?"

She looked up at him. She had a serious look on her face.

"Tom, do you like children?"

"Yes, of course," he replied as he looked at her wondering what was on her mind.

"Would you like to be a father?" she asked with a smile.

A smile came over his face and he said, "Yes. I would like to live and work on your ranch, and I would like to raise cattle and children."

"Yes. I would love to marry you," she said softly.

Tom pulled her up to him and swung her around as he kissed her. But their moment of joy was interrupted by a knock on the door. Tom stopped spinning her around, set her on her feet and let go of her. He looked at her as he walked to the door, not sure who might be calling on him. He opened the door to find his mother standing there.

Tom's mother was smiling until she saw Tracy standing in his living room. She looked up at Tom as if to ask what she was doing there.

"Mother, come in. Just the person I want to see. I have some great news for you. I know how much you like to be the first to hear what is going on in our small place in the world, so here it is. Tracy and I are getting married."

There was a shocked look on her face. Her mouth fell open and her eyes got big. It was the first time Tom could remember when his mother couldn't speak.

"Well, aren't you going to congratulate us?"

"I - - I - - don't know what to say."

"Say, congratulations, Mother," Tom said flatly.

She looked over at Tracy and then back at her son. She found it hard to say anything.

"Mother, you are going to have to get used to us being married. I would suggest that you show Tracy the respect she deserves, and that you treat her as my wife. If you choose to do otherwise, I doubt that you will be seeing either of us very much."

"Does, your father know?" she asked ignoring Tracy.

"Not yet. Why don't you go tell him," Tom suggested.

"Yes. I should do that," she said as if she wasn't sure what to do.

With that said, she turned and left Tom's apartment.

"That wasn't very nice," Tracy said with a slight grin.

"You're probably right, but she has to know that we are in charge of our own lives. She is not going to run our life or the lives of our children."

Tracy couldn't help but smile. Tom walked over to her. He took her hand and led her to the sofa where they sat down together.

"Tom, what are we going to do? I mean, are you going to continue to work at the bank?"

"While I was out at the barn in the north pasture, I found out that what I really like doing are the things that ranchers do. I want to be a rancher, full time. I would like to live with you on your ranch, and help raise cattle and work alongside you. Would that be okay with you?"

"Yes. You know how much I love the ranch. I would love to live there and raise cattle, and a few children. I didn't think you would want to give up your job at the bank."

"I have a little money saved up. We could use it to pay off the debt on the ranch. That would give us a good start, and the freedom to build up the ranch the way we want."

"What about the natural gas under Spiny Ridge?"

"We could drill for it, if you want, but we don't have to."

"We can think about it," she said as she looked into his eyes.

"I do want to keep the little valley in the ridge a secret for as long as we can. It can be our private little place to go when we need to be alone together. How does that sound?" Tom asked.

"It sounds perfect."

* * * *

Over the next few months, Tom and Tracy spent most of their time working on the ranch. They made a lot of the necessary repairs to the ranch that had been put off because of a lack of money.

However, they did take time to get married. Tom's mother had a great time helping to arrange the wedding and showing how proud she was of her new daughter-in-law. It didn't hurt any that she put on a lavish reception after the wedding. It was the talk of the town for weeks.

While they were working on the ranch, Mr. Norbert arranged for more testing for natural gas along the northern edge of Spiny Ridge. When the tests came back with good results, Mr. Norbert loaned Tom and Tracy the money to drill for the natural gas.

It took several months before Mr. Blaine and his two thugs finally stood trial. It only took three days in court to find them guilty of all charges.

Shortly after the trial was over, natural gas had been found and the natural gas well was tapped. Within a few months, Tracy was able to hire back the men who had to leave when she couldn't afford to pay them. Jacob returned to work on the ranch as the foreman. Two of the other ranch hands that had quit were rehired, plus another ranch hand was hired.

Will Strong had recovered enough to be released from the hospital. He returned to the ranch to finish recuperating. Tracy had told him that he had a permanent place to live on the ranch for as long as he wanted it. Will moved back into the bunkhouse and spent most of his time taking care of the horses. As he regained his strength, he did whatever he could to help around the ranch.

* * * *

It was a quiet afternoon when Tom and Tracy were sitting on their horses looking at the drilling rig as it was drilling a second well. It was not what Tracy had wanted to see on the land, but she knew that the money from the natural gas would support the ranch no matter what the weather did. She also knew that once the well was in place and working, there would not be that much of it to see. It was the first time in years that she had felt that the ranch was finally financially secure, which relieved a lot of pressure for her. She turned and looked at Tom.

"Tom, I think it is time that we go on a honeymoon. Don't you?"

"Yes. We have Jacob to look out for the ranch. I see no reason not to go. Where would you like to go?"

"I would like to spend a week in the little valley. Just the two of us."

"No trip to some place miles from here?"

"No. There would be no one around except you and me if we go to the valley. I just want to be alone with you. We could start working on those children we talked about," Tracy said with a grin.

"That sounds good to me. We could bathe in the creek we found near the northeast end of the valley, and lay around in the soft grass and in the shade of the big oak trees. And we could just spend some time getting to know each other," he said with a grin. "In the biblical sense."

"I don't suppose that your mother will be too happy with us for not going some place fancy and expensive."

"My mother will never change," Tom said. "Her idea of anything is, if it's not expensive, it's nothing."

"I don't think she will be much of a problem," Tracy said. "After all, you are married to one of the richest women in the county. I'm sure that will make her very happy."

"I'm sure it will," Tom agreed with a laugh.

"I think the ranch is in good hands now with Jacob and the others back on the job. I think we can take some time to spend for ourselves."

"I'm sure we can."

"I was thinking that we should get some gear together and head out for our honeymoon tonight."

"I think we should, too," Tom agreed.

Tom leaned toward her from his saddle while Tracy leaned toward him until their lips met in a loving kiss. As she drew back and sat up in the saddle, she smiled then spurred her horse and headed toward the ranch house to pack up what little they would need.

Once they had enough food for several days packed on a packhorse, they saddled up a couple of fresh horses and headed for the narrow canyon that would take them into Spiny Ridge. They found the canyon, then looked around to make sure that no one could see them. When they didn't see anyone around, they entered into the canyon and disappeared, not to be seen or heard from for seven days and six nights.